World Planetary Defenders
and the Hidden Menace

GW00726054

WORLD PLANETARY DEFENDERS
and the hidden menace

All rights reserved; no part of this publication may be
reproduced or transmitted by any means, electronic, mechanical,
photocopying or otherwise, without the prior permission
of the publisher

First published in Great Britain in Great Britain in 2013
Ercall Publishing, 2 Mile Oak, Maesbury Road, Oswestry,
Shropshire, SY10 8GA

This paperback edition first published in 2013

Copyright text and cover illustration © F. W. Tart 2013

Cover illustration by D.R. ink (Emil Dacanay)
www.d-r-ink.com

The right of F.W. Tart to be identified as the author of this book has
been asserted in accordance with the Copyright, Designs
and Patents Act 1988.

A CIP catalogue record for this book is available from the British Library

ISBN 978-0-9926851-0-2

Printed and bound in Great Britain by Clays Ltd, St Ives plc
Typeset by Dorchester Typesetting Group Ltd

World Planetary Defenders and the Hidden Menace

F.W. Vann

Ercall Publishing

*for Elaine who never stopped supporting me
and Sarah, Jamie and Matthew who give
me much hope for the future . . .*

Chapter 1

'You will not beat me, Marduk, even if you fight for ever.'

Galileo ran his fingers through his short, fair hair and turned away from his opponent to stare across the frozen wastes of the Antarctic landscape. Although the temperature was minus thirty, he felt no cold through his simple white shirt.

Marduk took a few paces away from him and stared across the azure sky towards the ice floes. 'There's nothing on this planet for you, G. It's small, uninteresting – and the natives are busy destroying themselves and their environment. Great Creators! It's even got a stupid name – the planet *Earth*… They may as well have named it the planet Rock or Soil. Bit of a comedown after our own Aurea Cura, isn't it!'

'Then why are you so interested in it, Marduk, if it's worthless?'

Marduk turned towards Galileo and took a few steps until they were face to face, his leather boots squeaking with each pace across the shimmering fast ice. 'Let's just shake on it and part company. We both have to find a new home. The Creators need us to spread as widely across the universe as we can. You have your strengths, G, and I have mine. I'm better suited to this planet, and…'

'And what?' Galileo said quickly, watching as Marduk's

eyes flicked from right to left.

'It's nothing. We should leave our enmity behind us, make the most of the fact that we both got away from home before the asteroid hit. Think of all our compatriots who weren't so lucky.'

'I do, I do. On a daily basis. The burden of our race's survival weighs more heavily upon me than I can say. It's almost more than I can take. But my mission is Earth; yours is not. I intend to fulfil my purpose, to share the knowledge of the Creators with the Earth people, teach them the lesson our race was wise enough to learn: that there's no higher purpose than goodness, knowledge and working together as one.'

'In that case, I'll have to fight you for it. I marked out this planet for my own ends over two thousand years ago.'

'What?' Galileo asked, his voice raised in shock.

A huddle of Adelie penguins to their left were squabbling and squawking, the sound echoing across the vast, glittering landscape.

Marduk went on. 'Beneath your feet, buried under the layers of ice and the frozen continent below it, is a hidden memento of my last visit.'

The penguins continued to squawk, and the sun shone down from cloudless blue, the brilliance of its reflected light almost too intense for eyes to bear.

Marduk said, 'There are three mementoes of my visits to Earth… secret weapons that have been carrying out my will for two thousand, two hundred years. No-one knows of their existence, no-one knows exactly where they are – and no-one can stop them doing their job for me.' He threw back his head then and laughed, a deep, malicious guffaw that shook his dark shoulder-length hair and reverberated eerily around the frozen landscape. 'They're part of my little campaign to make sure the inhabitants of planet Earth don't get above themselves.'

'Why here? Why Earth?' Galileo asked incredulously.

'The Creators drew my attention to this planet when they were seeking out places where our race could be preserved – because the Earth people seemed to be so like us in intelligence and reliance on energy. And the planet has many natural resources... I knew it could be useful to me. So give up on this one, G. Find yourself another planet in another galaxy – this one is already mine.'

And far beneath their feet, unseen and unheard, Transmitter 001 (Sub-Antarctic) continued to send out its unending, evil signal into the world.

Chapter 2

'I don't care what you think anyway – and I'm still going!' Angie shrieked at the top of her voice, striding across the tiny apartment and slamming her bedroom door behind her.

Her dad put his cello bow down in the music case listlessly, and ran his fingers through his greying hair. He knew he needed a haircut, and he felt tired and old.

'I can't afford the price of a holiday, Angie – the divorce is costing me every penny. I'm doing my best, but it isn't easy…' Her dad's voice tailed away, and he knew she wouldn't hear him anyway, because music was already blaring out of her room. He picked up his cello bow and tried to practise despite the noise, working on the piece he would be performing with the rest of the Johannesburg Philharmonic Orchestra the next night.

Suddenly the music from the bedroom stopped, and a moment later Angie appeared, this time carrying her school bag and the overnight bag she had brought with her only an hour earlier.

'I'm going to Mum's,' she yelled, tossing her long fair hair over her shoulder dramatically.

Her dad put down his cello bow again and leaned forward. 'Your mum's away, Angie. That's why you're staying with me.'

'I'm fourteen, and I'm old enough to look after myself. I hate it here, I hate you, I hate my life!' she shouted, dragging her bags as far as the front door of the apartment.

'Angie! Angie!' Her dad stood up, although his back and shoulders were bowed as though he were still bent over his cello.

Angie opened the front door.

Stepping carefully between the piles of musical scores, books and newspapers on the floor, her dad came towards her. 'Let's compromise. I'll take you to Mum's and you can stay there until bedtime, as long as you keep your phone on all the time. Then I'll call for you later and bring you back here. Okay?'

Angie let out a dramatically noisy sigh, dropped her overnight bag on the floor and ran down the apartment staircase, carrying her school bag over her shoulder.

'I'll take that as a "Yes" then,' her dad said quietly as he pulled the front door closed behind him.

Angie's mum's apartment couldn't have been more different than her dad's. Six months ago, when her parents had split up, Angie and her parents had moved out of their house in an expensive northern suburb of Johannesburg. Her mum took Angie to live with her new man, a wealthy computer games programmer. He lived in a huge, modern apartment in Fourways, which Angie's best friend said was the poshest place to live in the city. The apartment complex had a security gate and a gatehouse staffed by full-time guards. Meanwhile, her dad had moved into a one-bedroom apartment in the eastern suburbs, where the buildings were old and nestled among the Jewish and European communities. He slept on a sofa bed in the living room and left the tiny bedroom for Angie when she stayed.

Her dad borrowed his neighbour's car so he could drive Angie home, and as he pulled up at the gatehouse to the luxury apartment complex he let out a deep sigh.

Angie showed her pass to the guard, the electric gates swung open, and she got out of the car at her Mum's and Steve's front door. She didn't say goodbye to her dad.

Once inside the apartment, she dropped her school bag, crossed the huge, shiny floor to the open plan kitchen and pulled an ice-cold cola out of the fridge, which was nearly as big as her dad's entire home.

She slumped down on one of the cream sofas from where she had a bird's eye view through enormous windows of the city bathed in afternoon sunlight. Her stepfather said it was the most expensive view in South Africa. There was a haze across the skyline, with the familiar skyscrapers standing between the lower rise buildings, interspersed with trees and the hills beyond the edge of the furthest suburbs. She squeezed her phone from the pocket of her skinny jeans and texted her best mate. *I'm so lonely. Mum and Dad both hate me. Dad just kicked me out for the night and Dom duzn't fancy me either.*

Then she entered a ☹ into her social network status, and slouched further down into the sofa cushions. None of her friends were online.

She updated her status again. *Why is the world so rubbish? Why do people get divorced? Why don't parents love their kids? Life stinks.*

Minutes later she got up, took a long swig of cola from the can, which was now covered in condensation like in an advert, and walked towards the study. Although her mum had a desk there, this room was very much her new partner's territory. Steve was a massively successful businessman and he was black. Some of Angie's friends were shocked about that. 'Don't you mind that your mum's got a black boyfriend? Will they have a kid together? Would that bother you?' Those had been the kind of questions.

Angie touched the keyboard in front of the massive flat-screen on Steve's desk and it sprang to life. It was only one of the bank of screens and computers he had in the vast study. As a games programmer he needed all of them for his job. Steve had a cupboard full of games consoles, remote controls and game DVDs, but he insisted that these were always tidied away. He detested mess. His cleaner (whom he called his 'daily') made sure everything was polished and tidied and cleaned, although Steve took care of dusting and wiping the computers on the desks himself.

Angie put down her can of cola on the small table by the study door – she knew better than to put it anywhere near the precious technology. She stared at Steve's screensaver – a lifelike image of a gunman that he'd told her was a character from one of his company's recent games.

'Do you write all the games yourself?' Angie remembered asking him.

Steve had smiled. 'Not any more, honey. I used to, but now I have people to do that. But I play every single one to make sure it's good enough, and I keep an eye on every programmer's work.'

Angie clicked on the internet icon. When the browser logo appeared, its letters were interlaced with fat red hearts and cartoon flowers.

'Oh God, 'cause of Valentine's Day. Great!' she said aloud. For a moment she stared blankly at the screen until a tear brimmed in the corner of each of her blue eyes. But she wiped them away harshly, sniffed and selected a game icon from the bottom of the screen.

The title page loaded at once. *A Better World*. The images weren't of guns or aliens or cars, but views of planet Earth from space. Angie was surprised and intrigued. Perhaps this game was going to be a bit more girlie than all the other ones. She clicked on 'New Game' and entered her usual ID, 'Sexychick'.

Angie waited a second for the game to start, but instead of the expected request to select players, or a game level, in the centre of the enormous screen there appeared a face.

It was a white man in a crisp, open-necked shirt. He had soft, fair hair and a little bit of stubble. Angie thought he looked younger than her parents, but older than twenty. He had a kind smile and his eyes were slightly narrowed because of it.

'If that's a digitally made image, it's a brilliant one,' she said aloud.

'I'm not an image, Angie, I'm real.' The face spoke in a clear, authoritative tone.

Angie pushed the chair back from the screen on its wheels. Her heart started to beat fast. 'How do you know my name?'

'I will explain everything in time, Angie. My name is Galileo and I have travelled the universe looking out for a girl like you for a long time – hundreds, if not thousands of years. The time is now right, and the signs propitious for you to be brought together with the others who have been called.'

'Stay away from me and my computer, you creep.'

Angie rolled her chair back to the desk, dragged the mouse to the X at the top right-hand corner of the screen, clicked and exited the game. She sat back in the chair and let out a long, slow whistle of breath.

To her horror, a moment later the face reappeared in the centre of the screen.

'Wait, Angie. I am not going to hurt you in any way. Just listen to what I have to say – not about you, but about the world. When you have listened, it is your choice how you respond. You can ask me to leave and I will never contact you again. You have my word on that, on the honour of the Creators of my race. There is no deeper or truer promise.'

'I don't trust you,' Angie said quietly.

'Of course you don't. How can you? But listen and then decide. Before I say anything else, I want you to go and get your phone, and have your dad's number ready to dial. If at any point you feel worried, you can call him right away.'

Angie stared into the lovely face. It was kind and gentle.

She got up from the chair slowly, and without taking her eyes off the screen she backed into the living room to retrieve her phone. She selected her dad's number, then placed the phone down by the keyboard and sat.

'Thank you, Angie. This is a kind of story, but it's a true one. To begin, I'll ask you a question. Have you ever felt disappointed with the world? And with the people in it?'

Angie paused before she answered. 'Er, yes, I suppose so,' she said quietly, her hand on her phone.

Galileo continued. 'Many, many children across the world – and some enlightened adults – are dissatisfied with the way the world is. They feel limited, held back somehow, and although they have genuine intentions to have a happy family or do good in the world, something always stops them. Do you ever feel like that?'

'Go on...' Angie said cautiously.

'Some people believe they are only limited by their own negative thoughts, as if a person is always their own worst enemy. But, Angie, the real truth is that there are far worse enemies and dangers present on this planet, threatening not just the human race, but the rest of the universe.'

Angie's eyes were as wide as pools now.

'But another truth is that if a few are brave enough to act as warriors against the present enemies and dangers, there is nothing to stop the human race reaching for the stars and bringing about a time when people will be judged not by what they have, but by their good actions. I have been sent by the Creators of my race to find six brave young people who can be those warriors. The Creators are the lords of our part of the universe, and they have powers of sight which are far beyond those of myself or my people.'

Galileo paused and leaned forward a little further, so that it seemed as though his face would almost touch Angie's own. 'Will you be one of those brave young people?'

Chapter 3

Sasha poked the lazy, fat fish in the river pool with a stick. He had done this a thousand, thousand times in his fourteen years of life. He was careful, slow and gentle so that the fat fish wouldn't see his shadow or notice a flicker of movement. Since his earliest days in school, Sasha had known that the local city of Cuiaba was named after the ancient tribes that had lived here and had fished for fat fish just like this one, shooting quick arrows to kill them in the water.

When he was small, Sasha had played in the river for hours with his two younger brothers, pretending to be Ykuiapá hunters – wild and free. As the eldest, Sasha was always the best hunter, the best warrior and the best fisherman. Here, beside the slow-moving waters of the river tributaries that flowed through his father's farmlands, he had learned to love the red earth, stubby bushes and the open prairies just as much as he loved the rocky ravines and clear river waters.

Whenever it became too hot and humid in the spring months, Sasha would lie on his back in the cool shade of the trees and stare through the branches at the clear blue of his native Brazilian sky. And whenever school closed for the holidays, Sasha begged his Spanish mother and Brazilian father to allow him to travel with the cowboys as they moved his father's vast herds across the savannah. These were his happiest times, sitting excitedly beside his dad in the front of the jeep, speeding across the landscape to the agreed meeting point where one of the cowboys would be waiting for them. A horse would be prepared for Sasha, and he would be in the saddle before his father had turned off the jeep engine, a cowboy hat on his head and bending forward to whisper into the glossy chestnut ears of the horse that would carry him across hundreds of kilometres of savannah. Sasha loved to tell his friends how you could travel for thirty days on horseback, moving the herds, without ever leaving his father's territory. Many other farmers used vehicles to move their cattle, but Sasha's dad believed that the herds and the ranchers were happier moving at walking pace, trotting under the bowl of the sky, as farmers had done for hundreds of years before them.

There would be days of moving and days of rest when the animals could stop, feed and roll in the red dust. At night Sasha would sit with the guys around the fire and hear tales of their glorious land, tales of fighting with hustlers, tales of women and love and long ago. At dawn the men would get up before daybreak, check the herd, eat a quick meal and saddle up at first light. Sasha could never tire of watching the creamy broad backs of the swaying cattle as they meandered ahead of him to the next farm station, nor tire of watching the ranchers racing along the edges of the herd to keep the animals moving in the right direction, hollering as they went.

He loved the land, the young calves close to their mothers, the sounds, smells and tastes of the great outdoors, and the feeling of closeness to the Earth as the sun moved above them in a great arc from east to west, each day exactly like the last, but no two ever the same. Only the other cowboys understood what that meant.

This evening the ranchers were camped beside a waterfall at a bend in the river where the cattle could come down to drink, and yet where the view was open enough for the guys to see the herds and watch out for any trouble.

'This is an old gold mining pool,' one of the older cowboys murmured in his soft mother tongue.

Sasha waited for more.

'The gold diggers used to pan their piles of earth here, looking for tiny nuggets which would show 'em there might be a gold seam that would make 'em rich. This was never the best gold rush country, but it was still full of gold hunters. D'you know the money from all our gold went to pay for the industrial revolution in Europe?' said the cowboy, then added wistfully, 'There's a different kinda robbery going on here now though…'

'Don't go downbeat on us, Luiz,' another guy joked.

'Nah! It's the truth and you know it,' the older man went on. 'Here we are in the very centre of our continent, the very heart of South America, and we're losing our forests and our resources every day that sun comes up. Just hurts my bones to think of it. I fear there'll be a time when our kids will hate us for what we've gone and done. Our trees, our gold, our minerals – all going west. Makes an old man weep.'

Sasha couldn't help speaking up. 'But things are getting better, aren't they? With the national parks and the government and everything?'

Luiz smiled in the firelight and the worn lines of his face deepened, lines that told the history of sixty-five years of sunburn on brown skin. 'Well, boy, you're the strangest looking rancher I've ever seen, with your big specs and your baggy clothes. Not like your pa, eh?'

The men smiled and some of them laughed kindly.

'Guess you're gonna be a city businessman, not a rancher!'

'I love the land, sir, and I hate being at school 'cause I can't see the prairie from there.'

'Never went to school myself. Where's yours?' Luiz asked.

'Cuiaba. A Catholic school in the city. I have to stay with my aunt all week 'cause it's too far to go home at night. But I love chemistry and photography… and music,' Sasha said enthusiastically.

'You'll never run out of sky and earth to photograph out here.' Luiz smiled. 'What kinda music?'

'Rock. I play in a band – I'm the drummer, but I'm not very good. I think they only let me join the band 'cause I have a drum kit.'

'And where's all that gonna lead? A photographer-chemist who drums?'

The men laughed softly and one patted Sasha on the back.

'I don't know. But I always win the general knowledge quizzes at school.'

'So you'll know you can enter the very centre of the Earth from just near here then, won't you?' Luiz asked.

Sasha leaned forward and hugged his knees, his eyes wide. 'No, sir!'

'True as I'm sitting here,' Luiz went on. 'We're only a few metres from the cavern hole in the sandstone cliffs where the Brazilian natives came and went to the centre of the Earth. It's hollow as an empty nut down there underneath us, sonny.'

'Don't tease the boy, Luiz,' said the rancher beside him.

'This ain't teasing, it's the sober truth. Those ancient tribes knew their ancestors were down there, and they went there at the end of life. Forget all the nonsense about the Earth having a molten centre; it's hollow. That's where the ancestors came from and returned, and where the secret places are. And this ain't mumbo-jumbo – it's a proper scientific theory. Makes me wonder what they teach you in school, Sasha!'

'Where's the cavern hole?' Sasha asked, his dark eyes reflecting the yellow and orange flames that still licked around the red-hot logs.

Luiz paused. 'Round that bend on the right. With this moon you could pretty much see your way there.'

Later, when Sasha turned onto his side on his sleeping mat and pulled the woven wool blanket over him, he knew sleep wouldn't come. The fire had subsided into a glowing mound of ash, and the moon was turning the white backs of the cattle to silver. All around him he could hear the herd breathing, jostling, chewing – and occasionally a cow calling her calf closer.

Sasha rolled onto his other side, and blinked as he thought about all that Luiz had said. A hole at the centre of the Earth. It had to be nonsense, of course; he had seen diagrams in geography about the super-heated outer core of molten lava, and the solid, impenetrable inner core of the Earth. The planet was dense matter all the way through, of course it was. But as the moon shone and made everything ethereal, he began to doubt all that he thought he knew. Perhaps there was a mystery deeper than science or geology could reveal, something the natives had known that had long been forgotten.

He sat up. The men were sleeping around him. Sasha

moved as silently and slowly as if he were spearing fat fish in the river pools at home. He crept noiselessly away from the little camp to the river bluffs formed by the erosion of the water as it had meandered this very same course over thousands of years. He looked back at the men, but no-one was stirring. He walked more quickly now, stepping silently along the bluffs, his way brightly lit by the moon. The bend was very close to the camp, and he didn't feel afraid, his curiosity and sleeplessness leading him on step by step.

Immediately after he rounded the curve of the river he saw the entrance to the cavern of which Luiz had spoken – a low-arched entrance in the red sandstone rock. But Sasha gasped when he saw that he wasn't the only one there – one of the men was standing in the entrance. He ducked down behind a bush and tried to make out which of the cowboys had beaten him to it, but he didn't recognise the figure in the cavern entrance. It was a Westerner, a white man with the fair hair of a tourist, slim and dressed in a plain white shirt.

Sasha peered gingerly from behind the bush. He knew that in the dark colours he was wearing he wouldn't be too easy to spot, unlike the guy in the white shirt. But he also knew that in this moonlight any sudden movement would give him away.

The man in the entrance to the cavern seemed to be sniffing the air, in the way that a dog does when it's first let out after being cooped up indoors. His head was tilted at an angle and his senses seemed to be fully alert. Then suddenly he called out softly into the chill air. At first Sasha couldn't make out what he was saying, but then the sound reached him through the stillness.

'Don't be afraid.'

Sasha tensed; it felt as though the man were calling to him

personally. Then he froze as he heard the next call.

'I won't hurt you, Sasha.'

He shrank down behind the bush in pure terror. How on earth did this guy know him?

'My name is Galileo and I am part of the old race – an ancient race that has existed for thousands more years than you can imagine.'

Sasha knew he had two options: stay hidden behind the bush and listen, hoping that the guy didn't know exactly where he was hiding, or run for it and be caught. The ranchers weren't far away, and he felt pretty sure they would wake if he yelled, but they wouldn't get there in time to save him from the man called Galileo, so he crouched and listened. He hoped Galileo didn't have a gun or a knife, and that he wasn't a nutter.

'The old race is like your people, but we have evolved far beyond mankind in science, technology and personality. And we're different from you in one very important way. Long ago our race realised that even though we were all individuals, we were connected to each other by intricate, invisible bonds. We came to our senses and realised our race was damaging itself through negativity and greed. We understood that if we worked together, we could achieve so much more than our people had ever dreamed. After that, our progress was super-fast.'

The voice paused and Sasha was aware of the light breeze stirring through the leaves, as well as the sound of the water running below them in the creek.

'Let me ask you a few questions. You love the Earth, don't you, and all its creatures, wonders, expanses and beauties? But why don't all humans feel the same? Why do they destroy the rainforests and send toxic gases into the atmosphere? Humans can be so noble and compassionate, but they can also be the cruellest creatures on the planet. When will you wake up? Will it be before you have made the Earth so broken that it'll never mend?

'You probably know the saying "There's a light at the end of the tunnel". I was thinking about that as I came up through the darkness of the cavern and saw the moonlight shining in at the entrance. It's a true saying, because despite all the negativity of humans, you have the power to unite and achieve wonderful, beautiful things.

'Young people like you understand this so much better than most adults. You still have the threads of energy and goodness and hope that came with you into the world – and those threads can be joined together to weave a strong and exciting future for the Earth.'

Galileo paused and then began again in a serious, deeper tone. 'Sasha, you are someone very special, and you have a secret title which has been yours since the day you were born.'

Sasha's eyes were wide in the moonlight. Despite his fear, every word was sinking into his mind and taking root.

'You are a WPD, Sasha – a World Planetary Defender. One of six young warriors who have been chosen by the old race to fight against the present evil. And not only that, you are chosen to be the greatest of all WPDs on Earth.'

Through the branches in front of his face, Sasha could see that Galileo was now walking towards him, slowly but surely.

'I need you to step towards me now, Sasha, because then I can show you the truth of what I am saying, and prove that you are specially chosen.'

Galileo stood still again. Sasha knew this was a moment

when he had to choose: either stay fixed in fear or step forward and take his chance. The ranchers would hear him if he yelled, and would come running to help him. After all, they worked for his dad and were responsible for taking care of him. So, very, very cautiously, he got up from his inadequate hiding place. A twig fell from his hair onto the dusty ground.

Galileo was holding out his hand in the moonlight. 'All you need to do is touch my hand, with just the tip of your fingers, and you will understand.'

Sasha took one tentative step and then another. He realised now that Galileo was far taller than he had first thought. He was holding out his hand, palm uppermost. If he had a weapon, Sasha didn't know where he could be hiding it beneath the white shirt and slim-fitting trousers. He took the final step and lifted his right hand to touch Galileo's fingertips.

Immediately an almighty jolt of energy shot through him, starting from his hand and shooting through his body, like a bolt of lightning in a storm. As the power increased, Sasha saw a bright light, and then a flash of an image that was gone before he had a chance to identify it. He thought it had been a face, but he wasn't sure.

The after-effect of the power surge was strange. Sasha felt warm and confident and courageous.

'What are you feeling?' Galileo asked him kindly.

'Erm, not afraid any more... Warm... Funny,' Sasha said.

'Come and sit by the water for a while. You will be able to understand me better for the next few moments,' Galileo said, and he led Sasha to a flat red rock above the creek.

Sasha sat down. He was aware that he was smiling

broadly. He looked across the waters at the silvery backs of the herd in the moonlight and he felt tears well up inside him. But he didn't feel sad. In fact, he felt exactly the opposite.

'They're beautiful, aren't they?' Galileo asked.

Sasha nodded and wiped his face with the back of his hand.

'And you're seeing them and the landscape with new eyes. It's compassion, Sasha, for the beauty around you. My people have that compassion. We're filled with it, and we've discovered that the more of it we have, the more love comes back to us. Science and technology are marvellous things that improve our lives, but it's only since my people have been at one with each other that we've become true conquerors. The warmth that you feel now will fade, but will never leave you.

'This is what will happen next. I have already met with Angie. She is a WPD just like you, and there are four others who don't yet know their real purpose. I will go to them now, and then you will travel to meet each other. It's time for you all to discover your dormant powers! Your journey will be the most exciting of the six, and will involve a ride, but far more exciting than any you've known.

'And if you need me, I am always available. Whenever you touch the fingertips of both hands together and say my name, I will be there for you. Remember that.'

Sasha hadn't been able to tear his eyes away from the moonlit land, and when he was finally able to turn his head towards Galileo, he was shocked to find himself alone on the rock. He stood up and looked all around him, but no-one was there.

In panic, he touched his fingertips together. At once he

noticed a smooth white pebble on the rock where Galileo had been sitting a moment earlier.

Sasha picked it up and put it in his pocket.

Chapter 4

'If you want me to go to this place you call *Celestxia* without using one of my father's jets then you can get me there first class. I'll only fly Emirates, and I need a cabin suite with the full TV, games and entertainment options. So that means I'll only fly on the A380.'

Although Galileo was a full head taller than the twelve-year-old Jamal, he stepped back with an almost fearful look in his eyes and let out his breath in a slow whistle.

The boy standing in front of him was short for his age and a little on the tubby side, with olive skin. He wore Western-style jeans and a designer T-shirt but with a traditional headdress of red-and-white-checked ghutra, fixed in place with a black band.

Jamal continued, 'And I need to know more about who I'll be meeting, and the arrangements for me when I arrive.'

'Anything else?' Galileo said with smiling sarcasm.

'Plenty, but that's all for now.'

Galileo turned to look across the lobby of Jamal's home in Dubai. The floor was polished marble, with pillars to the right and left supporting a ceiling so high that there were two levels of balconies overhanging between them. One outside wall was made entirely of glass, and through it the Dubai sky looked a deep royal blue. The door to the gardens was shaped like a temple arch and was decorated in rich golds and yellows. Galileo knew that although this was the place Jamal called home, he had an even bigger house in Mumbai near the head office of his father's property development business, as well as a seafront apartment near the Jebel Ali racecourse, and a country home in India. Although not yet a teenager, Jamal owned several racehorses, and had already learned to drive off-road.

When Galileo had opened up Jamal's profile on the World Planetary Defender database before making his first appearance to him, he'd thought the boy's credentials were unpromising.

Jamal is an only child. Father is Indian-born, mother a member of the UAE royal family. A highly intelligent boy, obsessed with horse racing and Formula One. The seven homes owned by the family are staffed by a total of one hundred and nineteen employees, and transport is well catered for by a fleet of vehicles and private jets. Jamal is privately educated, cynical and is dismissive of females, particularly girls his own age.

When he had first read this, Galileo couldn't understand why Jamal was scoring so highly on the Creators' list of initial WPDs. In the end, he knew he would have to accept that they knew best and give the boy a chance.

'This has to get better,' Galileo whispered under his breath.

'Don't mutter,' Jamal scorned, 'and tell me more about Celestxia.'

Galileo paused, biting his tongue before beginning. 'I think I will begin by telling you a story…'

'I drive a jeep and I have my own servants. I am too old

to hear a story,' Jamal interrupted.

But Galileo continued as if he hadn't heard him. 'Once upon a time there was an enormous planet on which lived a race of people so intelligent they made human beings seem like chimpanzees. On that planet, this house of yours would be considered a hovel, and every pupil in every school was fifty times more knowledgeable than the greatest human genius who's ever lived.'

Jamal got his phone out of his pocket and began to play a game.

Galileo appeared not to have noticed. 'But while the people on the enormous planet lived and invented and evolved, all the time a massive asteroid six hundred kilometres wide was heading for the centre of their world at colossal speed. From the moment its course was discovered and plotted, every single scientist, inventor and leader turned to work on the problem, trying to find a way to avert disaster. They knew if it hit, the force would be the same as their planet being hit by a million megaton bomb, and all life would be destroyed.

'Even worse, their destruction would affect life throughout the universe, because more knowledge was stored up in the minds and memory boards of this planet than anywhere else. Its people had discovered solutions for environmental problems and cures for fatal diseases, and they had enough natural resources to save thousands of smaller worlds.

'And the planet was home to a species that was unique in the created universe, a race called Space Glowbabies, or sometimes Solar Glowbabies, but they are more often known as Glowbabies. Every one of them was different to the other, a race of highly developed, affectionate creatures, all less than a metre high. They were far more advanced than humans, but very fun loving, and their greatest desire was to see humans develop into all that they can become. When the planet was heading for destruction, the Glowbabies believed that there was a race of creatures out in the universe with the potential to develop the powers and abilities to save the universe and bring about good. They insisted these creatures were called Earthlings. So, in a very real sense, I am here with you now because of the Glowbabies. They are highly intelligent life forms from other parts of the galaxy where evil has already been eradicated. Without the presence of evil, these creatures developed a child-like innocence, a quality almost unique in the known universe.

'On Aurea, the scientists tried to divert the course of the asteroid, but nothing could stop it. So they tried to move their own planet out of the way, by developing a molecular shift program, but in the end they had to admit defeat. In order to preserve as much as possible, they began to build a miniature replica of their planet in a safer part of the galaxy. They named that replica Celestxia.'

Jamal looked up from his game and appeared to be listening.

'Celestxia was only small, and it housed the very best of the home planet's inventions and technologies but only had room for a handful of the planet's people. So the Creators chose to send only those who would be able to pass their knowledge on to the universe.

'Meanwhile, plans were made to divide up the rest of the race and send them to new homes on other planets... including planet Earth. Finally a secret entry route was constructed from each of those planets to Celestxia, a route that would be known only to the Creators and to their messengers. Because of Celestxia, everything and everybody from the mother planet would remain connected until a new planet might be discovered that was large enough for them all to reunite in the future.'

Galileo paused. After a moment he said, 'Do you want to know how you fit into this story, Jamal?'

Jamal said, 'Tell me more about the Glowbabies. I want to meet a Glowbaby.'

'All in good time. On Earth, a few special humans were chosen to travel to Celestxia where they would learn the knowledge and the ways of the mother planet. For reasons that we don't need to understand, you are one of those chosen to enter Celestxia from Earth, Jamal.

'So you see, this is a true story, and you have a starring role in it. Along with the other young people who have been chosen, you will be travelling to Celestxia, and your journey will be the first part of your education.

'But I have two warnings for you: first, that you must watch out for the evil one whose aim is to destroy the World Planetary Defenders, and second, to remember that you will never receive more than you give. If you give much, you will receive much, but give only a little and all will be taken away from you.'

'At least show me a picture of a Glowbaby so I can decide whether I want to go to this place you're on about,' Jamal ordered.

Galileo held out his hand. 'Pass me your phone.'

'There isn't a picture on my phone, stupid!' Jamal replied.

But Galileo continued to hold out his hand until Jamal handed over his phone. He swiped the screen a couple of times and passed it back. There, in the centre of the screen, Jamal saw an image of a short, rotund creature covered in fur, with sharply intelligent yellow eyes.

'That's Beepee,' Galileo said, 'and he's one of the funniest. They are found in all sizes, shapes and colours.'

'I want him as a pet,' Jamal said determinedly.

A shadow of anger passed across Galileo's face. 'NO Glowbaby will ever be a pet, or belong to anyone. They are proud and amazing creatures.'

'Well, I'm having one, and bringing it back home with me,' Jamal insisted.

* * *

Marduk tuned in three of the screens on the wall of his control room in Beijing. It took a few moments before he got clear pictures from all three. Then he sat on the swivel chair in front of the screens and put his left hand up to his chin in concentration.

He had been gleaning information on the young recruits from every possible source, by fair means and foul, and used his communication devices to track their every move. In the past there had been other young people he'd suspected were WPD candidates, identifiable by their above-average energy levels. But these final six had stood out a mile, their molecular energy levels way higher than those of any humans he'd ever seen.

He now saw Angie in the middle of a class at her music college. She was leaning back in her chair, tapping into her phone, and the teacher appeared to be losing her patience. Marduk turned up the sound.

'Angie, this is a performing arts class, not a kindergarten! I will confiscate your phone unless you stop texting.'

'Will you, miss?' Angie replied without looking up. 'I think my stepdad will have something to say about that.'

The teacher ran her hands through her long, straight hair

and pressed her fingers to her forehead in despair.

Marduk turned his attention to the second screen to see Sasha editing a set of photographs he had taken on the recent ranching trip. He was hunched over his computer keyboard in the sitting room at home on the farm, and was trying to ignore the calls and pokes of his younger brothers who wanted him to join in a game of football outdoors.

On screen three, Marduk saw Jamal at the Jebel Ali racecourse. One of Jamal's horses was winning, and two of his father's horses weren't far behind. A light breeze was lifting the edges of his traditional red and white ghutra headdress, and his eyes were hidden behind a pair of gold-rimmed sunglasses.

Marduk sat back in his chair and closed his eyes for a moment. He had already managed to discover the travel plans for getting Jamal to Celestxia from the flight confirmation in Jamal's email inbox. First class to Florida via London Heathrow.

He also suspected he'd guessed the method of transport that was being planned for Sasha. A new horse had appeared at the family ranch in Cuiaba, a stunning Mangalarga Marchador stallion, larger than any of Sasha's father's horses. It was far too big to be saddled up for Sasha, but Marduk knew that would be resolved in an instant if G chose to use it as Sasha's mount. The Mangalarga Marchadors were famed for their classic beauty, intelligence and excellent nature, and the new one in the stable was a stunning, rare Palomino colour, with a gold coat and pure white mane and tail.

But what confirmed to Marduk that the horse must have come from Celestxia was that not one of the many ranchers and grooms who went in and out of the stables and paddocks every day could see it. In fact no-one seemed to be able to see the new horse except Sasha. And it responded only to him. When Sasha went to the paddock, the horse trotted right up to him and let him nuzzle it. The ranchers seemed to think Sasha was going mad when he asked them about the new Palomino stallion. They clearly didn't know what he was talking about.

Now Marduk was monitoring Angie's time online to find out how she may be transported to Celestxia – he suspected G would contact her again in the same way as he had introduced himself, via the online game in her stepdad's office.

If he was honest, the entire concept of Celestxia was driving Marduk mad. He had tried every possible way to gain entry, but the Creators' security systems were impenetrable. He knew that there was an access route to Celestxia somewhere on Earth, and he knew that watching and following the WPDs was the best way of getting there himself. He also suspected that there were other WPDs not yet known to him.

'At least my transmitters are safe if Angie, Jamal and Sasha are the ones up against me.' He laughed sinisterly to himself, staring at the screens once again. Angie was still in class, picking at a loose thread on her right trainer, Sasha was now outside with his brothers in the Brazilian sunshine and Jamal was kicking the front of the royal box as his horse came in second.

* * *

Mitchi Wang was taking apart the digital radio that her brother had brought home from school. She wasn't exactly sure where it had come from, or whether it was stolen, but she certainly wasn't going to ask any questions in case someone took it away before she had examined its electronic insides.

Her mother worked at the state electronics company in the city and cycled there each day from their cramped family home in the suburbs. Ever since she first learned to talk, Mitchi had been asking her mum about what was made in the factory. She could recite the product catalogue by heart, and knew the purpose and specification of every item – the pin headers, reel cables, wire harnesses, D-Sub and centronics. She had taken apart radios and TVs, phones, microwave ovens and circuit boards, using her tiny screwdrivers and miniature tweezers. All her friends and relations knew that if they had a broken electronic item, Mitchi would want to take it to pieces, to learn what ran through its wire veins and what microchip powered it like a tiny electronic heart. As she sat cross-legged on the living room floor, every movement of her fingers was as careful and precise as any made by a surgeon in an operating theatre.

There were many things that thirteen-year-old Mitchi had never seen – the sea, a film at the cinema and the inside of an aeroplane, for example – but she had examined the tiniest workings of a circuit board, and that supplied her with as much joy as she ever longed for.

She knew her parents were poor, and that her mother couldn't afford medical treatment for their father who'd been sick now for many years. There was never enough money for food or rent or clothes, and her mother was waiting for the day when she and her brother were old enough to finish school and start work. Everyone knew that Mitchi was very, very clever. Clever enough to go to college and university, even to study for a doctorate, but that couldn't happen because she must go out to work and earn money as soon as she could.

Some of the girls at school laughed at Mitchi because her clothes were so old-fashioned, and they called her Grandmother Mitchi or Antique Doll. While her friends wore jeans and trainers, Mitchi went to school in the straight, plain ankle-length dresses that her mother made for her on the sewing machine, with lapped openings from her neck to her right underarm, and simple mandarin collars. Her mother called them her qipaos, even though Mitchi knew that most Chinese qipaos were made of beautiful coloured silk and were richly embroidered, while her own were made from hard-wearing dark-green linen.

She was thankful for the slits at each side of the straight skirt, so that she could cross her knees and bend over the electronic surgery she deftly performed every night after the chores were done.

This evening her mother was checking to see whether the lunch box in Mitchi's school bag was empty when she came across a piece of work the class had been doing in Ancient Mandarin class. The instruction at the top of the sheet was, *Describe Mitchi as a person, and explain why you like her.*

Underneath, another pupil had written in wobbly Ancient Mandarin script, *Mitchi is very clever and kind and thoughtful. She always listens when I have a problem, and she is very helpful. I think Mitchi is shy but she can be fierce when somebody is cruel or unfair. I hope she will be a famous scientist one day when she is older.*

Her mother raised her head from the piece of school paper and looked at Mitchi hunched over the dismantled digital radio in the corner of the room, utterly absorbed and completely at peace.

* * *

Marduk retuned the monitors. He switched the first to the buried camera that never slept. It was focused permanently on Transmitter 001 (Sub-Antarctic). In the natural cavern deep beneath the Antarctic ice cap, the transmitter pulsed out its evil purpose. As long as it did so, Marduk knew the people of Earth could never reach their true potential. For over two thousand years its unseen signal had ensured that the noble purposes of mankind were polluted by greed and selfishness.

He retuned the next monitor. Transmitter 002 (Xi'an) worried him. In Earth date 1974, three clumsy farmers had stumbled upon bits of pottery while they were digging for a well in Xi'an, China. Marduk had hoped they would keep quiet about their find, but before long hordes of archaeologists had swarmed to the site and started digging around and nosing into his two-thousand-year-old tunnels. When they began to dig up the warriors that they called the Terracotta Army, the experts believed the figures were guarding the tomb of Emperor Qin Shi Huang Di, but of course that was exactly what Marduk wanted them to think. That was the decoy to stop them understanding that the army were actually protecting his transmitter.

He switched to another camera. The diggers were now within seventy-five metres of his transmitter. When they got to within fifty metres the fun would start. Each of the warriors within that zone was radioactive and loaded with chemicals that were fatal to mankind. It was vital that they protected Transmitter 002 because its work was proving to be so successful. Recently its invisible signal had achieved more than Marduk had hoped or dreamed. He had programmed it to make the people of Earth careless of their planet and its resources.

For the first few hundred years he had wondered whether the signal was actually working at all. But then, many centuries later, mankind had discovered the power of fossil fuel and started to build steam engines, factories and motorcars. Marduk had watched with delight as all the good intentions of the inventors had turned to dust. He watched tons of carbon emissions stream into the planet's atmosphere, and knew that Earth was being slowly choked to death.

It particularly amused him to see that the greed caused by Transmitter 001 (Sub-Antarctic) was helping to make the work of Transmitter 002 even more effective. He noticed that the faster people were travelling and manufacturing, the more money they wanted, and the more forests and resources they needed to gobble up. It was all very satisfying.

And then of course there was his favourite – Transmitter 003. He fine-tuned the third monitor to check that his finest creation was doing its job.

* * *

The surf curled and rolled along the expanse of beach in Santa Monica, California. The three strips stretched as far as Lotty's eyes could see: one of sea, one of sand and the thin lip of surf that separated them. Above all three was the arching roof of cloudless American sky, as blue as cornflowers, as blue as her own two eyes.

This was the place Lotty came whenever she was happy, whenever she was excited and whenever she felt as all-out miserable as she did today. Mascara had run in streaks down her face, and she had made it worse by smearing it with the backs of her hands as she sat on the sand, hugging her knees to her chest. The beach was quieter than usual, the winter wind keeping most people away, apart from hardy dog-walkers and a few joggers. A cold breeze lifted her curly strawberry-blonde hair and blew a fine sprinkling of sand across the surface of the beach.

Every few moments Lotty reached inside the pocket of her hoodie and took out her mobile phone. But there was no text. Now the realisation hit home – maybe Scott would never text or call her ever again. But she might have to see him at high school and every day until she was ninety-three without them ever having another conversation, hug or kiss. Maybe he really was dating Alicia from 10th Grade, and worst of all, maybe he had never loved Lotty at all.

Now she understood why there were so many songs about heartbreak and loss and pain. She had lived fourteen contented years in the world, followed by six months of heaven crammed with precious memories – meeting Scott, speaking to him for the first time, biking past his house, seeing him smile at her in the main corridor and finally him asking her out for a date. And now, at only fourteen, she knew any possibility of happiness was over for ever.

Her phone bleeped in her pocket and Lotty's heart leaped, but it was only a text from her best mate saying, *Just seen S in town with A. He's a loser*.

Pain shot through Lotty like an electric charge, and left her with a pulling, dragging ache in the well of her stomach. She scrolled through the screens full of texts that Scott had sent in the past weeks: *Luv you, U make me laugh & u make me happy, I need to c u…* Nothing made sense any more – she couldn't accept that this relationship had ended so suddenly and painfully. Scott had said he was crazy about her – he loved her energy, her sportiness, her sense of humour. He'd said there was no girl in high school who could compare to her.

Lotty couldn't face going home to her mum, dad and younger sister. They had teased her mercilessly about being smitten and 'soft in the head' over Scott. Now she couldn't face their taunts or their sympathy. She got up from the sand and began to run, fast, furiously into the wind. And she carried on running.

Her mind went back to the day before. Now she thought about it, Scott had been texting her much less since last Saturday night. And she had started to be naggy with him, sending a string of texts saying ???? and Where r u? into the silence. But last night the bombshell had fallen.

Lotty had cycled the three blocks to his house, planning to surprise him. She had a bar of chocolate in her pocket for them to share, and she was going to invite him to the movies at the weekend. But after she skidded her bike onto his drive and jumped off, wheels still in motion, she noticed another bicycle leaning against the garage wall. It clearly belonged to a girl because it had cerise pink lettering on the crossbar.

Lotty knocked on the front door. She waited a long while before there was an answer, and it wasn't Scott who came to the door but his younger brother, Jake. He opened the door only a crack and said, 'Sorry, Scott's busy.'

'Can I come in?' Lotty asked.

'Er, no, not really. He asked me to tell you he's busy.'

Scott's mother appeared behind Jake. 'Come right on in, Lotty. I'll fetch Scott for you.' She forced Jake to open the door fully.

'Mom, he'll kill me!' Jake whined.

'Whatever's wrong with letting Lotty come in? Ignore my son,' his mother went on.

Jake looked genuinely uncomfortable. 'Mom, he's up there with... with...' He flicked his head in the direction of the staircase.

'With whom?'

Lotty thought of the bike she had seen and she asked flatly, 'Who is she, Jake? It's okay to tell me.'

His mother took a couple of steps back from the door.

Jake said, 'It's Alicia Meyers from 10th Grade and he'll kill me for telling you, and I'm only doing it 'cause I like you and my brother's stupid.'

Lotty put her hand on the door frame to steady herself.

There was a pause, quickly filled by Jake's mother. 'Well, come right on in, Lotty, and have a cupcake with me in the kitchen.'

'Thank you, but I'll be off now if that's okay. Th-thank you,' Lotty stammered as she walked back towards her bike. She understood what was happening perfectly. If this had been an innocent visit then Scott wouldn't have forced his brother to lie to her, to stop her coming inside the house. On the ride home Lotty stopped every few metres to send a text to Scott. He never answered.

The thoughts were not getting any less painful. Running so feverishly had made her out of breath, and she felt hungry for the first time in twenty-four hours. The bar of chocolate was still in the pocket of her hoodie from the day before, the gift she had planned to share with Scott in his room. She pulled her curly red-blonde hair out of her eyes and took the chocolate out and turned it over so that she could tear the wrapper open. Written clearly across the back of the wrapper in large capital letters she saw the words, DO NOT CRY. YOU ARE VERY MUCH LOVED. YOU ARE COMING TO CELESTXIA.

* * *

As far back as he could remember, Yury had always had a tough life. He had never forgotten the actual moment on the actual day when he'd decided to change the course of his own future. He'd been ten years old, and was standing outside the school gates waiting for his mother to collect him after her shift at the hospital. All the other kids had gone home and the teacher was getting more and more frustrated, saying under her breath, 'I'm not paid to stand here in the freezing cold looking after other people's kids.'

Yury wondered if she thought he couldn't hear. He was imagining himself as a soldier escaping from the enemy. The snow underfoot was flattened into a sheet of hard, white ice. He thought he may have spotted a sniper behind the warehouse across the street.

'I'm going to make a phone call,' the teacher grunted.

Yury followed her automatically, weaving his way towards the main school entrance in a zig-zag motion, checking all the way that enemy fire wasn't trained on him from behind the tall buildings.

The teacher was gone a long time. While he waited outside the main entrance for her to reappear, Yury's thoughts turned away from gun-fighting to his own situation. He was usually the last kid to be collected from school. He often came last in tests, and was almost always the last to be chosen by his classmates for any team games in sports. And even worse, he was the shortest pupil in his school year. Even shorter than the girls.

Yury kicked his foot against the brick pillar beside the main doors. He decided it felt horrible being last. Horrible, unfair and hurtful.

He looked above his head and tried not to cry. There was a butterfly clinging to the sheltered wooden rafters beneath the arch above his head. Its wings were folded shut and Yury wondered whether it was alive or dead. He figured it must be dead, as the temperatures in St Petersburg this winter had regularly dropped to minus twenty degrees. But while he watched, the miracle butterfly spread its wings and revealed brightly coloured markings. Then it closed them again and returned to stillness.

Something about the butterfly touched Yury deep inside. Something about its resilience and toughness that had made it survive through all the bitter cold days of winter. And something about its generosity in opening its wings to show him their beauty.

In the flash of a moment, Yury decided that he was going to be like that butterfly. From that day forward he would choose to be strong and generous, tough but kind.

'I'm going to start coming first instead of last,' he whispered to the butterfly. And he was as good as his word. That very evening he'd asked his mum if he could start staying after school for sports clubs. She had been shocked at his change of heart. 'But you hate sport, Yury, because you say the other kids all pick on you because you're so small.'

He'd started to do his homework and listen in class instead of day-dreaming. At the next maths test he came twenty-sixth out of twenty-nine in his class. At the next history test he came twenty-fourth. The teacher wrote a note on the bottom of his test paper: *Well done – you are making excellent progress*. Yury pinned that piece of paper to his bedroom wall.

Before the end of the year he was picked for the year's soccer team.

And then he started to grow – almost overnight. At first Yury thought he was imagining it, but after only a few weeks his trousers were six centimetres too short, and his sleeves weren't much better. Then he banged his head on a tree branch that he'd always been able to walk underneath.

He never forgot that butterfly. Now, three and a half years after he'd seen it and decided to change his life, he swam for the school, played football in the under-fifteens team, taught the younger boys baseball and always came near the top in tests. And he was the tallest boy in his class. His last school report had made his parents so proud that Mum had stuck it to the fridge with a magnet. *'Despite being so talented at academic subjects and in sport, Yury is one of the most popular boys in the school. He always has time for other pupils who need support or development and he plays an active role in the anti-bullying initiative and our buddy programme.'*

Since he'd grown tall, his mum had started accepting second-hand clothes from his aunt who lived outside the city and whose grown-up sons wore combat gear and baggy workwear. Immediately Yury seemed to have set a fashion trend for the guys at school. They all started wearing similar clothes. Sometimes he smiled to himself in the evenings at home when he remembered how the same boys used to tease him for what he wore and bully him for being so bad at ball games. Now they wanted to be like him *and* be liked by him. That gave him a warm feeling inside, and he wanted to make sure no younger kids in school ever felt as lonely or scared as he'd done when he was younger.

Today when Yury turned up at the Be a Buddy Not a Bully group, he noticed a new boy. He was very short and Yury guessed he must be new as he'd never seen him in the playground or corridors. They were paired up together for an exercise.

The younger boy was quiet and timid. Yury gave him a

high five and said, 'Hey, kid, if you ever have any trouble here, they'll have me to deal with,' and winked.

The boy replied with a shy smile and seemed to want to speak. Yury leaned his head down nearer to the boy's mouth, in case he wanted to say something private.

He whispered into Yury's ear, 'I have a message for you. Galileo says you've proved that the last can become first. You are the last World Planetary Defender to be chosen, but you will become the protector of the six.'

Yury wondered whether the boy was living in his own little fantasy world, but his words affected him deeply and he treasured the message. Before the next class he wrote them down in his school diary. He never saw the boy again.

Chapter 5

Galileo looked around him and smiled. Celestxia was ready for the arrival of the WPDs. Just before he sent the email to the six chosen ones, he spent a moment thinking about each of them.

Angry, lonely Angie in South Africa who couldn't forgive her parents for splitting up. Tough but geeky Sasha who loved the ranch and the open prairies of Brazil – the Creators had specified him as physically strong despite his geeky appearance. Yury was destined to be the protector of the group, but Galileo was still questioning the reason for selecting wealthy Jamal, who seemed to be wholly unsuitable for the mission ahead and would be lost outside his life of privilege in the United Arab Emirates. But Galileo already had a soft spot for Mitchi, whose love of electronics kept her cocooned from the hardships of her life in China. He couldn't understand Lotty's emotional American mind at all.

Galileo read through the email before he sent it, to make sure it was just right.

You are about to begin your training as a WPD. There are many things that will only become clear to you while you are in Celestxia, but it will help to understand the basics before you arrive.

First, don't worry about being away from home. Time in Celestxia is different from time on Earth, and the Creators have arranged that however long you are away, it will be as though no time has passed when you return. Although the work you do here is vital to secure the safe future of mankind, no-one at home will realise that you have been away. There is a lot we will teach you about the reality of time, but that will come later.

Now for the important things:

All humans have special abilities, but centuries of greed and selfishness have squashed and squeezed these wonderful skills. Children have the ability to be mini creators and – given the right practice – their powers can be almost limitless.

When the right children become WPDs and act together, those powers are magnified. You will need all these collective abilities to overcome the one who is trying to destroy human potential on Earth. His powers are stronger than your fledgling abilities, and he can be overcome ONLY when you act as one.

As a team, nothing will hold you back but your imagination and your belief.

The world needs your help. Mankind is destroying its home planet, and you already know about the dangers of deforestation, over-population and global warming. You will learn that our best ally is nature, and that we are all interlinked. When we work together, amazing things start to happen.

This mission will be the first of many as there are future threats coming from outside this planet.

This comes with my love. The Educators and I are excited about meeting you here. Be ready – your journey will begin at a time when you least expect it.

Galileo

Galileo pressed 'send'. Moments later, he received six replies.

Wow – that's so exciting. I hope I can help the other WPDs settle in at Celestxia. I'm happy to do anything to help. Are the other five girls or boys? Yury (St Petersburg).

Hello, Galileo. Thank you for your email. I'm not sure why I have been picked to be a WPD and I am very, very nervous, but I will be able to help if there are any things to do with electronics – and electrics (probably). I'm very glad my mother won't notice I'm away – she would worry a lot. Best regards, Mitchi.

Hi, G. Can't wait. I totally agree with what you say about nature. I love nature. Will I be allowed to take some photos in Celestxia or is this not okay? I totally understand if it's not okay. C U soon, Sasha.

Your comments about greed show you have no head for business. And scientists have proved there is no such thing as global warming. Only coming so I can collect a Glowbaby. Jamal.

Dear dear Galileo, this trip has so come at the right time for me. I just can't stop thinking about Scott and getting away from home. Are there any other girls on the trip? It all sounds really scary and I'm not sure what I can do to help, but I am very sporty and I usually get on with everyone – adults as well as people my own age. I did get a text from Scott but it really broke my heart 'cause he was saying he wants to be friends, but anyway we can chat about this in Celestxia. Tons of love and thanks again, Lotty ☺ ☺

Hi. What clothes should I bring? Is there wi-fi? Anywhere has gotta be better than here right now. Angie.

* * *

Sasha had become deeply fond of the huge Mangalarga Marchador stallion in his father's stables. By now it was completely obvious that no-one else could see the horse, not even his two younger brothers. Every day, before or after school or at the weekends, he groomed, patted and spoke to the horse, and whenever he would allow Sasha, he stood on a box and nuzzled his nose. His desire to ride Unicornio was almost more than he could bear.

He was amazed and fascinated by the horse's rich, gold coat and the contrasting pure white mane and tail. He could tell he was a rare and remarkable animal, and whenever he set eyes on it, the stallion reminded him of a golden unicorn. So he had named it in his native language – Unicornio.

Today the first rays of the rising sun had burst into Sasha's bedroom as always, but unlike other mornings he knew that sleep wouldn't return. Sasha felt a burning desire to see Unicornio, and to ride him for miles across the prairie. So he jumped out of bed, grabbed his specs and pulled on a T-shirt (which he had almost out-grown) and his baggy chinos (which he hadn't grown into yet). As he went through the back door towards the stable yard, he tugged on his leather riding boots. As an afterthought, he went back to the boot room and grabbed a sleeveless puffa jacket (which came down almost to his knees).

On the way to Unicornio's stable, he wondered whether he might be able climb onto the stallion's back, just for a moment. He was so placid and gentle this morning, maybe it would be possible.

As always, the first sight of the horse took Sasha's breath away. He had his body turned away as he nibbled from the hay net on the wall. For a second, Sasha was sure he saw a silver-white horn coming from the front of the horse's head.

He blinked and stepped forward, and the horn was no longer visible. But he had been so sure.

Sasha called, 'Here, here,' softly, as he always did. Unicornio stopped eating and turned to face the boy. Sasha ran his hand along the golden flank and patted the warm, muscular flesh firmly. Then he fetched an upturned wooden box and placed it beside the stallion. What happened next was strange and inexplicable to Sasha. As he reached up to put his hands on Unicornio's back, either the horse became very much smaller, or Sasha became very much bigger. With ease he slipped his right leg over Unicornio's back and sat upright.

The sensation of being on the stallion's back made Sasha's heart flip over in his chest, and he leaned forward and kissed the horse between the golden ears. He had ridden bareback many times of course, and he began to wonder. 'Could I...? Should I...?'

Unicornio's ears pricked up. He began to breathe out and snort noisily in the excited way that horses always did on the ranch when they got the scent of action.

Sasha dearly wished that he had opened the stable door, and wondered whether if he got down and opened it now, Unicornio would let him climb on his back again.

But before he had time to move, Unicornio was backing into the corner of the stable. Suddenly, miraculously, he leaped in a single stride, from a standing position, over the stable door, which was as tall as a man, and bolted through the yard towards the prairie.

Sasha clung on to fistfuls of white mane, clenched the horse's body with his knees and flattened himself forwards along the animal's back.

And Unicornio galloped. He galloped as if he were free for the first time in his life, as if he were racing for the finish line on the Hipódroma da Gávea racecourse in Rio de Janeiro, as if his life depended on it. Everything rushed past Sasha in a whirl, and he thought of nothing but hanging on. He wasn't sure how long the gallop lasted, but his legs were aching, his back was hurting and his hands were sore from gripping the mane.

And then he heard a voice. 'Loosen your hold, Sasha. Put your feet into the cleft space behind my front legs. Sit forward. Loosen your grip.' It was as if Unicornio were speaking to him.

Very, very gingerly, Sasha let go of the mane slightly. Immediately his arms felt better. Then he released the fierce grip of his knees a little. He shifted his legs around until he found the cleft behind the muscle of Unicornio's shoulders and tucked his feet there. His sitting position shifted forwards naturally and he was able to sit upright. He wasn't at all sure how or why this was working, but it seemed to be.

'Now release a little more,' the voice in front of him said.

Sasha felt truly afraid. And then a thought pushed itself in front of the fear. I am doing what I always dreamed of, he thought. I'm riding Unicornio. This feels amazing.

'*ALLA VAMOS!*' he yelled. 'Here we go!'

He released his grip until the touch of his fingers and legs on the stallion was light and gentle. Immediately Unicornio doubled his pace, so that prairie, trees, sky and earth were flying past Sasha almost faster than he could see.

'*Alla vamos!*' he shrieked again in joy and delight.

* * *

However many times Marduk fiddled with the monitors, he couldn't find Sasha. And the Mangalarga Marchador stallion had disappeared from its stable too. He kicked the wall and cursed.

To cheer himself up he tuned into Transmitter 003. He was so proud of this one. It had been a very late addition to his plans, as he'd completed the installation of Transmitter 001 (Sub-Antarctic) and 002 (Xi'an) over two thousand years earlier. But the opportunity for 003 had been too good to miss – Marduk had seized on it as soon as the enthusiasts began planning to build a reproduction of Shakespeare's Globe Theatre in London.

He sat back in his swivel chair in front of the monitors and remembered. With each memory a wider and wider grin spread across his darkly handsome face. He'd always fancied siting a transmitter in London. The English were much too inventive and unpredictable for his liking. With their fierce island pride, and their love of the underdog and the weakling, they had a tendency to be tolerant, and some-times even heroic. He wanted to get a transmitter into the heart of their land to start sending out signals that would replace these undesirable qualities with individualism, ambition and intolerance.

The theatre project was perfect for his needs. The strip of land beside the river had been offered to the project quite quickly, but then the money had run out. It looked as if the theatre would never be built after all. And then the archaeolo-gists had got distracted by a timely discovery of the original Globe Theatre two hundred metres away. Marduk didn't need long. The site on the bank of the Thames was cordoned off and empty while the project team were raising funds to carry on building. It was almost too easy. Marduk let himself in and tunnelled underground beneath the diaphragm wall the builders had already installed to keep the River Thames out.

He needed only a small transmitter this time, to send out the very specific signal required to undermine the people of England. Where there was ingenuity, it would bring red tape; where there was self-belief, apathy; where there was nobility, pettiness; where there was tolerance, prejudice. And he knew that what happened in England would spread like a disease into Europe and further afield, as so many people in America and Australia and faraway countries still saw this small, cold country as 'home'.

Marduk tuned in the monitor to the view from the Thames of the little round theatre with its quaint flag on top. It looked so small beside the twentieth-century buildings that surrounded it. He smiled to think that beneath the cute reconstruction of the Shakespearean theatre was his hidden secret, sending out its unending signal into London, into England – the land of inventors and poets.

* * *

Ever since Galileo had met her at the electronics store, and ever since she had received his email, Mitchi had been excited but very nervous. She had noticed the blond westerner immediately, standing behind the till in her favourite city store, Everything Electronic. She'd wondered whether he was a visitor, or perhaps a volunteer.

He spoke fluent Mandarin and had been most helpful with her questions. And he'd been so courteous when giving her the booklet at the till entitled *Everything you need to know... from Everything Electronic*. He urged her to read it as soon as she got home, and then crossed his hands and gave her a slight bow. She had been surprised and touched by this, as it was a gesture she would normally make to show her respect for her elders, and not the other way around.

As soon as she got home she had slipped off her outdoor shoes and put them on the rack in the lobby outside the entrance. Then she hurried to her favourite spot on the floor of the main room.

'Is that a new book from school?' her mother called from the kitchen area.

'It's just an electronics catalogue, Mother.'

'Oh, Mitchi, is there anything more you *don't* know about electronics?'

But she'd guessed all along that this booklet would be about something quite different. When she opened it, she found maps of Celestxia and the mother planet, masses of information about the amazing knowledge of Galileo's race, which excited and thrilled her, and facts about the world which made her sad.

One paragraph made her deeply concerned.

It is a disappointing truth that some world leaders are not what they appear to be. You may have wondered why presidents and governments do certain things, and why they seem to tell lies. Part of your mission will be to expose truths and enlighten people. You will need to be very open-minded and have great faith, about whether UFOs are real, about whether badness is sometimes disguised as goodness. You are a WPD and that means that your special qualities of trust and vision have already been recognised.

Mitchi tended to trust people, and she certainly trusted the government and figures of authority. She doubted whether she would ever be able to 'expose truths and enlighten people'.

But she was fascinated by all the detailed explanations about the need for a WPD mission, and about what had happened to Galileo's planet. She wanted to help if she could.

She read the booklet all the way through again carefully and with an open mind. Then she realised how hungry she was. The apartment was strangely quiet.

Stretching her numb legs, she crossed the floor to the archway that led straight into the kitchen. She was startled when she saw that the table had been set for one, with dishes of her favourite foods and a thirst-quenching drink of juice. Beneath the glass was a note. *Eat and drink your fill. It is time to make your journey.*

Mitchi's heart began to beat faster. She paused for a moment with her hand on the back of the chair, then fetched from the lobby her shoes, her coat, and her backpack, into which she tucked a bottle of water. Only then did she sit down to eat.

After she finished, she washed her plate in the sink, and sat down again on the chair to wait.

It didn't take long. In a surreal movement, her chair began to sink down through the floor, as if it were on a hoist. The movement was steady and slow. Mitchi found herself in a pure white room, and it took her eyes a few moments to adjust to the brightness after the normal electric light of home.

After a few seconds, she realised that the walls of the small chamber were not actually white, but clear like glass. The outside space beyond must have been white at first but was now turning into different colours – lavender, mauve, purple, turquoise and the green of new spring leaves.

Her chair stayed still but the outside view, seen through the clear wall, began to move past her at a faster and faster rate. It reminded Mitchi of being on a train at home, but she had no sense of herself moving at all.

Suddenly a small creature appeared at the left-hand wall.

It was standing at floor level and knocking on the glass. Its vivid green fur was being pinned back from its face in the rushing wind of travelling at high speed.

Then it opened a section of wall and stepped into her chamber, smoothing its fur and smiling at Mitchi. 'I'm Teeto – welcome aboard,' it said in perfect Mandarin. 'I am a Glowbaby and I have come to bring you this.'

The strange talking creature passed her a small hand-held device attached to a belt. 'This is your communicator. On it is stored all the information and knowledge gathered by Galileo's race over millions of years. With it you can contact the other WPDs and download data about the rest of the known universe. It contains all the resources you will need in your quest.'

Mitchi nodded her head in a bow, and ran her hand over the device in her lap.

'But how rude of me, that was no proper introduction,' Teeto went on, 'especially as I am the first Glowbaby you've ever met – although you are well known to me, as are all human children. Most children only see us when they are asleep, and they don't seem to remember it. That surprised us until we discovered that our molecules, like most matter in the universe, vibrate much faster than molecules on Earth, and since then we've been trying to get on a wavelength that will allow us to be seen by children, because we love children!'

Mitchi was having trouble keeping up with Teeto's stream of words.

'We love fun, too! But we've noticed that, unlike us, humans get less fun-loving the older they get. That's such a pity. But we still like humans better than absolutely any other race – human children, that is, until they are about fourteen or fifteen… or some even sixteen… or some only nine…'

Mitchi nodded her head again.

'Oh dear, I talk too much, but there is so much to say, and it's all so interesting,' Teeto said, rubbing the spiked-up green fur on his head. 'There are many of us – all different, but all the same.

'Farewell then, and don't be surprised if the other WPDs haven't met a Glowbaby as they will need to change their wavelengths first. But when you need us, you only have to ask for us by name and we will come to you, or if we can't get there ourselves, we will send help.'

Teeto saluted, which looked amusing to Mitchi, with his short, furry arms.

'Teeto, here to help you save your planet,' he said, and with that he let himself out through the same place in the wall. The last image Mitchi had of him was a blur of green fur streaming back from his smiling face.

A strip of running text appeared on the wall in front of her.

You have arrived. Welcome to CelestXia.

Chapter 6

Yury was on the way to the school gym for circuit training. He pushed the swing door in the corridor and walked through. But instead of finding himself in the next section of walkway through the centre of the main building, ahead of him he saw a dark and mysterious multi-coloured passage. He looked back through the swing door, confused and bewildered. Behind him school life was continuing as before. Kids were milling around on their way to class, and a teacher had stopped to pick up a scarf that had been dropped on the floor. Yury looked ahead again.

That's when he noticed the motorbike. A vintage Harley Davidson parked to his right, with a label pinned to the helmet on the seat.

Enjoy the ride. You already know that you can be whatever you want. Positive thoughts are all-powerful.

There were keys in the ignition.

Yury put on the silver and black helmet, which fitted as if it were made for him, and lifted himself onto the seat. Before he even touched the keys, the bike began to move forwards, almost as though he were caught on a wave of air or water, flowing forwards with great force.

After that everything began to happen very fast and felt

utterly dreamlike. Yury wasn't afraid and leaned forwards, turning up the throttle and whooping at the top of his voice as the bike accelerated yet faster.

The tunnel seemed to be like the inside of a kaleidoscope, and after a while Yury noticed other tunnel exits to his left and his right, each with a sign above it: *Brasilia – 15 minutes*; *Galapagos Islands*; *This way to the Strait of Gibraltar*; and *Next stop: Sydney Harbour*. But the bike was now travelling forwards along the main tunnel at even greater speed. It felt almost as if it were being pulled and sucked forward by a giant vacuum cleaner, and Yury knew there could be no turning back.

Without warning, the tunnel began to incline a little and, to his shock, he popped out over a ramp, leaping several metres through the air like a stunt rider. Although he didn't intend it, the rear wheels skidded round towards the front and threw up a flurry of dust – just like in the movies. He was in front of a burger bar. Yury felt a million dollars, and knew all the girls inside were looking at him.

'But I don't think this can be Celestxia,' he said to himself.

* * *

'I have priority check-in,' Jamal insisted. 'Get me the airport manager.'

The steward looked tired and hassled. 'I'm afraid we have a major security incident so all passengers have to proceed through the standard check-in. We're sorry for any inconvenience.'

'You will be sorry – very sorry indeed,' Jamal said in English. 'Do you know who I am?'

'Er, no, but it won't make any difference, sir. Every passenger has to go through standard check-in today.'

'I'm a VIP, a first-class passenger,' Jamal carried on, raising his voice for effect, 'and my mother is a member of the royal family. You will regret this.'

The other passengers just stared at him and then whispered to one another. The steward walked back to his duties and no-one else spoke to him. Jamal got out his mobile phone and began to tap out a text to his father. Then he remembered Galileo's email about this being a secret trip, and – although it sounded unbelievable – that his parents wouldn't notice his absence.

He swore in Hindustani and scrolled to the picture of the purple Glowbaby to remind himself of his reason for going through this inconvenience.

After the problem with check-in, everything about the journey annoyed him. Although he did get priority boarding at the gate, there appeared to have been some kind of mix-up with his booking and he hadn't been allocated a place in first class. Instead, he had a seat in business class between a fat businessman and a woman with a young child. The child had an ear infection and kept screaming about pain in his ears. Every time he squawked, the mother apologised to the fat businessman and tried to quieten the child.

Jamal called the stewardess. 'I need to be moved,' he said.

'I'm sorry, sir. As you can see, this flight is full and there's nothing we can do. As I've already explained, we will be able to offer a free upgrade to first class on your next flight with us because of the problem with your booking today, but for now we can only offer you first-class meals.'

'This is a total disgrace!' Jamal said. 'It's the worst case of bad service I've ever had. The royal family will hear about this. And I've got to put up with this for sixteen hours. You wouldn't expect an animal to put up with these cramped conditions and shocking surroundings.'

The people in the row in front of Jamal started peering between their seats to get a better look at him.

When the plane landed at Orlando International, Jamal was exhausted and very, very cross. People who had been sitting nearby were staring at him as he queued to leave the aircraft.

There was a very long wait for cases to appear in baggage reclaim. Jamal had instructed the housekeeper about all the essentials that were to be packed for his journey: clothes, games, laptops, designer shoes, designer boots and toiletries. They had filled two large cases. His first case came off the carousel quite quickly, but his second didn't appear. Everyone else took their bags and left the building, while Jamal watched a pushchair, a purple holdall and a golf bag going round and round and round forlornly. There was nobody to complain to, and no sight of his designer suitcase.

He was almost at the point of walking away without it when the case finally rolled through the plastic flaps and onto the carousel.

When he emerged from the terminal building into bright sunshine, he had no idea what to do next. All his life Jamal had been surrounded by people who organised his life and made it run smoothly. There were staff to run the home, drivers to take him wherever he wanted and personal secretaries in his father's office who arranged every aspect of travel, purchasing and planning.

He suddenly felt alone for the first time in his life. It was a horrible, empty feeling. He stood at the kerbside and blinked into the sun, not knowing whom to ask, or even what to ask.

Just then there was a tap on his shoulder. Jamal turned his head and saw a taxi driver holding a piece of paper that said, *JAMAL – CELESTXIA*.

'Welcome to America!' the driver said. 'Had a good journey?'

Jamal stared at him – he seemed genuinely happy and friendly.

'No, I did not. It was hell,' he said in English.

'Well, it's over now. Hop in, kiddo.'

Jamal pointed at his two enormous cases on the trolley.

'You won't be needing those, they'll be sent straight back home on the next plane. No personal belongings needed in Celestxia.'

'WHAAAAT?' Jamal shouted. 'I have dragged those cases, waited hours for them to come off the plane, pushed and pulled them, and now you say they're not needed. This whole thing is a JOKE!'

The taxi driver opened his eyes wide and led Jamal to the car.

* * *

Marduk was becoming increasingly anxious. Not only had he lost sight of Sasha and the stallion, but his monitors were no longer picking up Yury or Mitchi.

He'd always known there may be secret routes to Celestxia from Earth, but he'd been certain he would discover at least one of them by tracking the six WPDs on their journeys there.

Now he was focusing all his attention on the remaining two: Angie in South Africa and Lottie in Santa Monica, USA. He knew he was down to his last two chances. Once they were all holed up in Celestxia, he suspected he would have no way of knowing what Galileo was up to.

He selected the monitor showing Lotty's home and turned up the volume.

* * *

Lotty had waited fourteen days after receiving the email from Galileo telling her she would soon begin her journey to Celestxia. He hadn't said the time would be soon, just that it would happen when she least expected it... but the trouble was that Lotty was expecting it *all* the time.

She expected it when she sat down in class, when she was doing her homework, biking to school, getting into bed – every moment. She even dreamed about how it would happen while she was asleep.

After the fourteen long days of waiting, Lotty decided to start the journey herself. She searched for 'Celestxia' on the internet and could find no entries about it. The closest she could find was 'Celestia':

> *Celestia is a 3D astronomy program, used by NASA and ESA as part of their educational and outreach programmes, that allows users to travel through an extensive universe, modelled after reality, at any speed, in any direction and at any time in history. Celestia displays and interacts with objects ranging in scale from small spacecraft to entire galaxies in three dimensions from perspectives that would not be possible from a classic planetarium or other ground-based display.*

It was also the name of a book and a princess doll and a computer game. None of these entries were the least bit helpful. She checked every few days, and on day fifteen she found a new entry on the first page of search hits.

Finding Celestxia. Wherever you start from, you will always need to head due east. Follow the signs for Land of the Morning Sun. Celestxia is close to the ocean but you will not need to cross seas to reach it.

Lotty opened up online world maps. She placed one finger on her home in Santa Monica, California, on the far west coast of North America. With the forefinger of her right hand she traced a line due east across the screen, through Arizona, New Mexico, Texas, Louisiana, Mississippi and Alabama to the eastern coast in Georgia. Even the names of the states excited her. The distance was over two thousand, five hundred miles.

'Phew,' she whistled softly to herself. Next she checked out coach and bus fares and travel times, and composed an email to Galileo.

Hiya.

Please don't think I'm too impatient – which I am – but it's really 'cause I'm so excited. I'm going to catch a Superbus interstate coach out of town tomorrow and head due east 'cause that's where I think Celestxia is.

I'm just sooooo keen to get there and forget all about Scott and school and stuff, and I just wanted to let you know, and also check that it will be the same as if you were arranging the travel. i.e. (or is it e.g. – I'm never sure which one it is) my folks won't notice I've gone.

Is that okay? Oh, and can you promise that my dog Mifty won't notice either, please? Will keep my mobile phone on all the time, obviously! LOL. I reckon the journey to the coast will take me about three days – hope I find it?!

Tons of love, Lotty xxx ☺
PS – Will watch out for the signs.

* * *

Marduk leaned forward in his chair towards the monitor showing Lotty. This was going to be extremely interesting.

* * *

Angie threw her school bag at her dad's car as he pulled away from her mother's apartment.

'You rat! You toe-rag! You scumbag!' she yelled at the departing car. 'You promised!' she cried out, determined that her anger wouldn't turn to tears. Her mum and Steve were away on a conference, and her dad was supposed to be looking after her. But he'd said the principal cellist of the orchestra had pulled out of a concert trip to Capetown and that this was his big break and he simply couldn't turn it down.

'Who's going to look after me then?' she had yelled back.

'I'll arrange somebody. All your things are at Mum's, so I'll drop you there. You're plenty old enough to be on your own in the daytime, and I'll get my sister or someone to pop over at night. It's only three days till Mum gets home anyway.'

'So I'm officially home alone? Abandoned, unwanted… It just about sums up my life!' she shouted back.

'Angie, please! I've never done anything for myself. I never ask for anything.'

'I bet you're going with HER!'

'Don't start…'

'Mum's got Steve and you've got this new hussy from the orchestra but who have I got? Nobody! I hate you, I hate Mum and I wish I was DEAD!'

A look of doubt and worry passed across her father's face. 'I know the last few months have been tough, Angie, but you'll get through it.'

Now she stood on the pavement and watched the taillights of her dad's car disappear out of sight. There was nothing else to do but collect her bag and let herself into the apartment.

Just as she did every time she arrived, she flung her bag on the floor, helped herself to a cola from the giant fridge and went into Steve's study. A screensaver message was flashing on his largest monitor. She slumped into the plush chair and read it.

Welcome, Angie. It's time to play A Better World, and then you will help us create one.

The screensaver disappeared and the game start screen came up. The choices were 'New Game', 'Saved Game' or 'Exit'. She clicked on 'New Game'. Immediately she saw a graphic of a forest, so lifelike that she could actually smell moss and dampness. At the bottom of the screen was the message, *Collect your first jewel*. An arrow pointed to a tree stump near the centre of the screen.

Angie wasn't at all sure what happened next: whether she had reached forwards and entered the graphic forest herself, or whether the monitor had moved towards her and engulfed her. It had all happened in an instant. Either way, she suddenly found herself in the quiet dampness of a shady wood, with the sweet sound of birdsong ringing through the trees.

'Angie,' a voice called from behind her.

She turned to see Galileo. Then she burst into angry tears.

He stepped forwards and hugged her for a long time, until her choking sobs subsided into sniffs, and then he passed her a tissue. 'I know how hard it is, Angie. I know how it feels.'

'I wish I had a brother or sister,' she said, blowing her nose noisily. 'Then it wouldn't seem so bad.'

'But that's not what you wish for most of all, is it?' Galileo asked gently.

'No.' Angie paused and looked up at the tree canopy, where arrows of sunlight pierced between the moving leaves. 'No. What I really want is a true parent.'

'That was hard to say, wasn't it?'

'Yes,' she sniffed. 'And I dunno why. It should be easy to say because my parents are both scumbags, but I want a true parent like in books.'

Galileo waited patiently.

'I want a mum who doesn't leave my dad, I want a dad who isn't weak and pathetic, I want a mum who doesn't go off all the time on business, and a dad who can stand up to me when I'm having a tantrum.'

'Perhaps most of all you need someone to listen to you and help fight your battles.'

'Yeah, that would be a start!' Angie said, and she raised her eyes to Galileo's and met them for the first time. 'Is this my journey to Celestxia?'

'It is. But you'll need to change your shoes,' Galileo said, pointing down at her designer platforms.

'I'm fine in these – I wear heels all the time. I wouldn't be seen dead in anything else.'

'You'll regret that later, but it's up to you, of course.'

Galileo set off down the forest track and Angie followed. At first the path was wide and passable, but they were soon heading deeper into the woods.

After a while Angie asked, 'How much further is it?'

'A long walk, and then a long way further,' Galileo replied. 'How are your feet?'

Angie ignored the question. 'Aren't there any buses or taxis we could catch? Or maybe someone round here could lend us a jeep.'

'A worthwhile destination is only reached by an arduous journey,' Galileo said.

'Ouch! Something just BIT me!' Angie suddenly shrieked. 'A giant gnat or a mosquito or something! Ouch! OUCH!'

Galileo began to search in the undergrowth.

'Don't you care at all about my bite? It might be fatal, and if I die, the people back home will certainly notice THAT!' Angie complained, rubbing her calf with her hands and jumping up and down.

Galileo found what he was looking for and passed her a large heart-shaped leaf. 'We need to bind this around the sting.'

'Well, that's going to look great!' Angie said sarcastically.

'Suit yourself,' Galileo said as he raised his arm to toss away the leaf.

'Okay. I'll try it.'

'We'll need to use a piece of vine stem to bind it,' Galileo said, looking around them into the trees. 'Ah, that'll do the trick.'

He took a penknife from his pocket and walked a few metres to a tree that had a creeper growing around the wide trunk. He returned with a piece of stem a couple of metres in length. Then he knelt on the forest floor and pressed the heart-shaped leaf against Angie's calf, tying it in place with the stem, which he wound around her leg as many times as it would fit, then making a knot to secure the natural bandage.

'Well, let's hope I meet the boy of my dreams now, seeing how I look so totally wonderful,' Angie said with more sarcasm.

'Without the leaf, this bite will begin to burn and itch,

until you scratch the skin into blisters. This is the best way.'

She looked down at Galileo, who was kneeling at her feet on the damp forest floor, checking her bandage. Deep inside Angie there was a faint wish to thank him, but the familiar anger rose up from her belly and kept the wish buried. So instead she said, 'And my feet are KILLING me!'

'Pity we didn't think of that,' Galileo said quietly, and as he stood he held out his hand to lead her on.

Angie paused for a moment and then slipped her smaller hand into his warm, larger palm.

Chapter 7

The Superbus interstate coach pulled out of Broad Street at half past ten. Lotty had been waiting at the coach stop in good time and she had a small backpack for the journey. She was excited and positive about the adventure ahead. Even though this coach was a sleeper, she had paid a very low price for the ticket.

She spent the first couple of hours writing in the new journal she'd bought for the journey, jotting down her thoughts and feelings. She headed a page *Top five hopes*, which she listed as:

That I like the other WPDs and I'm not the only girl.
That I'll forget Scott.
That I can make a difference.
That at least one of the boys is fanciable.
That everyone at home is okay (especially Mifty).

She listened to music on her phone, texted friends, read a celebrity magazine and a sports magazine and then fell asleep with her mass of red curls flopped in front of her eyes.

When she woke it was four a.m. and there was absolute darkness outside the coach. She found it difficult to settle back to sleep and realised she was actually very hungry and thirsty. For the first time, a little bit of fear and doubt crept into her mind, and then a pang of loneliness hit her as she thought of Scott.

The hours until morning passed more slowly than early on Christmas day as a child. Although she couldn't see much in the darkness outside, she tried to imagine the towns, villages and houses that she was passing. It felt strange that everyone out there was in their own bedroom and their own routine, while she was setting out for an experience that she knew absolutely nothing about.

When the dawn came it was surprising and beautiful. At first she thought she noticed a paler hue to the sky, but she wasn't sure. Then undeniable streaks of pale lemon and pale turquoise spread from the east ahead of them.

'Oh, The Land of the Morning Sun!' Lotty said aloud.

After that came a full-on, full-colour sky show. The lemon changed to peach and then strawberry pinks, brightening to orange. After a few minutes the colours faded to plain sky-blue.

'Wow,' Lotty exhaled, and somehow she felt the entire display of utter beauty had been for her alone. She wrote in her journal:

I never really thought about it till today, but nature duzn't have to be so FAB. It seems to be FAB just for the fun of it. I mean dawn duzn't have to be that pretty, and Mifty's fur duzn't need to be that soft, it just IS! I'm glad about that.

A few hours later the coach pulled in at the bus station in Austin, Texas, and Lotty was exhausted. She tried to feel the same sense of excitement and confidence she'd had the day before, but only a shadow of it remained.

She spotted a diner across the street and decided to buy herself an all-day breakfast. Food always cheered her up. As she was waiting to cross the street, a silver limo pulled up. The dark window slid down and she was shocked to see a face smiling at her from inside.

'I'm Galileo,' he said, 'And I'm going to take you the rest of the way, Lotty.'

As her eyes adjusted to the dark interior of the limo from the morning sunshine outside, she saw a table spread with all the things she'd ever dreamed of eating for breakfast: croissants and cookies, pastries, every different fruit, fresh juice and yoghurts.

'How did you know where to find me?' Lotty said with delight as she dropped her backpack on the seat and planted a kiss on Galileo's cheek.

He smiled widely. 'Never mind how. You have proved that you're brave enough and committed enough to begin this journey alone. That will not be forgotten in Celestxia. Now feast. Is everything as you would like?'

Lotty smiled widely to see the spread of delicious food. 'Oh yes, thank you, but...'

'Go on.'

'Would it be possible to have the windows open so that I can see everything while we go along, please?'

Galileo laughed. 'We can do better than that, Lotty,' he said, and immediately the windows changed from smoked dark glass to transparent. 'You will be the first person ever to take the journey to Celestxia by road, and in style. You deserve it.'

* * *

At that precise moment, Lotty disappeared from Marduk's monitor.

He cursed as he had never cursed before, and kicked the

wall, the door frame and then the wall again. 'I will NOT be defeated by this,' he yelled.

Angie was still clearly visible on-screen, making her painfully slow progress through the temperate rainforest of South Africa. Marduk was tracking her every step along a hidden track in the Garden Route between Cape Town and Durban, across the south-facing slopes of the Drakensberg Mountains by the Indian Ocean.

The problem with her sore feet and the insect bite was now being compounded by the heavy moisture and fog that rolled in from the ocean. It amused him greatly that of all the WPDs, the one least likely to cope with the rain and moisture of the forest was Angie, what with her hair extensions, make-up, designer clothes and poor level of fitness.

Marduk wondered how long it was going to take to reach Celestxia the way Galileo was taking her. He had watched Mitchi disappear from China, Yury from Russia, Sasha from Brazil and Lotty from the USA. Their start points were so far apart that he couldn't begin to calculate the location where Celestxia was accessed on Earth.

He'd tried converging the WPDs paths to a probable central point, but that gave so many possible options it didn't help him at all.

Using his communication devices he switched view to focus on Jamal, who was still in the taxi in Florida.

'Take me to World of Splenda!' he was saying.

'I have orders to take you to Celestxia, sorry,' replied the taxi driver.

'Look, I've had the flight from hell, so they can wait for me in Celestxia while I take a detour to enjoy myself. I need to go to Splenda Mountain. Pull in at the gate and get a one-day VIP pass.'

The taxi driver looked over his shoulder with an expression of amazement on his face. 'Okay, kiddo. If that's what you want.'

'I do.'

'But you can get your own ticket.'

Just as Jamal got out of the taxi at the drop-off point for World of Splenda, he disappeared from Marduk's screen.

* * *

Yury climbed off the motorbike and left it where it had come to a stop. He didn't have much choice, and hoped it wouldn't be damaged or stolen. The girls in the burger bar were still looking at him. When he took off the helmet, his short, blond hair looked stylishly ruffled, and with his height and baggy combat gear, he looked distinctly like a young film star. His ice-blue eyes were shining after the exhilarating ride through the kaleidoscope tunnel.

He glanced around. Excited screaming was coming from somewhere nearby, and loud music from a short distance away, and families were streaming along the tarmac paths from every direction. Most of them were carrying World of Splenda merchandise. Yury was far too embarrassed to ask them where he was, but he was certain he hadn't left planet Earth.

Then he noticed a very small dark-haired girl, of Chinese appearance, who was standing beside a wall away from the thronging walkways. He wasn't sure, but he thought she might be crying. She didn't appear to be with anybody. Her clothes were unusual, and Yury thought her outfit was either a very old-fashioned Chinese kind of dress or a very new fashion. He hadn't seen anything like it worn by girls back home. He moved towards her to see if he could help.

'Hi, I'm Yury from Russia. Who are you?' he asked in English.

The small girl lifted her head and fixed her eyes on his jaw. She shook her head slowly.

He thought he would try again in Ukrainian, which he spoke a little. 'Вітаю! Я з Росії. А звідки ти?'

She shook her head more firmly.

So he pointed to his chest and said clearly, 'Yury!' Then he pointed to her and raised his shoulders questioningly.

The girl pointed to herself shyly and in a quiet voice said, 'Mitchi.'

This seemed to be working, and he held out his hand to shake hers in greeting. But the girl immediately took a step back from him. He felt hurt.

Mitchi must have noticed as she raised her eyes to his jaw again and said slowly, 'Yoo-ree?'

'Yes!' he said in English. 'Yury... Mitchi!' and he made a playful bow.

At once Mitchi responded with a small bow made with her upper body. Yury smiled, not sure what to do next. Mitchi looked inside her cotton bag and produced something a little like a mobile phone, but not exactly. She turned the screen towards him and indicated that he should look. There was a world map on the screen. Mitchi scrolled with her thumb and forefinger to zoom in until China was clearly seen. Then she scrolled again and focused in on the province of Sichuan.

'You're from Sichuan, China! I see!' Yury grinned.

Mitchi smiled for the first time.

Yury pointed to himself again. 'Russia!'

Mitchi repeated, 'Rush-ya.'

Yury glanced again at her unusual hand-held device to

see who had manufactured it, and noticed a tiny logo at the bottom right of the casing which read *WPD*. His heart missed a beat.

He gesticulated excitedly. 'Mitchi, Galileo? Celestxia?' Then he pointed at himself again, bursting with excitement this time. 'Yury – WPD! Mitchi – WPD?'

Her face broke into a smile as wide as his own and she nodded enthusiastically.

* * *

All the time that Sasha rode Unicornio, the scenery flashed past so fast that he had no idea where he was. He guessed the journey had taken three or four hours already, and he felt certain they were travelling at several hundred miles an hour. Once or twice he glimpsed an iridescent flash of blue and realised they must be close to the sea, and he assumed Unicornio was racing up through his home continent of South America, and heading into the USA.

He enjoyed every second, and felt exhilarated rather than tired. Without a saddle, the stallion's own joy at the ride transmitted through his body into Sasha's own. He felt that even if he never reached Celestxia, this would be the best experience of his life.

Suddenly the pace slowed, and now Sasha began to be aware of his surroundings. He was in a heavily built-up area, and there was some sort of castle ahead. Just as he focused on this, Unicornio slowed to a halt. Right in front of them was a huge blue sign saying, *World of Splenda Monorail*.

'Wow,' Sasha whistled. 'I've nagged Mum and Dad for years about coming here.'

Unicornio turned his head and whinnied.

Sasha said, 'Okay, friend, I guess that's it. Please let me

see you again, even if I can never ride you.' He had a heavy heart.

It was a long jump down to the ground, and he ran his hand all along the stallion's flank and neck, then laid his cheek against the horse's golden side. Unicornio looked enormous now, and Sasha couldn't imagine how he'd ever been able to mount him.

He looked up at the blue sign and, when he turned round again, Unicornio was nowhere to be seen. But in the exact spot where he had been standing, a great silver limo pulled up and stopped right beside Sasha.

He lifted his specs and rubbed his eyes for a moment. He watched in fascination as the car door opened and a smiling girl with curly red hair bounded out. She was dressed in sports gear and carried a backpack. The limo pulled away immediately and left the girl alone.

'Hiya, I'm Lotty,' she said, holding out her hand.

Sasha turned his head to see whom she was talking to, but no-one else was close by. He wondered with surprise whether she was speaking to him.

The girl giggled and her red curls bobbed. 'G told me to say hello to the first person I met when I got out of the car, and that's you!' She smiled.

Sasha spoke in his best classroom English. 'Hello, my name is Sasha and I come from Cuiaba in Brazil.' He felt shy and short and geeky beside her.

'Great to meet you, Sasha. I'm Lotty from Santa Monica, right here in the US, and I've just had the journey of my life.'

'I also had a wonderful journey.'

'Did you come by limo, too?'

'No, I have ridden on a stallion that I see but no person else sees. I have ridden on the bare back of the horse and the speed was very fast. I have been laughing and shouting for happy feeling.'

Lotty spoke slowly and carefully so Sasha would understand. 'Sounds like a trip of a lifetime! Galileo just gave me breakfast and it was the best I've ever tasted!'

'Excuse me, did you say the name called Galileo?'

'I sure did. I call him G. Do you know him?'

'I have meet Galileo by the river and he tells me about... mission? I do not know how to say.'

'Mission! Hey, Sasha, do you know about Celestxia?'

'Of course. I am Defender!' Sasha beamed.

'Well, that's just so cool! I'm one too, and I've got instructions and two entrance tickets to the World of Splenda. We have to climb aboard the monorail and head towards the burger bar closest to Splenda Mountain. And then we wait for further instructions.'

Sasha laughed out loud. 'We have lucky to be WPD!'

'We have BIG lucky. This is gonna be a blast!' Lotty said, pulling the tickets out of her pocket and linking arms with Sasha.

Chapter 8

Galileo was almost at his wit's end. After four and a half hours trekking with Angie through the South African rain-forest, he messaged the Educators in Celestxia.

> *You will need all your resources with this one. It is only fair to tell you that during this journey I have not noticed any qualities that may be called noble, unselfish or honourable. Will keep you informed as we go on, G.*

'I want to go back. I don't want to be a WPD any more. This isn't funny and I need to go HOME!' Angie burst out.

Her clothes were soaked through to the skin, the attachments of her hair extensions were visible through her blonde hair and every trace of make-up had rubbed off.

Galileo added a PS to his message.

> *To say that her shoes are ruined is something of an under-statement. I am led to believe that they were rather expen-sive.*

Angie stopped walking, and burst into hysterical sobs. 'I'm so unhappy. Life at home is rubbish, but this journey is a nightmare. Just tell me what I have to do to get out of here. I'm begging you, Galileo, begging you… And I've never begged in my whole life.' She sank to her knees and shook uncontrollably through heaving sobs.

For the very first time, Galileo felt a wave of sympathy flow through him for this girl who looked like a little lost child, slumped on the forest floor in the pouring rain.

He said softly, 'If you want a way out, it is so easy, Angie. It couldn't be easier.'

She looked up immediately. 'Where? Where? Show me!'

'I can't show the way; you must find it within yourself.'

Angie began to sob again. 'You know I can't find my way – geography is my worst subject, I've never even done orienteering and I have no map or compass or ANYTHING to help me.'

'But you have a heart,' Galileo said more softly still. 'What is it saying to you?'

'I don't know, I don't know, I don't know,' she cried.

Half a minute passed, a minute, two minutes, and her sobs lessened. Her shoulders stopped heaving, and her breathing returned to normal. Then Angie looked up.

'My heart is telling me that somebody is watching me, watching us,' she said, sniffing.

'Good! That is good, though it may be more accurate than I care to admit. What else?'

'Nothing else. I'm just empty and really, really sad.'

Galileo waited.

'I don't want to be here, and I don't want to be at home and I don't actually want to be anywhere right now. I don't want to exist at all.' Her tears began again, but this time there was no sound of sobbing; the tears flowed noiselessly. 'There is nothing to look forward to… nobody is good… nothing is good…'

'Nothing is good? Nobody?' Galileo asked.

Angie had her head in her hands, shielding her face from

Galileo. Her gaze settled on her bandaged leg. 'But thank you for what you did to my leg. It isn't hurting any more, so that's one good thing,' she said quietly.

'Look up, Angie,' Galileo said.

As she did, she noticed an old wooden door right in front of her eyes. At first it seemed to be only a door, standing there without frame or hinges, but then she saw there were sides of a building. It seemed to be a wooden shed or maybe even an outside loo.

'That wasn't there a minute ago!' she said in surprise.

'You created it. Your thoughts created it.'

'Pardon?'

'What was the feeling in your heart when you thanked me just now?'

Angie looked confused, and pressed one hand to her forehead. 'Erm, I don't know… A sort of small, warm feeling. I can't describe it.'

'Well, that small, warm feeling created this door. You recognised a little bit of goodness, you felt thankful and the door was the result. I think you should walk through it now.'

Angie laughed dryly. 'Into a shed?'

'Just walk through the door.'

She rubbed her face with her grubby fingers, then stood and smoothed her soaking clothes. Glancing back at Galileo, she stepped forward and tried the door. It pushed open immediately – there was no latch.

'What do you see?'

'Darkness.'

'Walk through.'

As Angie stepped into the dark, two things happened. First she heard the noise of people screaming with excitement, and then the door slammed behind her. Frightened that she would get shut in, she pushed on the door to return to Galileo in the rainforest.

But he wasn't there.

And neither was the forest.

Instead Angie saw a burger bar, a wall, a very expensive motorbike and a group of four teenagers. She tried to retreat into the shed, but found that the back wall had moved forward and there was no way she could get back in. In desperation she thumped at the wooden wall, but the space inside was now so small that she lost her balance and fell outwards onto the grass.

'Oh no!' she said in acute embarrassment.

A tall blond guy stepped forwards from the group of teenagers. He looked like a model, a footballer, the lead singer of a boy-band or all three at once.

'No!' Angie whispered to herself. 'My hair! My shoes! My face! I want to go back to the forest... Galileo, help me!'

Yury smiled as he heard the name. He was getting used to this and he spoke in his heavily accented English again. 'I think you may be a WPD. You said, "Galileo".'

For the first time in her life, Angie was unable to look a guy in the face. And yet she had never wanted to as much as she did at that moment. She rummaged in her pocket and found a scrunchy, pulled back the wet rats tails of her hair and hoped the clips of her extensions would now be less obvious.

She glanced at the three other teenagers. One was wearing some weird kind of green tunic and seemed to have stepped out of a film about poverty; one had tanned skin, geeky specs and clothes that didn't fit him; and the other looked like an annoying version of Annie from the musical – but a few years older. She seemed irritatingly cheerful. Angie hoped these weren't the other WPDs.

'Welcome – you must be the fifth WPD!' laughed the red-haired girl, lunging forward and trying to put her arm around Angie.

'Are there any shoe shops around here?' Angie said, turning away.

* * *

Jamal was having a fight with the shop assistant.

The child in front of him in the queue of the World of Splenda had picked up a soft toy that Jamal was sure was a Glowbaby. It had huge eyes and a label tied to one arm which read, *I love children*. The fur was lime green and the face looked highly intelligent.

'I saw it first,' Jamal shouted at the assistant.

'I'm sorry, but this kid was ahead of you,' said the assistant. 'There are plenty of other toys.'

'Not like that one. I'll pay double – triple – just give it to me. Get the manager!'

* * *

Mitchi was pointing at something. Nobody had noticed her. Yury was talking to Sasha about his journey through the kaleidoscope tunnel, Angie was asking passers-by if they had seen a shoe shop as she'd got soaked on the water flume and Lotty was texting on her mobile phone.

Mitchi looked at her communication device then continued to point, wait and point again.

Eventually Lotty looked at her. Above Mitchi's head was a very small sign stuck on the wall. Lotty moved towards it and nodded to Mitchi. In very small letters, the sign read, *WPDs this way* ➤.

'OMG, look what Mitchi's found!' Lotty announced. 'She must have recognised the initials WPD.'

Yury and Sasha rushed over, but Angie continued to speak to the passers-by.

In the direction of the arrow was a narrow gap between the wall and the next building.

'What do you think?' Yury asked the group.

'We go the way,' Sasha said immediately.

'Angie!' Yury called.

The others could see she was saying goodbye to the people she was talking to, and then she called across to them, 'I'm just going to do a bit of shopping.'

Yury walked towards Angie but she immediately turned away from him. They had a short conversation and he returned to the group.

'She won't come with us yet, and says she'll follow on later, now she knows where we're heading.'

'Should we wait for her?' Lotty asked.

Sasha shook his head. 'We must hurry. The mission important. Need us.'

Yury nodded and said, 'She's determined to go shopping. She can follow us,' and he indicated that Sasha should lead the way.

The gap between the wall and building was narrow and nondescript. Ahead of them there appeared to be a dead end, but as Sasha approached he saw a chink of light to the left. He pressed on the wall and it gave way to allow them to walk through. Lotty took Mitchi's hand and squeezed it.

Immediately the sounds of music and screaming in the World of Splenda faded away. The WPDs found themselves in a very small space, on a carpet of lush green grass, the ground sloping away from them as if it they were on the top of a perfectly round hill.

'This isn't what I expected at all,' said Lotty, 'but then I don't know what I *was* expecting. Maybe something high-tech or modern… not this.'

Sasha walked a few paces to his left, then his right, and returned to the group. 'It does go nowhere. Just stop.'

Yury went to check. As soon as he descended from the rounded summit, the grass ahead of him looked paler and faded out, and then vanished. Yury took a few more paces, but his feet became so heavy that he couldn't lift them. He could go no further. 'I guess we just wait for instructions,' he said to the group.

Lotty said, 'Perhaps this is some sort of holding area on the way to Celestxia?'

Mitchi was reading her communication device. Then she nodded urgently to the group, and spoke excitedly in Mandarin.

Yury held out his hand to ask whether he could look at the device. He scrolled the screen but couldn't understand the Chinese characters and raised his shoulders at Mitchi. The group gathered round her.

Mitchi looked crestfallen and frustrated. She pressed both her hands to her temples and tried to communicate what she felt. Then she began to make gestures, pointing first at her head, then at the grassy knoll, then making big movements with her arms as if she were suggesting large structures or mountains.

'It's like charades,' Lotty said.

'What is she-rards?' asked Sasha.

'Oh, this is hopeless!' Lotty giggled. 'How are we ever going to understand each other?'

Mitchi continued to point at her head then at the miniature landscape around them.

'She's telling us to think,' said Yury.

'Think about the grass. Think big?' Lotty suggested.

Sasha was pacing up and down. He seemed to be concentrating hard. After a few moments he stepped forwards. *'Entiendo entiendo'* Then he spoke in English. 'Me understand! We imagine something and it happen here on the grass!'

The others looked at each other in turn and back at Sasha.

'Si, si, si, we imagine, it happen if we think it,' he said urgently. Then he motioned to Mitchi to borrow her device, and immediately he began to jump up and down. *'Si, si, si!'* He laughed.

Mitchi passed the device to Yury, who was surprised to see that the Chinese lettering had been replaced with English. He read aloud to the group.

'"Celestxia is about precision and surprise, in equal measure. Celestxia is not created; it builds itself in response to the imaginations and desires of those who enter. It is in part a scientific park, in part a store-house of all the information in the universe, but all those who come here will have a personal and unique experience of it. This place will give you what you ask of it, but in return Celestxia will ask you to sacrifice a part of yourself, in the mission to save the Earth.

'"You can achieve much more than you believe, and you will achieve things that now seem impossible. This is a place of creation, where your imagination will birth a living world. Celestxia is part of you, and part of everyone."'

Yury looked up. 'This next bit is in capital letters. "DO NOT IMAGINE WHAT YOU WANT, BUT WHAT THE WORLD NEEDS. DO NOT WASTE THIS CREATIVE

ENERGY ON FOOLISHNESS, BUT USE IT SPARINGLY WHILE IT LASTS."'

Mitchi, Lotty and Sasha looked at Yury seriously.

Yury said quietly, 'We need to be careful what we wish for. This is a big responsibility.'

Lotty burst out, 'Angie should have come with us! She could have imagined a shop for her shoes!' Nobody was smiling and the smile faded from Lotty's face. 'Sorry, that was meant to be a joke!'

Mitchi began to speak, very slowly and thoughtfully, in English. 'What world needs.'

Lotty jumped up and down. 'Mitchi that was amazing! You spoke English!'

Mitchi grinned from ear to ear.

Lotty went on. 'We need a list, guys, I think we really need a list.' She pulled her notebook from her backpack and tore out a page. Her pen was large and pink and had a pom-pom on the end.

'Good plan,' Yury said. 'Let's all suggest what we need for the mission. Lotty, you list everything down.'

'Knowledge,' Sasha began.

'Food and drink,' Lotty added.

Mitchi pointed at her communication device.

'Yes!' Lotty squeaked. 'We all need one of those with a translator and they all need to be able to contact each other. Good one, Mitchi.'

'Beds and clothes and showers and stuff,' Yury said.

No-one else had anything to add.

After a moment Lotty said, 'Isn't it weird? We've been told we can imagine anything and we've run out of ideas already. Why is that?'

'Too big. Too much,' Sasha replied.

Lotty nodded. 'You're right. If we were told to imagine just one thing it would be easy.'

'Okay, guys,' Yury said, taking the list Lotty handed to him. 'This is all good. We are here to learn how to save the Earth from itself. We need knowledge, but right now I am so hungry, I think we need to imagine where we are going to stay and sleep and eat. All of that. Shall we sit down on the grass and give it a try?'

'OMG, I've just had a terrible thought,' Lotty said, putting her hand on Sasha's arm. 'What if one of us imagines something bad? We could create an evil that comes into Celestxia and spoils everything. At the moment there's just fresh new grass growing, and it's so peaceful. I don't think I want this much responsibility.'

'We should promise each other that we'll never, ever bring evil here. Our first promise as WPDs, yes?' Yury asked.

Each of them nodded firmly, and one by one they sat down on the ground.

'Okay, guys, imagine a perfect place for us to live in. I guess we should just imagine it in our heads and see what happens.'

Chapter 9

Angie first noticed Jamal in the queue at the cashpoint. She had searched everywhere for a place to buy shoes, make-up and a hairbrush and had failed on every item.

Now, overwhelmed by hunger, she had queued for a burger, only to find that her South African rands were no good to her in the World of Splenda, USA. So she had found a cashpoint and was waiting in turn, still starving, and feeling more depressed about her appearance than she had ever felt.

The teenage boy in front of her was wearing Western designer labels and expensive looking sunglasses, but with the traditional red and white headdress of the Middle East. As he was obviously rich, Angie shrank back, hoping that he wouldn't look at her.

Jamal withdrew his money, turned and knocked into her as he was folding the notes into his pocket.

'Watch out! Don't push!' he said angrily in English.

Angie couldn't help herself. '*You* knocked into *me*, loser!' she said.

'There's only one loser round here, and it isn't me,' he barked back.

'Scumbag,' she said, pushing his arm.

'You've gone too far now,' he said, shoving her in the shoulder.

Angie raised both her arms and rammed into him, letting out some of the frustrated anger she'd been feeling since she'd arrived in the rainforest with Galileo. To her surprise, the boy wasn't very strong.

'Help, help!' he squealed as Angie grappled him to the ground.

'What's this all about? Stop RIGHT NOW!' shouted a security guard. He rushed forward, grabbed Angie's arm and lifted her off the flailing Jamal. 'Where are your parents?'

Jamal and Angie glowered at each other but didn't answer. Jamal stood, brushed himself down with his hands and straightened the collar of his shirt. He picked up his sunglasses from the ground and put them back on.

The guard looked unimpressed. 'Okay, if that's the way you want to play it, you can come with me to the security centre. We'll contact your families and your schools and make sure you never get into one of our resorts again.' He began to drag both of them away.

Jamal spoke first. 'Our parents are over by Splenda Mountain. We'll go back to them now, honest.'

The guard stopped walking.

'Sorry, sir,' Angie said. 'We were only messing. We'll go to our Mum and Dad.'

'Good. That's more like it. Any more fighting and I'll have you thrown out the park.'

He let go of their arms and both of them scooted away.

'Don't follow me, loser,' Angie called over her shoulder.

After a while she found the place where she'd last seen the other WPDs, but as Jamal was still on her tail, she carried on walking until she was sure she'd lost him. Then she retraced her steps to the burger bar. The motorbike was gone, but the small sign saying *WPDs this way* ➤ was still on the wall. Angie looked over both shoulders and scurried down the passageway, making sure she wasn't followed.

* * *

Mitchi, Lotty, Yury and Sasha sat in a circle of four on the very top of the round, grassy knoll. Each of their heads was bowed and Lotty was holding Mitchi's hand. No-one was speaking.

Unseen by them, behind Lotty a shoot began to sprout through the earth. It began as a small green point from which two, then four, then eight leaves unfurled. After that the tree grew as fast as the stalk from Jack's bean in the fairytale. Branches appeared, and new foliage opened along each emerging twig. Finally a bird began to sing on the topmost stem.

Lotty looked up as soon as she heard the sound. 'Holy crispy… !' she said loudly.

The others jumped up.

'I was thinking about the birds at home in my garden and feeling a bit homesick – I hadn't actually started imagining at all!' she added.

Mitchi just smiled and smiled.

Sasha walked around and around the trunk, running his hand along the bark in wonder.

Yury put his hand on Sasha's shoulder. 'Okay, guys, we must begin now. Let's think of a place where we can live and work and learn. It will be hard to keep our eyes closed, but that way we won't be distracted by whatever starts to grow.'

Lotty put a hand on her head. 'This is mad, crazy, nuts!' She laughed. 'Do you think four different places will grow, because we'll all be imagining something different? Or one, or what?'

This time the four covered their eyes when they sat down. At first each of them peeped, until they all realised they were doing it.

After a while, Sasha said seriously, 'Okay, no eyes, no looks, just thinks now!'

They bowed their heads. Nothing happened for quite a while, and then the magic started. Just as Lotty's tree shoot had done, something began to emerge from the grassy earth. This time it was four rows of small, square stone objects, quickly pushed up by a very large open square ridge. In the central square hollow the grass remained flat and still. On each ridged row, roof tiles rose up, followed by stone walls complete with windows.

Once the building reached three storeys it stopped rising. Oval pots of herbs and flowers sprang up in front of a door and a spurt of water came through the grass. As it rose higher a circular stone fountain followed. The water never stopped falling.

The sound of it was too exciting for the WPDs to ignore, and they opened their eyes. What they saw took their breath away.

Mitchi tried to stand, but fell back again onto the grass in shock.

'Ohhhhhhh wow!' Lotty whistled.

Her tree now gave shade to the area where the fountain played in front of the wide open doors of a four-sided sandstone building. Through the open doors, a grass courtyard could be clearly seen. Smoke was already rising from one of the chimneys.

'*Alla vamos!*' Sasha shrieked in delight.

'Yee-ha!' shouted Yury. 'Our new home!'

The WPDs could barely contain themselves. They rushed

into the building, exploring each corridor, room and passageway. There was a library full of books, DVDs, computers and a large screen. There were two spacious bedrooms each containing three beds – one room decorated in pale lemon with pastel stripes, cushions and toiletries, the other in black and white. There were showers, two baths, a choice of comfortable sitting rooms with plump chairs and an enormous kitchen where they found a fridge stuffed with food. The six kitchen chairs were set round a large table, and patio doors led out into the courtyard on one side and to the grassy world on the other.

Sasha came screeching into the kitchen from outside yelling, 'Unicornio! Unicornio!' and dragged the others outside, where they found an enormous golden stallion with a creamy white mane and tail, tethered to a paddock rail.

Sasha was beside himself with joy. 'This is horse bring me to Celestxia – very fast and faster. My Unicornio.'

Lotty had to wipe away a tear as she watched him nuzzling his face into the horse's golden coat.

A stable annexe had appeared next to the main building with an open horse box filled with fresh straw, a water trough and hay.

Once Sasha was satisfied that Unicornio was okay, the WPDs went back into the kitchen to have something to eat. The sight that met them was a complete shock. Angie was perched on a kitchen chair, cramming her mouth with cookies and juice, and in the kitchen doorway stood a short brown-skinned boy wearing designer gear and a red and white headdress with a pair of designer sunglasses perched on top.

* * *

As soon as she saw Yury, Angie flicked her long blonde hair in front of her face and looked down at the table. 'I tried to shake him off in the World of Splenda, but he must have followed me in. He's a nightmare and he's WPD number six,' she said in her South African drawl.

Yury stepped forwards across the stone floor and held out his hand to Jamal.

'Finally someone who knows how to behave!' Jamal said, holding out his hand and giving Yury's a firm, business-like shake.

'Tell us about yourself. How did you find out you were a WPD?' Yury asked.

Lotty, Sasha and Mitchi gathered shyly around the table. They were all looking at Jamal except Angie, who had her back to him and continued eating cookies steadily.

'Some guy who calls himself Galileo came to my father's house in Dubai and started droning on about how his planet got hit by an asteroid. It was so boring, but…' Jamal tailed off as he thought about the picture of the Glowbaby that had motivated him to come to Celestxia in the first place. He decided not to mention the creature, in case one of the other WPDs got hold of one before he did.

'We meet Galileo also,' Sasha said enthusiastically.

Lotty gushed, 'Yeah, G is like a dad, but he looks much younger – more like an uncle – and he brought me here in a limo and it was a kind of magic one. And it's great to meet you 'cause now you're here everything's ready.'

'So you're from Dubai?' Yury asked Jamal.

'One of my father's homes is there, but we have several,' Jamal replied. 'His family is Indian so we have places in India, beach houses, apartments – I can't even remember them all. My mother is a royal from UAE.'

Angie turned her head and said, 'Oooh, get you!' But no-one else spoke.

Sasha broke the silence. 'We all say who we are maybe? I'm Sasha from Cuiaba in Brazil and my home is a ranch. I love taking photograph and chemistry. And music also. I have two brothers.'

Jamal replied, 'And you're the group geek, obviously. There's always one total nerd in every bunch.'

Lotty looked upset and embarrassed, and butted in. 'Lotty, Santa Monica, USA. I just broke up with my boyfriend back home. It's been a bad time lately, but I'm happy to be here and I want to help G.'

Yury smiled at her. 'I'm Yury from St Petersburg in Russia. I travelled here on the coolest motorbike I've ever seen in my life.'

'Angie. Johannesburg. Having the worst time in my life. And looking the worst.'

'Time to eat!' Lotty grinned, heading for the fridge.

No-one had noticed or mentioned Mitchi who hadn't moved from her position by the large table.

Angie called across the kitchen to Lotty. 'Does this place have a decent bathroom? I need a shower. And can I borrow some make-up?'

'I only wear lip gloss, but you're welcome to that,' Lotty said over her shoulder as she investigated the contents of the enormous fridge.

'Lip gloss! Is that all? No other make-up?'

Lotty replied, 'I guess you could imagine some. We imagined this whole place and it appeared out of the grass.'

'Pardon?' Angie asked in a low voice.

'When we arrived there was nothing here except a sort of grassy round hill, and you couldn't even walk very far 'cause

Yury tried and got stopped. But then we all read something on Mitchi's mobile thingy… OMG, Mitchi! We haven't introduced you to Mitchi!' Lotty covered her mouth with her hands and felt her skin redden.

Immediately Sasha and Yury stepped forward towards the table.

'Mitchi, we're so sorry,' Yury began. 'This is Jamal, and, erm, Jamal, Mitchi is from China but she doesn't speak English, so we have to be extra… thoughtful…'

'*Have* to be?' Jamal said. 'Why? I don't have to be anything.'

Lotty added, 'Which we're totally not being. As you can see. Obv.' She rubbed her neck, which was now very flushed.

It was impossible to read the expression on Mitchi's quiet, still face. Her eyes gave nothing away. She made a small half-bow towards Jamal, and he raised his hand in return.

Angie steered Lotty to one side. 'Tell me more about this imagining thing. How does it work?'

The girls went out through the patio doors as Lotty began to explain what had happened earlier.

Yury pulled up two chairs at the large table and motioned to Mitchi to take a seat. 'You haven't told us about your journey to Celestxia yet,' he said kindly.

Mitchi looked at him blankly.

'Do you think this communication device of yours may have a translator on it?' he asked, and held out his hand palm uppermost.

Mitchi passed it to him. While Yury scrolled through menus and searched for what he wanted, Jamal turned to Sasha. 'I wish to see the rest of the building. Are we expected to sleep here, and if so, where? And are there any other people or… creatures here?'

'Not yet, but my special horse is outside. Come with me and I show you every room,' Sasha said, leading the way out of the kitchen into the main part of the building.

Yury was still scrolling on Mitchi's communicator, and after a moment he burst out, 'I have it!'

Mitchi watched him patiently.

Yury began to type in English, *Tell us about your journey here*. Then he selected the English-to-Mandarin translation option he'd found and pressed 'Go'.

Mitchi's face lit up as she read from the screen. She knew what to do and typed her reply ready for translation.

Yury read aloud in English. '"I came here in a small room that was a little like a train but not exactly. It had clear walls and I watched the outside world flying past me at great speed. Then a creature came to me through the glass and said it was a Glowbaby called Teeto. It was furry and bright green. It gave me this communication device and explained that there are many other Glowbabies like him and they all love children. They will help us save the Earth. When we need their help, we only need to ask and they will come to us."'

'Liar!' came a voice from hallway.

Both Yury and Mitchi turned in shock to see Jamal standing in the doorway. They hadn't realised he was listening.

'She's lying!' he said angrily.

A look of anger crossed Yury's face. 'Why would anyone lie about a thing like this?'

Jamal shrugged his shoulders and crossed the room to the fridge.

Yury said, 'I think you should apologise to Mitchi right now.'

'Think what you like, I apologise to no-one,' Jamal

replied, tugging the ring-pull on a can of cola and taking a deep drink.

At that moment Lotty burst in from the garden. 'I think Angie's going against the spirit of things – she's imagined some sort of beauty spa place and it has appeared in the middle of the grass. She's in there now having stuff done to her. I don't think this is what G had in mind when he told us to create. Didn't his message say something about not wasting the creative energy while it lasts?' She seemed genuinely distressed.

Yury put his arm around her shoulders and led her outside to see what was happening. They hadn't taken many paces before they reached an immense building occupying some of the ground that had faded out into a haze when they first arrived. The two WPDs pushed open glass doors and found themselves in a spa reception. Doors labelled *Treatment Rooms* led off from the lobby. Glass cabinets stood along the walls, lit inside and filled with jars and bottles of products and make-up. Soft, piped music was playing from somewhere within.

'This is bad, a very bad idea,' Yury said slowly, 'but it's too late to stop her now. We need to talk.'

Chapter 10

Mitchi walked out of the kitchen and into the girls' bedroom. There was a Chinese mat in one corner where she sat cross-legged once she had shut the door. Her expression didn't really change, but her shoulders drooped a little.

A few moments later there was a knock at the door.

Mitchi sighed and got up to answer it. At first she thought there was no-one there, but looking down she recognised the bright green fur of Teeto, and saw a second creature, of the same height, but with thick purple fur instead of green. Both Teeto and his companion had huge, sad eyes.

'May we come in?' Teeto said in Mandarin. 'This is Beepee, and he wanted to meet you.'

Mitchi gave a low bow and moved aside to let the Glow-babies in. Then she returned to her mat.

Beepee began, 'It's an honour to meet you, Mitchi, and we are so very sorry to see that the others are being bad already. Children can be bad...'

Teeto interrupted, 'We love children. Glowbabies love children.'

Beepee nodded enthusiastically. 'We do, but we feel hurt when they hurt.'

A small teardrop escaped from the corner of Mitchi's left eye and twinkled on her cheek.

'Don't cry,' Teeto said quickly, 'because then we will cry, and as our eyes are so big we produce buckets of tears and they run down our fur and make our fronts wet.'

Mitchi began to smile and then giggled, but the smile faded quickly. 'I don't fit in. I can't understand what the others are saying and I'm lonely, and the new boy didn't believe I had met you, Teeto.'

'I know. We know. It's all wrong,' the Glowbabies said in perfect unison. 'We have come to comfort you and also to warn the WPDs that you mustn't waste this creative energy while it lasts. You will need this time to imagine what you need later. The Creators want you to imagine all the things you will need in training, all the tools and equipment and facilities. It is an exercise in imagining and creating.'

'But as well as the things you imagine, you will have helpers, trainers,' Teeto said.

Beepee added, 'Educators, Teeto, they are called Educators.'

Teeto jumped up and down. 'They are, and it will be very exciting.'

'Teeto and I think you should go back and tell the others now what we have said. We are too shy to meet them today. Sometimes we have shy days, and this is one. Glowbabies can be shy, or fun, or both.'

Mitchi looked crestfallen. 'They won't believe me, and even if they did, they wouldn't listen. I'm not a lively person or a strong character like Lotty or Yury or Sasha.'

Teeto shuffled closer towards Mitchi and leaned his soft fur against her crossed knees. 'But you are a WPD, a special person, a chosen person, and we love everything about you! You were picked because of all your individual qualities. It wouldn't do if all the WPDs were the same now, would it?'

Teeto said, leaning forward so that his huge eyes looked right into Mitchi's own.

Mitchi paused for a moment, then said, 'Yes, you are right,' and stood up. She gave a small bow to the Glowbabies and they made an attempt to bow back, but their short height and round bellies made the movement comical rather than respectful, and Mitchi couldn't help grinning.

Teeto spoke again. 'Before we leave you, we have something to ask. We need you to sign our immigration papers.' As he said this he reached down into a pocket in his fur, which Mitchi thought must be something like a kangaroo pouch. He produced some crumpled formal papers and flattened them out on the ground in front of her.

Mitchi kneeled down again on her cushion and examined the papers respectfully.

Teeto went on. 'The fact is, we can't stay on Earth for long unless someone signs these papers, and that's a law of the universe.'

Mitchi asked, 'What do the papers say?'

'That unless you agree to look after us, we may never return to Earth. And agree to love us too. Which is a lot to ask, and a little bit embarrassing as we've not long met and we don't know you yet. But that's the way the universe decreed it, and so we hope you might feel able to sign.'

Teeto looked at Beepee and then back at Mitchi and his eyes were even bigger and sadder than before.

Mitchi looked into his eyes and said very seriously, 'But of course I will sign. Do you have a pen?'

'You don't need a pen!' Teeto giggled. 'At least, you couldn't write on this paper with a pen. You use your finger, and that's because with your finger you can only write the truth. Pens can lie – and in our experience they nearly always do – so we think you should never try to write anything important with a pen.'

Mitchi didn't hesitate and showed no surprise, but leaned forward from her sitting position and smoothed the paper with her left hand. For a second she hovered over the parchment with the index finger of her right hand and then she pressed it down, forming her name with a swirling movement. As she completed the final 'i', the signature suddenly became visible in gold. A second later the paper swirled into the air, rotating and spiralling towards the ceiling, and then vanished.

Teeto and Beepee jumped up and down, their long fur shaking as they bounced and shimmering as though it were made of optical fibres.

'You did it!' Teeto shouted. 'Now you will be able to see me whenever you need my help, until you stop caring for me. I hope that won't be for at least a million years! This bond will keep our molecules energised, and make us even stronger. Thank you, dear Mitchi. The papers have gone back to the legal department to be filed. I'm adopted by you, it's official!'

Mitchi bowed again and said, 'It is an honour, and I will never forget you.'

The Glowbabies waved enthusiastically as she left the room.

Mitchi walked back to the kitchen slowly. All of the WPDs were around the table except Angie.

Yury looked up at once when Mitchi approached. 'Oh, there you are. I was worried about you.'

Mitchi pulled up a chair and began to type into her communicator in Mandarin. After she had selected the function to translate into English, she passed it to Yury, who read it aloud to the others.

'"I have just been in our bedroom and two Glowbabies came to visit me, one purple and one green. Their names are Beepee and Teeto. They seemed to think it was important I came back and told you what they have said to me. We must not waste this creative energy while it lasts and we must imagine what we need for later, especially the things we may need in training. They suggested we imagine tools and equipment and facilities. We will have trainers to teach us and they are called Educators. This is what they told me."'

'She's a liar!' Jamal burst out. 'Of course she hasn't had a visit from some green and purple things that talk. She's just trying to push her own ideas on us because she can't speak English and this is some sort of power trip for her. It's so obvious.'

Lotty, Sasha and Yury stared at Jamal and Lotty's mouth fell open. 'Where did that meanness come from, Jamal?'

Mitchi was typing again and she passed the communicator to Yury who read, '"I guessed you wouldn't believe me."'

Yury spoke up. 'Mitchi seems to me to be one of the most truthful people I've ever met, and I choose to believe her. I don't know what your problem is, Jamal, but you need to stop this nastiness right now.'

Jamal stood up. 'Why can't you all see what she's doing? She hasn't got the strength of character to imagine something cool like Angie's beauty spa, so she's decided to control what happens here by being a sneak and a liar. And she's dreamed up some big-eyed Glowbabies to cover up her plan. It's pathetic.'

Nobody else spoke, but Lotty put her hand on Mitchi's shoulder.

Sasha got up and walked to the door. 'We only arrive and already there is fighting. I go see Unicornio. Animals are kind when human people are not.' He stepped outside.

Still no-one spoke, and after only a matter of seconds Sasha burst back into the room clutching a mobile phone. 'Jamal, you pig liar! You leave your phone in stable and on screen is picture of purple Glowbaby, like Mitchi say!'

As Sasha held out the mobile to Yury, Jamal lunged forward and tried to grab it, but Yury was far stronger and far too tall for him to be able to reach. He angled the phone down to Mitchi so she could see the image.

'Beepee!' she said immediately, beaming from ear to ear.

Jamal was jumping up and down now and hitting Yury on his back. 'Give me my phone! Give it to me NOW!'

Very slowly and deliberately Yury lowered the phone and placed it on the table, and Jamal snatched it up and put it in his pocket.

'You little rat,' Yury said. 'You nasty little rodent.'

'He gave himself away,' Lotty said. 'He said Glowbabies had big eyes, but Mitchi never told us that. She just said the colour of the fur. How do we trust you now, Jamal? We're supposed to be a team of six who help each other to fight problems and stuff in the world, and if we can't trust each other, we're bound to fail.'

At that moment, Angie walked in through the garden doors. Her long blonde hair was curled into shining twists, she was fully made up and she smelled of a summer garden after rain.

'Hi,' she said confidently.

Five startled faces turned towards her, and Jamal let out a slow whistle under his breath.

Mitchi's communicator buzzed. She typed quickly and passed it to Yury.

We must switch on the big TV.

Yury was glad of the distraction. He didn't know whether to feel angry at Angie for the wasted creative energy she had used to produce her personal beauty spa, or whether to sit and drink in how totally attractive she looked.

Sasha switched on the wall-mounted TV and all six WPDs turned to look at the screen.

Galileo appeared in the centre of a white background. He looked focused and stern.

'Welcome to Celestxia, all of you,' he said. He was not smiling.

Immediately Yury, Lotty and Sasha looked down at the ground as though they were embarrassed. Angie flicked her hair away from her face and grinned at the TV and Jamal skulked, fiddling with his mobile phone in his pocket.

Galileo said, 'I think you will know what I mean when I say that we are feeling disappointed in how this mission has begun. There are things you need to understand and accept if you are ever to fulfil the purposes for which you were selected.' All the time that Galileo spoke, Mandarin subtitles ran along the bottom of the screen for Mitchi to follow.

'First, you have been given the gift that Celestxia offers to all when they first come here – to join in the infinite creative possibilities of this place. We have allowed you freedom to use this gift and make your own choices, but some of you have abused that freedom already. However, there is one of you here who has an instinct for creativity, and that one WPD will lead the rest of you to make the right choices. It is up to you to determine who that person is.

'Tomorrow your training will begin. It will consist of three phases, and the first will teach you the physical and intellectual skills you will need to destroy the transmitters that are hurting the Earth and its people. Your Educators will be different in each phase, but you must heed their guidance.

'The film you are about to watch will demonstrate a little of what you are up against in your mission. And remember, you will achieve NOTHING if you do not learn to work together and with a harmony of purpose.'

The image of Galileo faded and a picture of another planet appeared in its place. While background music played, the WPDs watched images of nature and cityscapes that were different from anything they had seen on Earth. All of the people who featured in the film looked young, and certainly no-one seemed older than Galileo. The commentary explained that the film had been made during the last days on Aurea, before the asteroid blew their world apart.

When an image of an Aurean factory appeared, Mitchi leaned forward in fascination. She could see that the developers were using touch technology and robotics beyond anything that had ever been imagined on Earth.

Sasha was amazed by a piece about how crop growing had been perfected so that no genetic modification or chemicals were necessary, as the people of Aurea had worked together to avoid pollution and environmental damage so that optimum growing conditions were achieved naturally.

The next part revealed that Aurea had no monetary system and no governors or politicians, but that the Creators led the people of the planet justly and fairly, and that everything was achieved by teamwork. The more the people of Aurea did for one another, the more everyone prospered.

The children and young people didn't learn in schools, but with adults, because the highest value in their social order was considered to be learning. The phrase *Wisdom, justice and peace* was mentioned several times in the commentary.

A section had been filmed in a hospital. Here wounds were healed instantly with advanced tissue repair serum, and broken limbs and spines and even skulls were repaired by drugs stimulating rapid body regeneration. Lotty cried a little when she saw the before-and-after film of an Aurean embryo with a heart defect who was born perfect after being treated and healed in the womb. The Aureans had overcome ageing and many of them were hundreds of years old.

The next part showed scientists calculating the estimated time until the asteroid would hit Aurea. Images of other possible homes for the population were shown, including planet Earth.

The WPDs watched images of mothers hugging children and grown men weeping as they realised that not everyone on Aurea would be able to be saved in time.

Then Galileo reappeared in the centre of the screen. 'This film can only give you a hint of what the peoples of Aurea have faced. It is one of the greatest tragedies of the known universe that such an advanced and highly developed race had to face destruction. In the end, the cosmos and time overcame them. We hope that you will remember this tragedy when you are tempted to be selfish or when you're feeling afraid.

'Your job as WPDs is to help perpetuate the truths understood even by the youngest child on our mother planet: that nothing is impossible, that we are limited only by our own imagination, and that beauty and truth are achieved when we work together.

'But you have another more urgent mission. You are about to learn a little more about it now.'

Lotty exclaimed, 'Isn't that the Globe Theatre in London?' as a shot of the small, round, half-timbered theatre appeared on screen. It was quickly followed by a shot of the Terracotta Army in China, and then a frozen Antarctic landscape.

A deep voice began a commentary. 'You have just seen that Aurea was a place of beauty, advancement and learning. The accomplishments and achievements of its people evolved over thousands of years until almost every member of the race was gentle and selfless.

'But there is one notable exception. Marduk is one of the oldest living Aureans, and his birth coincided with that of Galileo. Marduk was as bright and fiery as a comet, and he was infinitely creative. But he desired personal power more than he desired the good of all people. The Creators were patient with him and his Educators encouraged his great talents, but over and over again Marduk turned away from them.

'It is a sad fact that although Marduk recognised the potential in human beings, he also saw a chance to control planet Earth and its inhabitants for his own ends. Over the last two thousand years he came to Earth and buried three transmitters that would carry out an evil purpose.

'Within mankind he had seen potential for infinite goodness, and yet seeds for evil and destruction. His transmitters had a simple purpose – to beam out a signal to interfere with any noble enterprise or creativity, so that human endeavours would always be destroyed from within.

'When the asteroid closed in on Aurea, the Creators selected planet Earth to become the gateway into Celestxia, where some of the remaining Aurean people would live and all their knowledge be preserved.

'The decision had been made and Celestxia was brought into being before the Creators discovered Marduk's transmitters. You may wonder why they did not destroy them, but Marduk had made it impossible for them. Not only do the transmitters emit a signal to human beings, but they also emit a type of electro-magnetic field which is impregnable to Aureans and to their technology.

'Only a human can deactivate the transmitters, and only a young person has molecular vibrations fast enough to penetrate the field. That is why the six WPDs had to be human children.'

The film ended rather abruptly.

'OMG,' Lotty said quietly.

Yury was shaking his head. 'I feel so bad about everything we've done since we came here. I honestly don't know why they picked us to be the six WPDs,' he said.

'Is that a dig at me?' Angie said with a laugh, tossing her hair to one side.

Yury replied, 'I think I was meaning myself most of all, but yes, it's a dig at all of us really.'

Lotty asked, 'You know at the beginning of the film G said one of us has the most creative energy and will help us make the right choices? Well, who do you think he meant?'

'I forgot that bit,' Sasha said.

'That's a great place to begin, thank you, Lotty,' Yury said. 'Why don't we all jot down the name of the person we think Galileo meant and see who gets the most votes?'

'Ooh, yes!' Lotty grinned.

Yury began typing the suggestion into Mitchi's translator.

'I think it will be the person who thinks of the thing we need most for training and the mission, the thing we must imagine to be here,' Sasha suggested.

Lotty was already tearing a page out of her journal and ripping it into six strips. She passed the papers round. Even Jamal and Angie seemed quite happy to take part.

'Good job we imagined pens!' Yury said, passing them round.

Yury collected the papers as soon as they were complete and shuffled them. He cleared his throat. 'Shall I look at them?'

'Yes, yes,' the others said all together.

'Okay, we have three names. One vote for Jamal, two for Sasha and three for Mitchi. So that settles it.'

Yury typed the result into Mitchi's communicator while Lotty and Sasha clapped.

Jamal said, 'I think we should do it again and each add a second choice as well as a first.'

'Why?' Lotty said, and sniggered. 'You've already voted for yourself once and you can't put yourself down a second time!'

'Lotty, that's enough,' Yury said quietly.

She coloured up and said, 'Sorry, Yury.'

'Okay, guys, let's get outside to the grassy place and sit down like we did earlier and start imagining what we might need to deactivate the transmitters and save the world. No sweat!'

Angie, Lotty and Sasha burst into a fit of giggles and Mitchi just smiled.

Chapter 11

All six slept deeply in their new beds that night. While they dreamed, a moon shone down on a locked glass building containing a selection of brand new items that they had imagined into being. The silver light lit up electrical and electronic components, wire, storage bags, water bottles, portable knives, lightweight rope, three tents and an array of tools and traditional scouting items, including compasses, flares, hiking boots, backpacks, ice picks and state-of-the-art polar suits. And by each of their bedsides was a communication device to match Mitchi's.

At dawn the next morning, all six devices rang and vibrated simultaneously.

In the girls' room, Lotty jumped out of bed immediately. Mitchi sat up and rubbed her eyes and Angie pulled the duvet right over her head and groaned.

One by one, the WPDs gathered in the kitchen, helping themselves to the juice, cereals, fruit and croissants that had appeared in the fridge overnight.

Not long after they began eating there was a loud, old-fashioned *ding-dong* from the brass bell inside the main door. Sasha ran to answer it.

There, standing in bright sunlight, was a man almost two metres tall, naked to the waist, bronzed, with enviable abs and carrying something that looked like a spear. On his head he wore a circlet of leaves.

'Erm, hello!' Sasha said shyly, stepping aside to let the man in.

'Well, hell-o,' Angie repeated, staring at the naked torso with her eyes wide open.

'Let me introduce myself,' the man began, taking a sweeping bow so that his left hand almost touched the toe of his brown leather sandal. 'I am Leonidas of Rhodes, and although my name may be unfamiliar to you, I am one of the most famous Olympic runners of ancient times.'

All six WPDs stared at Leonidas and Angie's jaw dropped a little lower. Although Mitchi couldn't understand the words he was speaking in English, she recognised from his coronet of leaves that he was an Olympian.

Leonidas went on. 'In 164 BCE, I was champion in three running events, and I went on to do the same in the next three Olympics, so that I had won twelve medals by the age of thirty-six. I mention this to explain why the Creators have asked me to be your Educator in the first part of your training.

'My events were the two hundred metre and four hundred metre sprints, and also the four hundred metre event wearing bronze armour and a shield, which required muscular strength and great endurance. I know much about training and fitness of mind and body, and I will be proud to share this with you.'

Yury stepped forward and shook hands with the man who towered above him. 'What will you be teaching us, sir?' he asked.

'The physical and mental skills you will need to reach your own true potential, and the techniques you will need to disable Marduk's transmitters. We will train on Mount Olympus, and you will learn the true meaning of endurance. You will learn to ride a chariot, endure heat and cold, swim and fight an enemy.'

'How do we get there?' Sasha asked.

'What do we wear?' Angie added.

'How much do we get paid?' Jamal added as an afterthought.

Leonidas threw his head back and laughed. 'Return to your bedrooms now and you will find an outfit laid out on each bed. This is your training suit, and you must change into it now. When you return, I will show you the transport that has been laid on for us.'

Before Leonidas had finished speaking, Lotty was already on her way to the girls' bedroom. Yury signalled to Mitchi by pointing at their clothing and using gestures to show her this was about clothing, and then all six went to change.

The outfits laid out for them were simple and practical. The boys had low-waisted, well-fitted combat trousers with several pockets and matching short-sleeved tops that fastened down the front and had a logo of a blazing sun. The fabric was different from anything they had touched before – extremely lightweight yet strong, and able to drape and yet fit closely to their bodies. Sasha's and Jamal's were matching blue, and Yury's was pale grey. On Jamal's bed was a matching guthra-style headdress.

The girls' outfits were very similar to the boys, but had a more feminine cut. The collars and cuffs of their short-sleeved tops were trimmed with silver, and their combats had silver tags attached to the trouser legs. Mitchi's outfit was pale grey, while Angie's and Lotty's were both maroon.

When the six returned to the kitchen, the first thing they

did was comment on how each other looked in the new outfits. It seemed strange to see Jamal out of his traditional red and white headdress, but he was still wearing his designer sunglasses.

The main door was open and Leonidas was nowhere to be seen. They walked out into the sunshine in the courtyard and saw three horse-drawn chariots waiting on the paved yard in front of the main entrance. The chariots had curved semi-circular fronts and open backs and were painted in grey, maroon and blue to match the WPDs' new outfits. Each was pulled by a pair of impressively tall and muscular horses.

'Jump in!' Leonidas said, appearing from nowhere and smiling with pleasure at the scene.

Sasha needed no further encouragement and leapt aboard the blue chariot. He lifted the reins and let them run through his eager hands.

'These are totally unsafe,' Jamal burst out. 'There are no guard rails, there's no protection from falling out and they wouldn't pass the most basic safety inspection. I'm not getting in THAT!'

Meanwhile Yury was holding out his hand and helping Mitchi into the grey chariot.

Angie said crossly, 'How come I have to go with Lotty? Why are two girls together? I'd be a much better partner for Yury.'

Leonidas said, 'I don't make the rules, I just follow them,' and gave his hand first to Lotty, who was bouncing up and down with excitement, and then to Angie. 'We leave in three minutes,' he said to Jamal, who was standing alone by the fountain, his arms folded.

'Now for a lesson in basic technique,' Leonidas went on.

'You will need to use all the strength in your legs and your arms. As you see, there are no seats, and the driver will hold the reins while the passenger holds on to the side of the chariot.

'These animals are highly experienced teams and will respond to a slight touch from the reins. Stand up straight and keep a soft tension on the reins, so that you and the animals can feel each other through the tautness of the leather. Command the teams saying, "Walk", "Trot" and "Stop" and pull on the right or left reins to go either right or left.'

Sasha asked, 'What about whips, sir, will you give us those?'

'These teams don't need whips, Sasha. They respond to every verbal command, and if they don't there is a good reason – it will be because they have seen some danger ahead that you haven't noticed yet.

'Make sure you always keep as still as you can in the chariot, because if you move around, the animals can't pull you safely.

'Now it's time to practise. Let's see whether you can drive around this courtyard – the turns won't be easy, but the horses will help you.'

Even though Sasha was alone in his chariot, he set off first, looking bold and confident. His pair of white horses pricked up their ears and set off at a trot.

Yury and Mitchi followed, with a cautious Yury at the reins. 'Not much suspension!' he called to Leonidas. 'I can feel every crack in the ground!'

Angie passed the reins to Lotty nervously and gripped the sides of the chariot. She looked pale and afraid.

The three teams followed each other along the length of

the courtyard, past Jamal at the fountain, and turning sharply at the far end to return to Leonidas, then they turned again and repeated the move. Sasha increased his speed to a fast trot, but Yury and Lotty remained cautious.

Leonidas shouted words of instruction and encouragement, then called to Mitchi and Angie to take the reins from their partners. Angie yelped and wobbled and let the reins fall limp, but Mitchi was surprisingly confident and her small face was intensely focused on the task as she leaned her body into the curve of the turns.

'She's far better than me!' Yury called out as she drove past Leonidas for the second time.

Leonidas shouted to Angie, 'Don't scream – you're frightening the horses. Concentrate and let them lead you.'

At that moment Jamal tapped him on the bare arm. 'I think I should try this. It seems easy.'

Leonidas looked down from his towering height at the top of Jamal's head. 'Training is over, boy, so you will have to learn as you go along now. This is your first lesson as a WPD: you must always seize the moment – it may not come again.'

He called out to the three teams. 'And now for my own chariot!' As he spoke, a sleek, lightweight silver chariot came into the courtyard from the far side. It was pulled by two perfectly matched chestnut stallions, trotting in perfect symmetry. They approached Leonidas, tossed their heads and came to a halt.

Jamal climbed up into the blue chariot beside Sasha, who passed him the reins and began to explain enthusiastically how to use them.

Leonidas leaped into his own chariot and called at the top of his voice, 'Olympia!'

He led the three WPD chariots out of the courtyard. The WPDs hadn't been outside the front of the house since they had arrived in Celestxia the day before, and they imagined that beyond the courtyard they would find themselves on the grassy knoll with only a view of the wall that had led them into Celestxia from the World of Splenda the day before. But as they turned out of the courtyard, they were shocked to see an unexpected vista opening in front of them. The horses were leading them along a dusty yellow track that cut through brown grassland.

Although Jamal, Lotty and Mitchi were concentrating intently on the horses ahead of them, Yury, Angie and Sasha were able to feast their eyes on the landscape ahead. Far away to their left was a view of shimmering blue sea. They were surrounded by grassy plains, and ahead of them were forested hills. As they approached the foothills, the horses led them to the highest of the hills ahead. To the left and right of the summit they saw a group of impressive buildings, with red-tiled roofs supported by white colonnades.

Leonidas called out from his chariot, 'You can see the gymnasium, and there's the stadium where my foot races took place, and the hippodrome where you will soon be racing in these chariots. Oh, it feels so good to come home!'

The bright Mediterranean sunlight shone down on olive trees and made the white columns glisten. Yury and Sasha let out their breath in whistles of amazement, Lotty cheered and Mitchi smiled.

'Have we gone back in time?' Lotty called to Leonidas.

'Yes and no,' Leonidas replied. 'Celestxia contains all knowledge and all the best of human endeavour, and that is how we have been able to come here.'

Leonidas led the three WPD chariots up the wide road

leading into the ancient Olympic site. All around them men and women were thronging the area, all dressed in the simple white tunics and loose-fitting robes and cloaks the WPDs had seen in books and films about Ancient Greece. Some tunics were decorated and edged with a boldly coloured band; others were perfectly plain. Some were belted at the waist, and others hung loose. Many people saluted and waved at the WPDs as they passed by.

In his chariot, Leonidas led them between the buildings to a stable complex where grooms were tending to horses and chariots. There were four empty bays for their own teams to be housed, and stable boys came forward to receive and tend to their animals.

'Time to eat!' Leonidas boomed. 'Follow me!'

The WPDs had to take two strides for every one of Leonidas's as he led them to a large building at the side of the site, where they entered a cool hall without windows in which simple wooden tables and benches were set up.

'The diet of an athlete is important,' Leonidas explained, 'and we eat mostly dried figs, fresh cheese and bread, with large quantities of meat, but no desserts. And absolutely no wine.'

They sat together at a table and immediately they were approached by boys dressed in half togas who came to the table to serve them.

'I had not realised how much hunger I have,' Sasha said.

'Nor me,' Lotty replied.

All six of them devoured the food brought to them on wooden plates. Each dish was fresh, tasty and filling, and was washed down with cupfuls of fresh spring water.

At the end of the meal, Leonidas wiped his mouth with the linen napkin and let out a satisfied sigh. 'Now it is time for you to learn about your training.'

The WPDs leaned towards him but Leonidas said no more.

'Hello!' called a voice from the other side of the hall.

'It's G!' Lotty exclaimed.

'Galileo!' Yury echoed, jumping up from the table and striding across the floor to shake him warmly by the hand.

Galileo smiled warmly at Mitchi, and indicated that she should get out her communication device. She passed it to him and he tapped the screen. Then he spoke into it. 'Testing, this is a test of the audio translator for Mitchi.' He held the device to her ear and she heard his words coming back to her in Mandarin. She beamed broadly and waited for him to say more.

Galileo turned to the whole group. 'Welcome to Olympia! You are in the heart of the ancient site where the Olympic games were born, around the temple of the god Zeus, in the most sacred place of ancient times. Here you will learn the physical skills that will help you in the mission to deactivate Marduk's transmitters. This will not be easy. The competitions Leonidas will prepare you for are real and brutal. Here your powers of endurance, courage and strength will be tested to their limits.

'Yury will compete in a wrestling bout, Sasha an individual chariot race, Mitchi the two hundred metre race, Angie the long jump, Jamal the javelin and Lotty the four hundred metre race. You will be competing against trained athletes, and your bodies will be pushed and tested. While you stay here, you will receive the best coaching and the best food, and there will be no time for excuses or complaints. Remember what I have already told you – that anything is possible when you work together. Be brave and focused.'

Galileo stopped speaking and looked thoughtful, rubbing his chin with his fingers and staring past the colonnades to the courtyard and the blue sky beyond.

'It is time to tell you more about why you have been chosen to be World Planetary Defenders,' he said, pulling up a wooden chair and joining them at the table. 'Some of you may have wondered why you were selected, and most of you will have asked yourselves why the rest of the group are here! You are from different nations and different backgrounds, and don't seem to have anything in common. From the outside you may not look much like a group of superheroes.'

Yury grinned at Mitchi, and Lotty giggled.

Jamal said, 'Speak for yourself.'

Galileo ignored him and went on. 'But you have already proved that you were selected for the right reasons. Can anyone tell me what you have already done that proves it?' He looked around at the group.

Lotty spoke first. 'Well, Angie had a really tough time in the jungle but she made it to Celestxia. And Sasha tamed a wild stallion. Is it that?'

Galileo shook his head.

'We haven't done anything much yet,' Yury said, 'except mess up the creating exercise where we had to imagine stuff and it became real.'

Mitchi began to speak into her communication device in Mandarin. Then she played the translation back to the group. 'Could it be the fact that we were able to do the creative thinking? Do we have special powers of imagining?'

'That's it, Mitchi!' Galileo laughed. 'Exactly.'

'But we only did that because you told us we should,' said Yury. 'And it only happened because Celestxia is a place full of creative energy, didn't it?'

'That is what we led you to believe, because it is so important that you don't misuse your powers,' Galileo replied. 'But if we had brought any other six children in the world to Celestxia, they would not have been able to do what you did.'

Angie raised her eyebrows at Lotty and even Jamal looked very surprised.

'The Creators have been searching for WPDs for generations,' Galileo said. 'Each of you came to their notice because you have powers of positive thought and the ability to create, destroy or change reality just through the power of thinking.

'What you were asked to do on the grassy knoll in Celestxia was a test of your undeveloped powers. And in some of you they are already highly advanced. Angie, you had no help or guidance but you imagined a whole building into existence on your own.

'But with power comes great responsibility. Now that we have made you aware of it, you have to learn the rules you MUST obey to make sure that you don't destroy yourselves. Firstly, Defenders must always think positive thoughts. Secondly, Defenders must only use their special powers for good, and not selfish ends. And lastly, Defenders must never believe that their special powers make them superior to other human beings.

'The world is full of troubles and problems. Some are natural, like earthquakes and tsunamis, and others are manmade, like wars and terrorism, and far more are caused by human greed. The powers you were born with mean that after training you will be able to change the course of history just by thinking and imagining.

'The most important quality of a Defender is a positive

attitude. As soon as you allow negative ideas to enter your head, you are just as vulnerable to evil as the rest of humanity. And more important than this, negative thoughts will mean you begin to lose your special powers as a Defender. But you have one other very special advantage over an evil agent, and that is that you can join forces and become invincible. Evil forces cannot join together – it is a law of the universe that evil has no friend, not even another evil being. Bad is enemy to good, but bad is also enemy to bad. Evil is the most lonely thing in the world, and that is its weakness.

'Your most important strength is that goodness unites. Unity is strength, and unity cannot come without friendship. Each of you has great powers, but you can achieve even more if you work as a team. As you face trials and assignments together, you will perfect your teamwork. Let this be your goal: that one day all human beings will be united as one in peace and amity, and then the human race will accomplish wonderful feats!'

Galileo paused and then patted Sasha on the back. 'So, let the training begin.'

Chapter 12

Jamal slept fitfully that night and had confused dreams. He woke at one a.m. sweating and shivering. Galileo's words had excited and worried him at the same time. Unlike the other five WPDs, he knew he hadn't yet imagined anything into being. He had no doubt he could do it if he chose, but knew he would feel much happier if he actually had proof. Like him, Angie had arrived at Celestxia later than the other WPDs, but she had immediately imagined an entire beauty spa with all its contents and facilities.

He knew sleep wouldn't come now, and he got out of the simple wooden bed with its straw-filled mattress and slipped on his training outfit. The courtyard outside their sleeping quarters was silent and empty. A bright moon shone down from the cloudless night sky, and somewhere an owl hooted.

Jamal sat beside the courtyard fountain and thought. Galileo had told them that Yury would compete in a wrestling bout, Sasha a chariot event, Mitchi and Lotty in running races, Angie the long jump and that his own event would be the javelin. Suddenly he had an idea, and he got up and walked briskly towards the stable block. He convinced himself that this was just an experiment to test his thinking powers and that no harm would come of it.

In the stables, he headed for the WPDs' chariot bays. Their horses stood peacefully, each with one back leg in the resting position. Jamal sat on the straw and stared at the grey and maroon chariots that had been driven by the other pairs of WPDs.

He pressed his hands to his head and pictured a large lead weight attached to the underside of the grey chariot, where it could not be seen. He imagined every detail of the weight – its size, shape and a heaviness far greater than a man could lift. He even imagined the heavy leather straps that would attach it to the underneath of the chariot floor. After a few moments, he felt a kind of power surge flow out of him.

That was the signal he needed, and he crawled under the grey chariot and began to feel with his hands. He knew immediately that his test had worked. A huge piece of lead was tightly attached by strong leather belts to the underside of the chariot.

'Result,' he said gleefully, and turned his attention to the blue chariot, which Sasha would ride in his event. This time he imagined a great, flat weight of stone, and again after a while he felt a surge of power leave him. When he felt the underneath of the chariot he was even more pleased with the result. The stone that was now fixed in place was smooth and pleasing to his touch.

The success of his experiment made Jamal feel triumphant and confident, and although he hadn't planned this part, he set off for the outbuildings where all the WPDs had been shown the equipment that would be used in the games and trials ahead.

Frustratingly he couldn't imagine anything that would hinder Yury in wrestling, or the girls in running, at least not until the events actually took place. But he knew he could imagine the perfect javelin for his own contest.

He sat on a wooden bench against the wall among the equipment and breathed in the strong scent of wood and metal and leather. He pictured the athletics events he had seen on TV, especially the Olympics. He knew that a javelin made of a strong, lightweight material such as carbon would be much more effective than the wooden ones leaning against the wall in front of him now. So he imagined a slim, light, strong spear – coloured in the blue of his training outfit, leaning amongst the ancient wooden ones. Closing his eyes, he imagined the touch and weight of it, and the speed with which it would fly through the air.

Then he opened his eyes. His javelin was in place. Jamal gave a high five into the air and then punched his fist. He knew that when he returned to his trestle bed his sleep would be deep and satisfying.

* * *

The next morning the Defenders rose at dawn and Leonidas led them to the training grounds. The sun shone down from a cloudless sky and the Olympic complex buzzed with excited boys, girls and athletes.

Before they parted to go to their individual training sessions, Leonidas gave a final speech. 'All the events that we perform at the ancient Olympic games are chosen because they prepare us for war, and for battles like those you will face on Earth when you return. For example, the long jump was designed to train warriors to jump across streams and ravines when they are in combat with an enemy. The javelin event is based on throwing a spear in battle. These competitions are serious and fierce. May the power of Zeus be with you.'

Mitchi and Lotty spent the day in the stadium where, under the fierce glare of the Greek sun, they were taught how to start a race, to sprint and to endure burning leg muscles until they reached the finish line.

Yury was taken to the gymnasium where he was shown how to wrestle with opponents who were stronger and taller than himself, and how to grip, unbalance and floor a man.

Jamal used his javelin for the first time in the open ground of the gymnasium and the trainers were amazed by his spear, which flew further and pierced the ground more easily than any they had ever seen.

Angie was close to Jamal as she practised the long jump, and she felt depressed and discouraged by his easy success. She had expected her event to be like the modern long jump, but instead she was allowed only a short running start and she had to carry a two-kilogram weight in each hand, which she was told to swing forward as she jumped, to increase her momentum. The experienced athletes threw their weights behind them in mid-air and let them go, to increase their forward momentum, but Angie wasn't brave enough to try that. One of the other contestants told her that the long jump was considered to be the most difficult event of the games, and that made her feel even worse. While they jumped, music was played on pipes to help the athletes find a rhythm for the complex movements of the weights they carried.

Meanwhile, in the hippodrome, Sasha was having terrible trouble with his chariot. Today it felt sluggish and heavy, and he couldn't get it to turn smoothly at the bends. It seemed to pull against the horses and destabilise them and, unlike the day before, Sasha noticed they were tiring very quickly.

By the evening, when the Defenders returned to the

refectory building to a meal of cured meats, fruit, bread and olives, they were all out of sorts.

'Today just made me feel like a failure,' Angie began. 'I know it sounds mean, but watching Jamal succeed made me feel useless.'

'And I have realise I'm not good chariot driver,' Sasha added. 'I was big head before today.'

Leonidas interrupted them. 'You are tired from the exertions and you must rest early tonight in readiness for tomorrow's training. Remember what Galileo told you about your special thinking powers, and imagine yourselves as victors wearing the garland of laurel leaves. Imagine your success, feel it inside you, and it will happen.'

* * *

During the next week of intensive training, the WPDs experienced the pain of aching bodies and searing muscles, as well as a constant and nagging fear of failure. Only Sasha had a body used to hard physical exertion. Every night they all practised positive thinking exercises together and imagined themselves as victors, even though winning seemed completely unrealistic.

When they woke on the day of the games, the Defenders were taken to the bathhouse where they soaked in steaming hot baths and then rubbed scented oils into their hot, pink skin. A masseur pummelled their bodies to take away the aches and pains left from the long week of training.

The Defenders were then given Greek togas to wear for the competitions. Mitchi, Angie and Lotty had white knee-length togas, clasped over one shoulder and belted at the waist, while the boys had white loincloths with simple leather belts.

After breakfast, Leonidas led them to the entrance of the Temple of Zeus in the Olympic complex. They stood together looking up at the enormous white marble columns and decorated portico above their heads.

In his booming voice, Leonidas asked them to gather round. 'This temple is one of the most sacred sites on Earth for my people. Before you begin your competition, you must take your oaths at the altar, which is in the very spot where Zeus is said to have thrown a lightning bolt.'

He led the Defenders up steps between the great pillars into the shaded interior. Ahead of them, half-filling the aisle, they saw an immense ivory and gold-plated statue, twelve metres tall, of a seated god. He was wreathed with golden carvings of olive stems, and seated on a magnificent throne of cedar wood inlaid with ivory, gold, ebony and precious stones. In his left hand there was a sceptre covered in gold on which an eagle perched.

Leonidas spoke again. 'This statue represents power and truth to all Greeks. Zeus is father of gods and men. Every game in the Olympics is in honour of him, and our triumphs are dedicated to him. They are not about selfish pride.' As he said this last bit, Leonidas's gaze settled on Jamal, who was moving a small stone around with the toe of his shoe.

One by one, the Defenders stepped forward to the statue. In turn, they bowed their heads. Leonidas passed each of them an olive stem, and without being told, Yury, Mitchi, Sasha, Jamal, Angie and Lotty instinctively took the few steps to Zeus and laid their branches at his feet.

'We compete in honour of you!' Leonidas said in a commanding voice.

'In honour of you,' the Defenders echoed.

When they stepped outside the dark coolness of the

temple, the sunlight seemed too bright for their eyes.

'I feel really emotional,' Lotty said. 'That was so amazing.'

Mitchi turned her face away from the other Defenders to hide the tears that were running down her cheeks.

Already athletes and competitors were massing in the paved areas between the buildings, and huge crowds of spectators could be seen gathering outside the Olympic venues.

'I so nervous, I think I will not win,' Sasha said.

'Courage!' Leonidas replied.

The Defenders joined the throng of athletes progressing from the temple to the hippodrome, the stadium and the gymnasium for the start of the games.

Yury was listed to compete first, in the wrestling bout at the gymnasium.

Angie asked Leonidas, 'What is the worst that can happen to him if things go badly?'

'Don't think that way, Angie. You must visualise Yury winning,' Leonidas replied.

As they passed through the entrance to the open gymnasium, Angie gave Yury's hand a supportive squeeze. He was staring straight ahead and his face showed no emotion or expression. Spectators were crowded around the perimeter of the open yard, and the noise of their cheering and clapping was almost deafening as the athletes entered the arena.

Yury knew he needed three points to win his bout. He could score a point by forcing his opponent's back, hip or shoulder to the ground, or if the opponent made a plea for submission. One of the most important things he had learned in training was how to prevent his opponent climbing on his back and trying to strangle or choke him.

As soon as the contestants had gathered in the sandy area

that filled the centre of the arena, the match referee read out the rules from a scroll. His powerful voice reached all around the gymnasium. 'Any athlete who breaks these rules will be eliminated, and if he does not cease the behaviour then he will be whipped until he does cease. No intentional hitting or kicking is permitted, no gouging the eyes or biting, and no grasping the genitals. All other holds intended to persuade the opponent to concede defeat through pain or fear *are* permitted. The referee's decision is final and the winner shall be the first to gain three points.'

From their position amongst the other athletes close to the gymnasium entrance, the Defenders could see that whoever Yury was matched with was going to be a fearful opponent. Although Yury was a match for the other men in height, their muscular strength and brutal competitiveness was obvious even from a distance. Their bodies were bronzed and shimmered with sweat under the heat of the morning sun.

The referee signalled for the pairs of contestants to move away from each other so that they were too far apart to touch. Each man crouched as if he were an animal ready to spring. All too soon, the referee raised his hammer and hit a sheet of bronze to signal the start of the bout.

The pairs of wrestlers lunged at each other, trying to get a hold that would enable them to throw their opponent to the ground. Yury was standing firm, resisting the push of the muscular, dark-skinned Greek athlete he had been paired with, deflecting the pressure he exerted by pushing his own foot and leg hard against the Greek. He had been quick to learn that keeping his balance was the key to winning.

Already some of the wrestlers were gaining points, one or two had submitted and others had been thrown to the ground.

Sasha was bouncing up and down. 'Go, Yury! He must score a point quick now if he win.'

Lotty covered and uncovered her eyes, Angie squeaked and shrieked by turns, but Mitchi kept her intense gaze firmly fixed on Yury. No emotion was visible on her small heart-shaped face.

Then, just as his opponent moved his feet to get a better grip on Yury's waist, Yury saw his chance: he pulled and flipped the Greek and forced him onto his back on the sandy earth.

'One point!' yelled the referee who had been assigned to their bout.

The Defenders cheered and hollered. The Greek opponent got to his feet quickly and brushed away the sand that had stuck to his sweaty skin. Yury wasted no time. As soon as the Greek lunged at him, Yury spun round, pressed his body to the other man's back and forced his neck into a painful hold. He leaned and tightened his grip with every ounce of his strength, pulling the man's head back in a choking motion. The opponent writhed and tried to twist, but after a few seconds raised his hand in submission.

'One point!' shouted the referee again.

'Yury will win!' Sasha yelled, jumping up and down more enthusiastically than before. Several of the wrestlers had gained two points now; some were two-one, others two-two.

Leonidas summoned the Defenders. 'Think positive thoughts now. You must will Yury to win with your minds.'

Lotty, Angie, Mitchi and Sasha leaned forwards and focused their thoughts on Yury. But Jamal hung back a little and looked uncomfortable. He was visualising the opponent throwing Yury to the ground.

Seconds later it happened – the Greek managed to loop

his leg around Yury's leg, unbalance him and tip his body until Yury's right shoulder touched the ground.

'One point!' the referee called again.

All the Defenders except Jamal winced but continued to focus their minds on the picture of Yury as victor.

In an instant, Yury flew at the Greek, tugged his long, dark hair and body, and rolled him to the ground. It was an impressive sight.

'Three points!' called the referee.

'Three points!' called another referee to the right of Yury.

The WPDs leapt into the air, dancing and shouting with delight. Jamal looked crestfallen. All around the ground referees were shouting 'Three points!' to the competitors in the various bouts. In the middle of the arena, one man's body lay limp and lifeless, and a couple of officials ran to examine him. Meanwhile, the referees formed a huddle around the match referee to discuss results.

'How do they decide the winner?' Lotty asked Leonidas.

'It is the first wrestler to gain three points, and if there is a tie, the winner is the one who did not lose a point himself,' Leonidas replied.

The Defenders waited for what seemed an age and watched the officials move the lifeless wrestler's body out of the arena. Some competitors were having difficulty breathing, and all of them were winded and exhausted. Yury stood with his head forwards and his hands on his knees, his chest rising and falling breathlessly.

At last the referee stepped forward. 'People of Greece, we have a victor, in the name of Zeus! In second place, with three points and one loss, is Yury!'

The crowd cheered as the referee lifted Yury's right hand and turned him to face the four sides of the gymnasium.

As the cheers died down, the referee spoke again. 'And in first place, with three points and no losses, is Agapios!' He raised the arm of a short, muscular Greek wrestler and the crowd went wild.

'What happened?' Angie asked Leonidas.

'To come second is a victory for Yury – an incredible achievement for someone so young and inexperienced. Your powers of thought achieved this. When you are more skilled then you will be able to achieve even more. Well done, team!' Leonidas said.

Jamal turned his face away from the others and smiled a small, wry smile.

Chapter 13

The stadium events were called next. Jamal appeared very confident and left the other Defenders without shaking hands or saying goodbye. He strode across the complex to the stadium and then crossed the arena to the throwing area, where he selected his blue javelin from the array of wooden spears being handed out.

While Jamal was preparing himself, an exhausted Yury returned from the gymnasium and shook hands with the group of WPDs and Leonidas. His naked upper body was dirty, sandy and bruised. Lotty and Angie tried to wipe the worst of the dirt away with the hems of their tunics.

Mitchi longed to step forward and help, and was angry with herself for being so shy in comparison to the other girls.

They all watched Jamal attach a leather strap in a loop at the centre of gravity of the javelin. In training he had been shown how to attach it where it would help him most – by making his grip secure, and to allow the best rotation in flight to stabilise the javelin and achieve a greater distance. When he threw the javelin, his fingers would release the thong at the very last moment

The competitors gathered at the starting line of the stadium. They left enough distance to allow them room to take a few steps before throwing. They had to aim into a central area delineated on three sides, and a throw would be disqualified if it fell outside the marked area.

When it came to Jamal's turn, he tied the thong as tight as he could to his javelin, put his index and middle fingers into its loop and pushed the javelin back with his left hand to tighten the thong and grip with the fingers of his right hand. Then, holding the javelin close to his head, he turned his body in the direction of the throw and started the run-up. A few steps before the starting line, he pulled his right arm back and turned his body and head to the right. He crossed his right foot in front of his left and drew his left arm back to help the turn. Bending his knees slightly, he stretched his left leg out in front of him to stop himself moving beyond the throw line. He hurled the javelin over his head and it flew almost magically into the marked area. In comparison to the other javelins it seemed to have wings as it sliced through the warm air. The Defenders could see that it was a remarkable throw.

Each athlete had three attempts to achieve the furthest distance. By the end of the first round Jamal was in the lead by a significant margin; the stone marker on the spot where his javelin tip had landed was clearly ahead of all the others.

In the second round, he was narrowly beaten by a tall Greek whose technique was masterful.

Leonidas turned to the group. 'I'm not sure what is happening here. Jamal's technique is very poor, but the distance he's achieving is quite remarkable. His javelin seems to be lighter and faster than anyone else's. You must be giving strong, positive thoughts. Well done!'

The Defenders looked at each other and said nothing.

The last round was an easy one for Jamal. The tall Greek was disqualified as his foot was just over the throw line when he let go of his javelin, and some of the others made poor throws. As soon as the last athlete finished, Jamal jumped up and down and punched the air with glee. The referee congratulated him and announced his victory. Immediately a fair-haired young boy dressed in purest white brought a palm branch to Jamal, and the crowd began to throw flowers. The referee tied red ribbons to Jamal's head and hands and he was told to wear them all day until the final award ceremony when he would receive his wreath crown.

Lotty and Mitchi turned to each other and gulped. The running races were next.

Lotty whispered to Angie, 'I know I should feel pleased for Jamal but I don't. I can't take any pleasure in his victory and that makes me feel bad.'

Angie nodded. 'I know exactly what you mean.'

Mitchi had been entered in the *stadio* event – a short sprint measuring about two hundred metres along the full length of the stadium. She would have to pass five staked markers: one at the start, another at the finish, and three stakes in between.

Lotty, who was taller and stronger than Mitchi, was entered in the *dialous* – a race making a single lap of the stadium, a distance of approximately four hundred metres. At each of the four corners was a turning post that the athletes had to pass on the outside before racing back to the starting line. Her race was scheduled first.

Lotty hugged each WPD in turn, and then made her way to the starting blocks – a long, flat stone etched with grooves for the athletes' bare toes. More than anything she wished she could have a pair of running shoes from home, any brand, which would give her a massive advantage over the other athletes.

When the hammer struck the sheet of bronze, she had a good start, and managed to keep up with the other girls easily. After the first turning point she was in third place, and at the two hundred metre turning post she briefly took the lead.

'Go, girl! Go, Lotty!' Yury, Sasha and Angie shrieked.

But the distance was too much for her, and in the third and fourth stages Lotty slipped further behind the pack, reaching the line in ninth place out of eighteen runners. As she finished, she stumbled and fell face down on the sandy earth.

Yury rushed over to her, pushing the referees and Greek officials out of the way, until he reached her side and kneeled down beside her.

'Lotty! Lotty, are you okay?'

Lotty groaned and rolled onto her side, too tired to speak. She pointed at her legs. 'Ow! Ouch!'

Yury rubbed her calves with his strong hands, still dirty from the wrestling bout.

'I've never felt pain like that,' Lotty said after a moment. 'My legs burning like fire... I did my best, Yury.'

'You did brilliantly, Lotty. You are a total star!' Yury smiled at her, helping her to her feet.

As soon as he had guided her back to the group of Defenders it was time for Mitchi to run.

'I worry about her,' Sasha said. 'Mitchi so small.'

'I know, she always seems so frail,' Angie added.

Leonidas patted Angie on the shoulder. 'Think positively team! You can do it.'

Yury put his hand over his mouth and looked up at Leonidas. 'I forgot to do positive thinking while Lotty was running. Lotty, I'm so sorry!' he said.

Sasha said, 'Me forgot also. Very sorry!'

Leonidas shook his head. 'Then Lotty's victory is the most important of all – she taught you the most valuable lesson so far,' he said.

Mitchi was already at the starting blocks in the centre of the entrance of the arena. Her course straight through the middle of the arena was half the distance of Lotty's. She looked still and calm. As the referee raised his hammer, she bent her legs and pushed back into the stone starting block.

After that, everything seemed to happen unnaturally quickly. The gong sounded, Mitchi flew out of the blocks, the twenty runners sprinted to their maximum pace and it was too close to call. But after twenty seconds, Mitchi seemed to be nudging ahead, and then she flew like a dart to the finishing line. She was a full metre ahead of the nearest athlete, and it was an astonishingly easy win.

Now the crowd really let rip – they had never seen a woman win by such a margin. Even the referee was waving his arms in delight. Mitchi leaned forwards for a moment with her hands on her knees and then turned to face the WPDs in their position near the entrance. She took a small bow from the waist in their direction and Lotty burst into floods of tears.

'She's so brave and proud and amazing! I'm so truly happy for her, happier than if I'd won. And she never complains that she can't understand us or speak English,' she said, sobbing through her words.

The referee attached the red ribbons to her head and ankle, and when the cheering had begun to subside, Mitchi returned to the group. Her face was radiant, and the joy of her victory was spreading like sunshine around her.

Already the long jump was being called, and Angie's

heart sank in her chest. Something had begun to happen inside her as the week of training had progressed. Something a bit like a thawing or a melting. The old, familiar anger that she had felt since childhood and that had become so much worse since her parents split up was beginning to fade. The feeling that was replacing it was new to her, and was made up partly of pride at Mitchi's victory and partly a desire to do well for the rest of the team. She realised she was thinking less of herself than she had ever done, and less about how she looked. The other new feeling was that she liked Mitchi and Lotty, even though she hated almost all the girls at her school.

As she walked across the stadium to the long jump area, these thoughts filled her head. 'I want to do it for the others,' she said aloud. 'I want to make them proud of me.'

Unlike Jamal in the javelin event, Angie would only get one chance to jump. She was listed as last to jump out of twenty-five competitors, which she realised wryly would at least give her a target to beat. Watching the others was a painful process, as a series of lean, muscular women from across the Greek world jumped further and further. The leader had jumped what looked like four metres.

Angie lifted the two weights she had to swing to give her more momentum as she left the ground. They were heavy and she found them more of a hindrance than a help. As she stood on the starting line, she looked up at the cloudless blue of the Greek sky and said aloud, 'For Zeus, and for the World Planetary Defenders. And for Galileo.'

The words had a remarkable effect. Her chest calmed and the sound of the crowd faded away. Suddenly there was nothing in the world but a long jump run and a pit of earth. Nothing existed but her legs and her mind.

Angie leaned back, bending at the waist and holding the weights behind her, arms outstretched. Then she began the very short run to the jump line. The weights came forward and, as she leaped, she threw them behind and away from her. It felt as though she was flying. When she landed, the crowd erupted and the referees rushed forwards to measure her mark in the earth. She had come second, missing out on victory by no more than seven centimetres, and it felt better than anything she had ever done in her life.

Tears streamed down her cheeks. All the occasions when her parents hadn't come to see her in school plays, all the times they had missed parents' evenings, all the loneliness of being an only child just faded away. She smiled as she realised that she was Angie, the girl who hated sport and had come second in the Greek Olympics. It was without doubt the best moment of her life.

Looking up, she saw Lotty running across the stadium, arms outstretched and with tears in her eyes. Lotty scooped Angie into her arms and they hugged and squeezed until they could hardly breathe.

'I'm so proud of you, so proud of you!' Lotty squealed. 'We all are.'

* * *

Leonidas spoke to the Defenders as they gathered around him. 'Today has been a great day for Galileo and the Creators. You have proved your worth beyond a doubt. Mitchi and Jamal will be crowned victors tonight and the rest of you have excelled in your events. It now only remains for Sasha to compete in the chariot race. I believe this will be the toughest part of the day for you all.' As he said this, Leonidas's gaze fell on Jamal.

The team joined the throng of competitors and spectators who were making their way to the hippodrome in the southeastern part of the site. One by one, the WPDs patted Sasha, or smiled at him by way of encouragement. Jamal did his best to appear happy. When Sasha left them to go to the stable block, he looked afraid and shy. Leonidas had explained that most of the charioteers would be teenagers, because their light weight gave them an advantage over grown men.

They entered the enormous, rectangular hippodrome with its high-banked sides where spectators were gathering. The central arena was divided in two along its length by a wooden barrier down the middle.

Before long, the procession of chariots began to enter the hippodrome, and a herald called out the names of the drivers and owners. When Sasha's blue chariot appeared, the herald called, 'Sasha of Cuiaba, for Galileo!' Sasha was dressed in the traditional charioteer garments, which were fastened high at the waist and strapped across his back to prevent them ballooning out dangerously during the race. Before he moved on, a referee checked that his feet were strapped into place on the floor of the chariot.

There would be six laps of the circuit, which meant Sasha would have to make a total of twelve horrifically dangerous sharp turns. That was when the casualties would happen, with crashes, vicious injuries and even deaths.

The hoard of chariots headed for the swinging gates that had been lowered across the start line. The horses were frisky and edgy and none of them wanted to be restrained by the gate. Charioteers jostled to get into the outside lanes where they would get a faster start. The tension in the hippodrome was palpable and the watching WPDs felt sick with nerves.

They knew Sasha was competing in the most dangerous event of all.

At last the starting gate was lifted, the competitors yelled to their horses and the crowd erupted. In a cloud of dust, the chariots pulled onto the track, but Sasha's horses were sluggish and accelerated at half the speed of the others.

Leonidas put his hand to his head. 'I don't understand what is wrong!' he whispered.

Being last actually proved to be an advantage at the first few turns, as Sasha was able to avoid the collisions that had already begun. At the second turn, one chariot deliberately ran into an opponent and caused him to crash into the central barrier. The chariot overturned, the horses fell badly and the charioteer could not escape as his feet were fixed in place. Sasha avoided the carnage and officials rushed to clear the track before the next lap.

Lotty couldn't watch any more and turned her face away.

After four laps, Sasha was so far behind that the leaders were catching up and threatening to overtake him from the rear.

'Think! Think, Defenders!' Leonidas cried out. 'Focus as you have never focused before. Give Sasha speed and strength and courage. Give his chariot wings!'

Almost immediately something remarkable happened. Beneath Sasha's chariot, the crowd saw a bright flash of light, like a firework or flame. Then something white flew out from between the wheels of his chariot. As it rose from the ground towards the sky above the hippodrome, it could be clearly recognised as a large white dove. It flapped its wings and dropped something from its beak to the ground.

Immediately Sasha's chariot doubled its speed. The horses now seemed to be pulling a weightless chariot, and they put their ears back and galloped for their lives. Within seconds Sasha caught the tail of the pack and he began weaving his way through the other chariots on the next two straights.

'How many laps to go?' Angie shrieked.

'One and a half,' Yury replied. 'Has he got time?'

'You can do it!' Lotty yelled over and over until she was hoarse.

Sasha thundered down the straight. He was now in third place. The two charioteers ahead of him had no intention of letting him pass and they worked together to prevent him coming through. As they came out of the turn into the last lap, the chariot in second place crossed into Sasha's path – a deliberate attempt to force a crash. Sasha was leaning forwards and it looked as though he was speaking into his horses' ears. As he approached the very last turn, the horses took the chariot as wide as possible.

'Oh no!' Yury called. 'Now he has too much ground to make up!'

The first and second chariots had gained several metres on him and were neck and neck. All they had to do was hold their line and pace and they couldn't be beaten.

But Sasha was on fire. Yelling to the horses, he accelerated up the outside track and gained a metre, then a chariot length, until he overtook one chariot and was parallel with the leader.

The crowd had never seen anything like it, and everyone in the hippodrome wanted the blue chariot to win – driven by the boy who had come from last place to joint first. The referees crouched at the finish line, six men with eyes like eagles who would decide which horses crossed the line first.

In a cloud of yellow dust the chariots thundered away

from the track, the horses lathered with sweat, the charioteers bent double with cramp.

First one, then another referee raised his hands to indicate that he had a decision. The crowd quietened so they would hear the result. A hush fell on the hippodrome.

The match referee stepped forward and the herald called aloud, 'The victor is Sasha of Cuiaba, for Galileo!'

Leonidas had his hands pressed to his head. He knew something remarkable had happened here, but couldn't imagine what it might be. He felt that if he knew what the dove had dropped from its beak, he would have the answer.

Chapter 14

At the end of the day, as the Greek sun began to descend in the crystal-blue sky, Leonidas led the WPDs to the Temple of Zeus where the award ceremony would take place. Many of the competitors and all of the winners were already gathered in the open paved area before the temple. On the elevated entrance at the top of the steps stood the senior games officials and the herald, who began to announce the names of the events in turn and then call the winners forward.

After a while he announced Mitchi's race, and in his clear, loud voice called, 'The victor is Mitchi of Sichuan, for Galileo!'

Still wearing her simple white tunic, Mitchi made her way forward and bent to kneel at the feet of the officials. They placed a circlet made from an olive stem, taken from the sacred tree, on her head. The official lifted her right hand and turned her to face the roaring crowd.

Soon afterwards, the javelin prize was called. The WPDs waited expectantly for Jamal to be summoned, and before the announcement was even made, he began to walk towards the steps of the temple. However, instead of calling Jamal's name, the herald spoke seriously.

'People of Greece, there has been mischief in this event

and the referee has declared that the javelin thrown by the apparent victor has been disqualified. It was not a javelin made by our people and it gave the competitor an unfair advantage. So, the victor in this event is Diokles of Sparta, for Lysander!'

At first the crowd remained quiet and then people began to boo and cheer, some clearly angry with Jamal, others delighted for the rightful victor. Jamal stopped in his tracks, just before the temple steps, then continued to walk forward and began to argue with the officials. They waved their arms angrily and indicated that Jamal should leave. He returned to the WPDs in a foul temper, mumbling under his breath about stupid regulations, foul play and injustice.

Moments later, the chariot event was announced. The herald called out in a clear voice, 'Sasha of Cuiaba, for Galileo!'

Yury and Lotty patted Sasha on the back and watched him make his way to the steps. One of the officials had turned his back to the crowd and was preparing an olive wreath for Sasha. As he knelt the official turned, and all the WPDs saw at once that the man about to place the wreath on Sasha's head was in fact their own Galileo. Lotty jumped up and down and Yury cheered out loud. It was not until Sasha raised his eyes that he realised who was standing before him.

Galileo beamed and spoke gently. 'Well done, Sasha, strongest of the World Planetary Defenders. Your event was the most difficult and you were bearing the weight of evil unseen beneath you.'

He placed the wreath proudly on top of Sasha's head. The crowd was already going wild, but Galileo had more to say.

'Sasha, there is something else I must give you. This is

what the dove dropped from its beak as it flew out from beneath your chariot. It is a pebble of purest marble, and although it was created in evil, when the Defenders willed you to win, their power changed it into good.

'Keep this with you always, and when you are in greatest need it will save you. Well done, my child.'

Now Galileo raised Sasha's right hand and turned him to the crowd. All around them, competitors and supporters were leaping in the air with delight. Sasha looked around and blinked into the rays of the setting sun. He knew he was just Sasha, the boy from the ranch in Brazil, not a victor or a hero. But he savoured the moment and he knew he would treasure it for the rest of his life.

He clasped his fingers around the pebble and began to walk back to his team.

* * *

Although the Defenders were physically exhausted, they chatted over everything they had seen and heard at the awards ceremony and talked about what would happen at the Olympic feast after sun-down.

Leonidas told them to retire to their dormitories and change into the outfits they found there, and that he would meet them in the refectory.

The girls were surprised when they saw their costumes; they looked nothing like anything they had seen the crowd wearing at the Olympics. Mitchi had a simple black floor-length gown with a bustle, gathered skirt and a high-necked white ruff at the neck. Angie and Lotty had feminine long-sleeved silk gowns, also floor-length, with sashes at the waist and scooped necklines. Angie's was pale blue and Lotty's white.

When they met the boys in the refectory, they giggled and stared, wide-eyed.

'You look like the Three Musketeers!' Lotty said, pointing at them and covering her mouth.

All three had wide-necked leather boots and broad hats trimmed with feathers. They wore tights with full breeches that gathered above the knee and ornate jackets. Yury's was yellow and trimmed with fur, Sasha's blue and Jamal's a rich red.

Leonidas beckoned to the Defenders from a doorway at the end of the hall. The six moved towards him, laughing and touching each other's outfits.

On the other side of the doorway they stopped still in shock. Ahead of them was no Greek courtyard, but a large grassy space between shining white buildings. The temperature was cool, and it appeared to be daytime.

'Where are we?' Sasha asked.

'What happened?' Angie added.

Yury said, 'I recognise this place. I'm sure I've seen pictures of it… Could it be England?'

Mitchi spoke slowly and in a thick accent. 'Cam-bridge Uni-ver-sity.'

Yury replied. 'She's right! That's the college chapel and yes! It must be Cambridge rather than Oxford because the buildings are yellower there.'

'Why do you think we are here?' Lotty asked.

A middle-aged man was striding across the grass quadrangle towards them. He had papers under his arm and was wearing clothes very much like the three boys', only he had a white cravat at the neck and his open jacket had a row of brass buttons down each edge.

He raised his arm to the Defenders and called, 'Welcome!' He seemed to be expecting them. 'Come with me, we have no time to lose,' he added, taking great strides across the ground. He led them through the courtyard, under an archway and towards a wide, smoothly flowing river.

Suddenly he stopped and turned to face the Defenders. 'But how rude of me,' he said. 'I am Isaac Newton, born forty-five years ago in 1642 in a manor house in Lincolnshire, to a mother who was widowed two months before I was born. I had no interest in the family farm, and came here to study in 1661. I was born just a short time after the death of Galileo, whom I believe is known to you as one of the greatest scientists of all time.

Angie whispered to Yury, 'Does he mean *our* Galileo?'

Yury whispered back. 'I don't think so. Our G was born on another planet and long before Galileo the scientist.'

Sir Isaac continued. 'Stop me if I am running away with myself. Galileo proved that the planets revolve around the sun, rather than the other way around. The grass is rather damp here but we will sit and watch the river. There is a wooden seat for the ladies, as you see.' Isaac motioned towards a bench and seated himself on the grass.

Lotty smiled at the intensity and the matter-of-factness he showed, and felt she ought to pinch herself because she was in the presence of a man she had learnt about at school.

'When I was a young man I thought about Galileo's discoveries and began to realise that the universe works much like a beautiful machine, governed by a few simple and yet masterly laws. I believed that mathematics was the way to explain and prove those laws.

'I have discovered nothing, only explained why the universe behaves in the way that it does. We all see that an apple must fall to the ground, or a quill from a desk, and I needed to understand why this is so.

'May I share this with you? There was a day when I watched an actual apple fall to the ground and it made me think – suddenly that apple made me ask myself why it did not rise to the sky, or float in the air. And from that simple apple, I calculated the force that is needed to keep the moon moving around the Earth. Although the apple is much smaller than the moon, the forces acting on them both are the same! Do you understand what a beautiful thing that is?'

Yury and Jamal beamed at the man sitting beside them.

'I apologise, sir,' Yury said. 'I cannot believe that I am sitting on the grass with Sir Isaac Newton, the greatest scientist who ever lived.'

Isaac looked bemused. 'That is not in the least bit important; what matters is that we understand the world that God has made and that we admire its wonder. Do you know that less than fifty years before I was born people believed the planets were held in place by an invisible shield, and not by the sun's gravity! All I pray is that after my lifetime, men will go on to make more discoveries and understand much more than my mind has been capable of.

'And now we must take a drink in the dining hall, as I have work to do with you.'

Isaac stood up at once and strode back along the path down which he had led the Defenders. His full coat swung out behind him and, despite their much younger age, the Defenders struggled to keep up with him. Mitchi, Angie and Lotty were following last as their full skirts made it much more difficult to walk.

Next he led them into Nevile's Court and into a small dining hall where a number of men were eating and talking.

Isaac turned to the Defenders. 'We will be left in peace here,' he said, then he raised his hand to Mitchi, Lotty and Angie. 'There are no women in Cambridge, but they will overlook your presence here.'

He banged on the table with his fist once and a porter appeared from a side door. 'A small beer for me and the new drink for all of us,' Isaac ordered. Turning to the Defenders, he said, 'I have a surprise for you. Those academics in Oxford think they have the better of us, for they have established a coffee house known as The Angel. The people of Oxford and the scholars are meeting and crowing over the place – calling it a university for the virtuosi – but we have brought coffee to Trinity College ourselves. Ha! Let them put that in their pipe and smoke it!'

Isaac beamed broadly as the porter brought a tray loaded with seven cups of steaming coffee. It was rich and dark and was served without milk. Isaac downed his beer first and then began to speak.

Mitchi noticed how Sir Isaac was thoroughly focused on one thing at a time, whether it was mathematics, walking or coffee. She turned up the microphone on her communication device so her audio translator wouldn't miss a word.

'Some drawings have been sent to me at the university. That is why you are here. I have already told you how I am devoted to, and indebted to, my forebear, Galileo Galilei of Pisa – the physicist, astronomer and mathematician. He died only fifteen years ago in 1642 and the world lost its brightest mind.

'Galileo used a telescope to confirm truths about the planets in our universe, and he developed new instruments like the compass and thermometer. You know what the word telescope means, I assume?' Isaac said, looking eagerly at the

Defenders. He didn't wait for an answer. 'It is from the Greek *tele* which means "far" and *skopein* which means "to look or see". Then he modified the instrument to make a microscope to look at the parts of an insect, the word *micron* meaning "small", and *skopein* again meaning "to look or see". Beautiful and useful – I am in awe of the man!

'It is only because of Galileo's work on the motions of bodies that I have been able to make my calculations and interpretations of the laws of motion in the universe.

'The drawings arrived by sea from the University of Florence, and were left by Galileo just before his death. He had been working on studying supernovas, but he had also left papers that we do not understand. The scholars in Florence have asked me to study the drawings and try to make sense of them.

'Among the papers I found this, a note in Latin which I will translate for you thus.'

Isaac pulled a rolled piece of yellow parchment from the folds of his robe, and began to read aloud, running his finger along the Latin script as he translated.

'"I desire that these papers fall into the hands of Isaac Newton of England. Written by my own hand, Galileo Galilei, twenty-fourth day of February, year of our Lord 1640, Florence.

'"The drawings and notes relate to an important discovery I have made that is unknown to any but myself. Before I leave this world the secret must pass to someone who will understand the serious nature of this information, and who will pass it on to men who will be able to vanquish the evils I have discovered.

'"It is many years since I discovered that the moment a man thinks negatively or doubts his abilities, those abilities begin to diminish. Positive thoughts are needed to oppose unseen enemies of this world, and indeed the enemies of the universe. The Earth faces many threats. Those who come after me and come after Isaac Newton must be ready and willing to challenge these threats in an instant. The evil has come from other worlds, as well as from our own.

'"There is one with great power who is seeking to control this Earth and its people. He is very dangerous, but he acts alone, and unlike those who will come after me, he cannot combine his power with another. Those who come after me, and who number six when they are together, are without any doubt the most powerful force in the universe.

'"When they teach the rest of mankind to think more of their fellow humans and fellow creatures than they do of themselves, then every enemy will be defeated.

'"Although the evil one stands alone, he is seeking to recruit others on Earth to assist him. Some weak people, including kings and leaders, will give in to his persuasive powers and will become formidable adversaries to the six, although they will never possess the strength of two or more of the six acting in unison.

'"His name is Marduk, which means "Mediator between gods and men". He is the one who has fallen from favour with the Creators of the universe. I have discovered drawings of the evil instruments he has buried under the surface of the Earth. Although it is impossible to be certain of the location of the instruments, one is buried under ice and snow in the land where the sun never rises, and one is protected by an underground army.

'"The drawings must be given to the six who will come after me, and who will disable the instruments. Great will be their trials and tribulations, but greater still will be their victory when the six who are to come learn to become true masters of their art."'

Isaac Newton looked up from the parchment. 'That is the best translation I can make of the Latin. Some of the words have become blurred. I think the paper has been dampened in its journey from Florence to me.

'There are many drawings here, and you must guard them safely so that they fall into no other hands but yours.'

Isaac looked at the six Defenders and went on. 'Now everything is in place, but there are only three of you. What are your names, please?' he said looking at Yury, Sasha and Jamal.

Angie spoke first. 'Pardon? There *are* six of us. I am Angie.'

'But you are not one of the six who will come. You are only a weak woman. We must await the other three men who are not yet in our midst.'

Lotty interrupted. 'But that's ridiculous!'

The men in the dining room looked up from their coffee and conversation and raised their eyebrows and shook their heads at Isaac Newton.

'Do not raise your voice, my lady,' he retorted. 'It is not seemly or right to do so. Ladies are not permitted in the college and it is only by the grace and favour of these good men that I may speak to you here now.'

Lotty couldn't help herself. 'But we are no different from boys. Angie and Mitchi and I have been chosen by Galileo himself to be three of the six Defenders. And Queen Elizabeth the First, the queen who beat the Armada and never married and ruled for years without a husband – well, she made a speech about being a woman to the troops before a battle. I learned it in drama and it went, "I know I have the body but of a weak and feeble woman; but I have the heart and stomach of a king, and of a king of England too." And she was the best ruler your country probably ever had. So there!'

Isaac Newton looked startled and fell silent for a moment. 'Are you expecting me to believe that the six of whom Galileo writes are three boys and three girls? But that is foolish nonsense.'

Yury spoke up. 'It's the way things are, sir, and the way Galileo ordered it.'

'Well, this is yet another fact about the universe I do not understand!' Isaac said. 'But my own part in this is done. We will look at the drawings and then you must leave me.'

One by one he unfurled the yellowed parchments on the oak table and showed the Defenders the maps and detailed sketches of transmitters buried under the surface of the Earth.

Chapter 15

Lotty and Angie were beginning to love the feeling of their full skirts sweeping across the floor as they moved.

Isaac Newton led them out of the masters' dining room and into Nevile's Court. 'I must leave you now,' he said. 'You should walk through the archway into Great Court, pass the fountain and go out through the Great Gate. It was a pleasure to meet you, and God speed with your endeavours. Fare thee well.'

And with that he walked swiftly away and disappeared through a doorway in a building at the side of the quadrangle.

'That was wow!' Sasha said. 'This is so much to take in – first the ancient Olympics and then Sir Isaac Newton. We seem to travel through time and to different places too, without making an actual journey.'

Lotty whistled. 'And I hope he will remember what I said about girls – it makes me glad I live in the twenty-first century!'

As they talked, the Defenders meandered across the quadrangle and the girls twirled their skirts.

'Where do you think our education will take us next?' Yury asked the others.

'Hopefully back to some decent facilities and modern

comforts,' Jamal replied. 'I'm starving.'

As the six walked under the arch of the Great Gate, they jostled and giggled. Yury had the papers given by Sir Isaac Newton safely stowed under his coat.

'Can you feel the ground moving?' Lotty asked.

'Er, yes, it's kind of swaying,' Angie agreed.

At the precise moment that the Defenders emerged from the gateway, two things happened.

First, they were surrounded by a swirling wind that seemed to tear their clothes from them. When they looked down, their outfits had changed. The girls' dresses had become closer fitting and the waistlines dropped from under the bust to a low V in front. Their heads were covered with wimples, which enclosed their hair that until now had been loose. The boys' coats had shortened into tunics, gathered at the waist with broad belts. Their wide-topped boots had become pointed shoes made of soft leather, and their legs were now visible in tight, coloured leggings. Unlike the girls, their heads were uncovered.

The second thing that happened was that they found themselves on the deck of a ship, which was rolling from side to side on an aquamarine sea, surrounded by waves topped with white horses of curling foam.

'Where are we?' Sasha asked, wide-eyed.

'Oh no, I'm going to be sick,' Jamal said, rushing to the side of the deck.

Beside them on the ocean was a ship with top sails, foresails and mainsails.

'Judging by our clothes, we're not in the twenty-first century!' Lotty said.

A tall, strong man of at least two metres in height was striding across the deck to meet the Defenders. He had reddish-blonde hair, skin burned red and light-coloured eyes.

He hailed them in Spanish. 'Welcome aboard, ladies and gentlemen!'

Sasha's ears pricked up to hear a language spoken which he could understand, after a long period of hearing only English. '*Estamos contentos de estar aquí!*' he said.

'Can you ask him who he is and where we are?' Yury asked Sasha.

The man and the boy had a long conversation in Spanish, with much gesticulating of hands and some laughter. While they talked, Sasha's eyes became wider and his face more full of amazement. The sailor summoned a man who brought a rolled map from down below, and he pointed at locations as he continued to speak to Sasha.

Eventually Sasha turned to the other Defenders; all except Jamal, who was leaning over the side of the deck and looked decidedly green.

'We are on the boat named the *Nina* with Christopher Columbus,' Sasha began. 'The date is January 1493. The other boat is the *Pinta*. This is his first voyage from Spain, and he is looking for the continent of Asia. He set off in three ships and he has been to San Salvador, which is in the Bahamas – but he is calling the Bahamas the East Indies. When he comes from Spain, he land first in the Canary Islands – where Spain belongs – and here he fill with food and make repairs to the three boats.

'After that he made a five-week voyage across the ocean to San Salvador where he says the native people were peaceful and friendly. He says many of the men had scars on their bodies, because other people from the mainland had tried to capture them as slaves. They had no weapons of any kind.

'Columbus also explored the north-east coast of Cuba, where he landed in October. He does not know it as Cuba and thinks he has discovered China. There he saw men smoking tobacco for the first time and his men tried it.

'His own ship, the *Santa María*, ran aground two weeks ago on Christmas Day and had to be abandoned. Columbus was received by the native chief and had to leave thirty-nine of his men behind as he had lost the largest ship. He set sail along the northern coast of Haiti on the sixth of January and he is now heading for further adventures in the New World. We are to sail with him, facing whatever dangers come!'

Yury let out a low whistle and Lotty covered her mouth with her hands.

'Where are we now?' Angie asked. 'I hated geography and I don't know any of the places you've mentioned.'

'I try my best on the map he shows me,' Sasha replied, 'but it is written by hand, and not like our modern maps. He crossed the Atlantic Ocean and reached the island San Salvador in east of Bahamas – I know this as I study it in school. Then for sure he has been in Cuba. Now we travel south and east so we will not be reaching North America. Maybe Puerto Rico, I think?'

Christopher Columbus was striding across the deck towards the Defenders, and he gave a low bow as he reached them. Lotty and Angie curtsied and Mitchi gave a respectful bow. Sasha and Yury stooped low to the deck.

Immediately a man in leather breeches appeared carrying three swords in halters. Columbus motioned to Yury and Sasha and ceremoniously slipped the halters over their shoulders. Their outfits now looked complete. The servant tapped Jamal on the shoulder but Jamal rudely pushed him away and continued to hang over the ship's rail.

'Venid conmigo a vuestros dormitorios,' Columbus said.

Sasha translated. 'We go to our bedrooms now.'

Lotty turned to Angie. 'I bet it will be all romantic, with bunk beds and brass candlesticks. This is so much fun!'

Columbus led them across the small deck through a tiny door in the stern. The girls gasped when they were shown into the dark, cramped space inside. Both Columbus and Yury had to stoop to get under the lintel and could not stand at full height inside. There were a few stools, a table and four hammocks made of rope. It took several moments for their eyes to adjust from the bright light reflecting off the sea outside to the darkness within.

Sasha translated as Columbus spoke to them. 'Welcome aboard the good ship *Nina*. My only sorrow is that I cannot welcome you aboard *Santa María*, my fine vessel, which is lost to the sea.

'I am happy to share my sleeping quarters with you. The ladies will sleep for six hours during the first watch and the three men will sleep during the second watch. I myself need little sleep. I am only happy on deck where I can look out for land in the hours of daylight, and for fires and candlelit windows by night.

'I am proud to have discovered the East Indies and China, places known only to us in stories and histories, but I know our greatest adventure is to come. Also, I am happy to live in the days of discovery when little is known of our world, and glad the prophecy came true.'

At this point, Columbus reached into a cupboard built into the wooden-panelled wall and pulled out a Bible. He took a crumpled piece of paper from between its pages and read it aloud to them. '"From the east will come those who will save mankind from the one who is between gods and men. The east wind will bring in the ones who number six."'

Mitchi tapped on Yury's arm and waited for her moment to speak.

'Yes, Mitchi,' he said. 'Sir, could Mitchi say something, please?'

She reddened a little and was grateful for the darkness which concealed her embarrassment from the others. 'The one between gods and men – Marduk. Isaac Newton named him so.'

Yury smiled. 'She is right! The letter Isaac read to us from Galileo named Marduk as the "mediator between gods and men". So we are meant to be here and the piece of paper in your hand is a prediction of that, sir.'

Sasha translated and Columbus nodded energetically. Then he spoke again. 'Now you must eat, and *Nina* is full of provisions as we have just left land. Be seated and my men will come to you.'

As he strode from the cabin he stooped to avoid hitting his head on the way out.

'I know it's amazing to be here, but what do you think we are supposed to learn?' Yury asked the other Defenders.

Sasha smiled. 'Maybe how to use a sword!'

The boys laughed as they removed their swords and halters and all five Defenders sat on the stools set beside the wooden table. Moments later, two men appeared with wooden plates stacked with provisions.

Sasha spoke to them and translated again for the others. 'There is no salt beef or pork meat as the ships have been away from Spain long time, but there is dry fruit and cheese, fish and ale. The ship's biscuit has not been spoiled by rats yet! The meat has been cooked on the deck by a kind of barbecue.'

'Rats!' Angie protested.

'I'm so hungry I could eat a rat whole just now,' Yury replied. 'That coffee we had in Cambridge seems a long time ago.'

Just as Lotty was asking, 'Should one of us go and check on Jamal?', he staggered in through the cabin door.

'Eeeuuugh, this is awful,' he moaned.

'Shall we get him in a hammock?' Lotty asked the others.

But Jamal was already on his way, feeling around the walls as he moved towards the back of the cabin.

Yury helped lift him into the hammock where he continued to moan and call out every few minutes.

The food was far better than any of the Defenders expected, and they ate their fill. Afterwards, they went out on deck and leaned over the rail and watched what they knew to be the north Atlantic Ocean. The motion of the boat was regular and quite extreme, but Lotty found it strangely comforting.

From the angle of the sun relative to the horizon they estimated the time to be somewhere near evening.

Columbus hailed them from the foredeck in Spanish. *'La hora de la primera guardia. Es hora de que la chichas vayan a dormir.'*

'The hour of the first watch,' Sasha translated. 'It is time for the girls to sleep now.'

Angie, Mitchi and Lotty said goodnight to the two boys and retired to the small cabin where Jamal now appeared to be sleeping soundly in the hammock.

Mitchi typed into her communicator and showed the screen to the others.

'Mitchi says we should stay fully clothed,' said Angie, 'for two reasons – modesty and in case the ship falls into danger.

Yes, good point, Mitchi.'

The girls helped each other into their hammocks. After she had sunk into the narrow space between the ropes, Lotty said, 'The movement of the boat feels a bit like being rocked in a cradle. I love it!'

'Do you think we'll hit a storm, though?' Angie replied.

'Not this close to land, would we? Or do they get tornadoes in this part of America? I know we see a lot of them on the TV, but maybe they didn't get so many in 1493, before global warming and all that.'

But no-one answered her. Mitchi and Angie were already fast asleep.

Chapter 16

The first watch hadn't yet come to an end when the girls were woken by a commotion from outside. They heard screams of *'Tiera ahoy! Tiera ahoy!'* accompanied by yells and shouts coming from above and below deck.

As the girls were struggling out of their hammocks, Yury rushed into the cabin. From the light of the single oil lamp they could see he was carrying a sword and three pistols.

'The sword is for Jamal and the guns are for each of you girls,' he said in an urgent voice. 'We're being attacked from the shore! Get Jamal on deck, but you girls stay inside unless it becomes impossible. Columbus is preparing the cannons.' Then he rushed outside and disappeared.

Jamal groaned, 'This is worse than being in a bad movie,' and turned over again to face the wall.

Lotty took hold of the sword that Yury had brought, slung the halter around her body, picked up a pistol and made for the door.

'Stay here,' she ordered the other girls. 'I'll come back and tell you what's going on as soon as I can.'

Out on deck she found chaos. The moon had risen and its light fell on a scene of conflict. As Lotty ran across the aft deck she felt and heard a sudden rupture beneath her feet. A few seconds passed before she realised it was the sound of a cannon being fired from the gundeck below.

Dodging between men, she made her way to the ship's rail and peeped over the side to try to see what was happening. She could just make out the shape of a shoreline, silhouetted against the moonlit sky.

As she crouched, an arrow flew through the air and landed on the deck behind her.

'Don't touch it!' She heard Yury scream from somewhere. 'It will be poisoned.'

Moments later she made out little lights leaving the shore, like a flurry of tiny fireflies.

'*Fuego! Fuego!*' men called around the deck as a series of flaming arrows began to land onboard.

The men were all fully occupied with shooting hand pistols towards the dark shoreline, while Lotty guessed others were manning the cannons below deck.

She needed no time to think. She hitched up her skirt, untied and tugged her thick petticoats until they came loose and dodged to a bucket of water hanging from the rail. Dunking her petticoats until they were wet through, she began to run around the deck, quenching each arrow that she found. But as fast as she extinguished one, another appeared.

'Watch out, Lotty! Watch out!' Yury yelled.

Breathless already, Lotty returned to the buckets and drenched the petticoats again. While her back was turned, an arrow landed in a wooden crate in the centre of the deck. As she ran back to continue quenching the flaming arrows, she saw sparks begin to fizz from the inside of the crate. Immediately Lotty made her way towards it.

A man yelled, '*Cuidado con los explosivos!*' and grabbed her arm to try to stop her reaching the crate.

'Let me go!' she yelled at him, flinging herself over the top of the crate and covering it with her wet petticoats. Beneath her body she felt and heard crackling heat.

'In the name of Galileo, I will not be beaten!' she cried. Leaving her petticoats in place, she darted back across the deck to the pail of water, which she heaved in her arms as far as the sparking crate. Her petticoats were now smouldering and thick smoke had begun to emerge from the container beneath.

With all the strength she had gained in the long jump from holding the throw weights, Lotty stood back and threw the water across the crate. Nothing happened for a moment, then there was a stifled explosion and a lot of hissing smoke.

'*Ella nos ha salvado!*' a sailor called.

Lotty heard Sasha's voice above the din. 'He says you have saved us!'

Moments later the chaos died down. No more arrows appeared from the shore. The cannon fire stopped in response. The sound of waves lapping against the sides of the ship could be heard. Men began to regroup and try to get their breath. Lotty sank to the deck in relief. Her clothes were soaked and she was shaking all over.

Sasha and Yury were by her side immediately.

'That was a crate of explosives, Lotty! If it had caught fire, we could have lost the ship in the explosion. You were amazing!' Yury said, putting his arm around her.

* * *

'What happened?' Angie asked when the Defenders had gathered in the small cabin.

Columbus came in, looking hot, dirty and exhausted.

Sasha translated as Columbus spoke. 'How can I thank

you, my lady, for what you did to save us tonight? I will be forever in your debt for your quick thinking and fast actions.' Columbus crossed the cabin floor and dropped on one knee before Lotty, who hid her face in embarrassment.

'It was nothing, sir,' she said. Sasha relayed her words. 'Anyone would have done the same.'

'How can I repay you?' Columbus asked in Spanish.

Lotty smiled. 'Actually, I'm soaked – would I be able to borrow some clothes until mine dry out?'

Columbus let out a guffaw of a laugh and slapped his bended knee. 'But of course! I will have your dress dried by the brazier on deck, and send fresh boys' clothes to you directly.'

He stood and turned to the group of Defenders. 'For many days we have been sailing along the coast of a new piece of land, heading in an easterly direction, and I intended to land tomorrow. Just after darkness fell we heard noises from the shore. You saw what followed.

'We will keep to our plans and take a party of men to explore the land in the morning. You boys should rest now.'

Columbus pointed at the sleeping shape of Jamal in the hammock, then crossed the cabin, drew his sword and poked its hilt into Jamal's buttocks. 'Get up, you lazy beast!' he said in Spanish. Sasha was barely able to translate through his laughter. 'You have slept through the first watch and the fighting. Now you will prove you are a man, not a foolish boy!'

Jamal shrieked and leaped up in the air, shouting, 'And now I'm being attacked! This is a disgrace.'

Columbus laughed from the pit of his belly and left the cabin. Moments later a boy appeared with a fresh, long white shirt and a clean pair of breeches for Lotty.

Yury and Sasha tried to persuade the girls back into the hammocks but they wouldn't hear of it.

'But, Lotty,' said Yury, 'you deserve to sleep more than any of us – you're the heroine of the night!'

'We should all rest as much as we can,' Lotty replied. 'It sounds as though tomorrow's going to be a full-on day!'

* * *

Just after dawn, Sasha came back into the cabin. He had woken and stepped outside to find out what was happening. Their watches over, Lotty, Yury, Sasha and Angie were in the four hammocks, Mitchi was curled up on the floor on a mat and Jamal was nowhere to be seen.

'*Hola!*' Sasha called. 'It's the thirteenth of January 1493 and Columbus says today will be his last stop in the New World before he returns to Spain. He has never met with violence or fighting on any of his landings before, so we arrived at the wrong time!

'He has named the place The Bay of Arrows and he plans to go ashore in one of the small boats in an hour. There is room for three WPDs.'

The five looked at one another nervously.

Yury spoke first. 'Does anyone want to volunteer? Or should we all stay on board?'

'I'm not keen, if I'm honest,' Angie answered, 'but I probably have the most to learn. Mitchi and Sasha excelled in the Olympics, and if I understand anything about the process we're going through then it's about being educated for our mission. I reckon I should go with Jamal and one other. What do you all think?'

Yury paused before speaking. 'That's an amazingly mature answer. I don't want any of us to be in danger but it makes sense... and if Jamal doesn't learn anything, at least he might get an arrow in his skull and never come back!'

They all spluttered and giggled at the thought.

Out of nowhere they heard a crack of thunder outside. The cabin shuddered.

Mitchi spoke into her communicator and played it to the others. 'Be careful. That thunder happened because we were being disloyal to Jamal.'

* * *

An hour later, Angie said goodbye to Yury, Mitchi and Lotty and joined Sasha on deck where a small boat was ready to be lowered onto the surface of the sea.

Jamal was in the middle of an argument with Yury.

'We have decided that you should go ashore. Sasha is there to translate, Angie has asked to go and it's time you did something for the group,' Yury said firmly.

'Suit yourselves,' Jamal replied. 'You can explain it to my parents if I die out there.'

'Stop being so melodramatic. And remember what we've been taught about positive thought.'

Jamal had a sword, and each Defender a pistol. Angie had a bow and arrows over her shoulders too. Her face was pale and her expression unfathomable, but Lotty gave her hand a tight squeeze before she dropped out of reach. While the small boat was lowered onto the swelling water, the Defenders could see that Jamal was still arguing with the sailor Columbus had put in charge of the shore expedition.

As the little boat was rowed away, everything around was peaceful. Ahead of the prow, the coastline was richly green with craggy rocks showing between the trees. The ship quickly became smaller behind them, until it was no more than a dot on the horizon. Sasha scanned the shore, looking for a place where the sailor may decide to land, and he spoke to him occasionally in Spanish.

'Everything seems too quiet,' Angie mused aloud.

As they approached the coast, the swell of the sea increased dramatically. Steep, looming cliffs could now be seen, formed of high ridges marked with a few palm trees, with surf crashing along the shoreline below. The sky had become overcast and Sasha instinctively felt that the conditions were not good for approaching a lee shore. The little boat was lurching dangerously.

Without warning, Jamal leaned over the side and was violently sick into the sea.

'Poor Jamal,' Angie said to Sasha.

Just as she was about to speak to Jamal, it happened. Two, then four, then eight canoes shot out of the trees along the shore, being paddled furiously towards their boat. Columbus's men were occupied with rowing and everyone knew they wouldn't have much time to react.

Angie let out a squeal when she saw that every canoe was being rowed by four natives with a single paddle each and contained two archers, arrows already notched in their bows.

She and Jamal raised their pistols, as did the other men, but their boat was rocking so much it was impossible to aim accurately. They knew their mother ship was far too distant to be able to protect them with cannon cover.

What happened next was dirty and ugly. Arrows began to fly towards them, and many landed in the boat. Angie and Sasha had only received brief instruction on how to load their pistols using gunpowder, a steel ball and lighting a touch-paper. With the darkness and the movement of the sea, they were all fingers and thumbs and neither of them managed to load their weapon.

Jamal didn't even try, but lay down in the bottom of the boat, retching and hiding.

The first two canoes were now almost alongside them. As each sailor fired, Angie could see the whites of the eyes of the native archers and the fear in their faces. She and Sasha ducked down while the sailors did battle, until they heard the sound of the fighting subside.

But the respite was only brief. Two more canoes were approaching them. Columbus's men were hurrying to reload their pistols, and meanwhile it was clear the natives were planning to board their small boat. Now the sailors began hand-to-hand fighting, using their knives to repel first the archers and then the paddlers.

Angie was trying to think clearly. A thought was pressing at her mind and she could hear a faint voice in her head saying, 'Focus! Imagine!'

With her hands to her head, Angie tried to obey. She didn't know what to focus on, but then out of nowhere she saw a shiny flash of white appear from the water nearby, lit up by a flash of gunfire.

In an instant she recognised the distinctive markings of a killer whale. That was the only prompt she needed, and she focused harder than she had ever done in her life. She pictured a whole shoal of them, adults and young, powering through the ocean in their shiny wetsuit skins of black and white. It was as though she were calling to them from deep inside her mind.

The scream of men made her open her eyes. There, arching out of the jet-black water, was a pod of killer whales, pursuing the native canoes with relentless purpose.

But in the chaos none of them noticed a single canoe

approaching from the starboard side. Just too late, Sasha turned to see two natives reaching into their boat, pulling Jamal from his hiding place on the floor and stowing him in their canoe before paddling furiously back towards the shore.

During the hand-to-hand fight, Columbus's men had hauled a couple of natives out of two canoes and taken them prisoner. Now the captain shouted, 'Get hold of the empty canoes before we lose them!' His sailors pulled the canoes alongside and tied them to the stern.

The sailors and the two remaining Defenders watched the whales drive the native canoes towards the shore. A couple of the natives were so terrified that they screamed and hurled themselves into the sea in despair. The last few stragglers finally made it to the beach and ran away, yelling.

Then everything went eerily quiet. No new canoes emerged from the shore, and there was no sign of the one containing Jamal.

Out of the silence, the whales returned. They passed within a whisker of the boat, and as the very last whale came alongside, Angie saw its eye blink at her, almost as if it were winking. Then they disappeared into the bosom of the night sea.

The captain turned his boat with the two captives back towards the Nina. He looked shaken and amazed by what he had seen. Columbus shouted to his men to find out what had happened, and Yury, Mitchi and Lotty were looking down over the rail. Sasha heard Columbus ordering that the three of his men who had been shot with poisoned arrows should be wrapped in the Spanish flag and thrown overboard.

Yury helped heave Angie and Sasha out of the small boat

and onto the ship's deck. 'What happened?' he gasped.

Sasha looked bemused and Angie was shaking violently. 'They took Jamal.'

'A native boat has taken him ashore,' Sasha added. 'They came alongside and we didn't realise what they were doing until it was too late.'

'A pod of killer whales came and chased the native canoes – it was amazing!' Angie said. 'I imagined them and they became real, out of nowhere. They didn't try to hurt us, just chased our enemies. I can't believe it!'

Columbus stepped forward and lifted Angie to her feet. He turned to Sasha, who interpreted for the others.

'Columbus says he will trade the native prisoners in exchange for Jamal. He will send the small boat out again under the cover of darkness tonight, and he won't give up until we find him.'

Angie spoke through chattering teeth. 'Jamal didn't help us, but I blame myself that he's been taken. I wasn't watching out for him.'

Mitchi stepped forward and put a blanket around her shoulders and Columbus led them all into the cabin. He spread a chart on the wooden table and the sailor who had captained the small boat pointed out the landmarks they had been able to observe from their position close to the shore. 'We saw a white beach to the left of our boat, and the native canoes appeared from a hiding place between that beach and the cliffs. We need to find a way to distract them somehow, so that we can surprise them by night. But we can't sail the ship any further away; we'll need to be close so that the small boat can get back quickly and safely.'

Columbus ran his fingers through his red-blond hair and looked frustrated. 'I don't know what to suggest. Until we came here we did not meet with violence and I fear we are ill-prepared. We have the two enemy canoes and we may be able to use them to our advantage, but I'm not sure how.'

Mitchi had stepped forward and was indicating to Yury that he should look at her communication device.

Yury took it from her and read from the screen. 'Yes, Mitchi, I think you've got it!' He turned to Columbus and Sasha, who translated into Spanish for him. 'Would you allow the five of us to speak together for a moment to talk about Mitchi's suggestion?'

Columbus and the sailor bowed and left the cabin.

'Okay,' Yury addressed the four remaining WPDs. 'First, we should really learn from what Angie did tonight. Just by imagining them, she called a pod of killer whales into being. Now Mitchi is suggesting that we all try the thinking exercise, to imagine and create a whole heap of fireworks. When the small boat sets off later this evening, the crew can let off the fireworks as a distraction – they'll be seen by the natives on shore, and they're bound to be fascinated and come out to watch. It gives us a chance to land without being shot at.'

'Brilliant!' Lotty said. 'We can imagine some powerful torches and better weapons too.'

'I can't shoot anyone,' Angie said, pulling the blanket tighter around herself. 'Please don't ask me to.'

Yury said, 'You're not going ashore, Angie, and that's final. I'm going with Sasha.'

'And me!' Lotty said.

'And me,' Mitchi echoed.

Chapter 17

By the time darkness fell, several things had happened. On deck there was now an enormous pile of fireworks, flares and safety lighters. In the small boat and both canoes were stun guns, torches and modern all-weather jackets. Yury, Mitchi, Sasha and Lotty were dressed in combat gear.

The stun guns had been a compromise: all the Defenders had suggested thinking modern firearms into being, but Angie wouldn't agree. 'We're not learning how to kill people; we're learning how to work as a team,' she had said.

'I can't disagree with that, Angie,' Yury had replied. 'It's so easy to forget what Galileo told us. Unless the team agrees about something, we shouldn't do it.'

At the last minute, Mitchi had asked the Defenders to think and focus on cloud cover, so that the pendulous moon over the West Indies wouldn't give light to their journey and allow the boats to be seen from shore. It had worked, and neither moon nor stars were visible in the sky.

Columbus had agreed to send four of his men in each canoe, under the command of the small boat's captain with another six sailors and the WPDs. Everyone was nervous and jumpy as they climbed into the boats being let down onto the black surface of the sea.

'At least the wind has dropped,' Sasha said. 'I hope it's

calmer near the shore this time.'

The sailors rowed in silence. As agreed, when the three boats were about fifty metres away from the ship, the first fireworks were set off from the *Nina*'s deck. No-one had anticipated just how brightly they would light the surface of the sea, and Angie watched anxiously from the *Nina*, hoping that the canoes and the little boat weren't as visible from the shore as they were to her from the ship's deck.

The sailors rowed on, and the Defenders watched the amazing display of fireworks coming from the *Nina*.

The captain led them further west than they had travelled earlier in the day. He seemed to know instinctively where to find the inlet between beach and cliffs that he had marked on the chart earlier.

As a bright white firework went up from the ship, Lotty was convinced she could see groups of people gathered on the beach far away to their left. Perhaps their plan was working. Their captain's course meant they wouldn't be easily seen from the beach.

They hugged the shore at the foot of the cliffs, then sailed into the uncharted waters of the inlet. The next time the fireworks lit up the sky, the Defenders spotted a row of huts along the left bank. They didn't see any natives.

Lotty whispered to Yury, 'Maybe they've gone to the beach to get a better view of the ship. That would be lucky!'

He nodded.

Their progress was much quicker in the still waters of the inlet. It proved to be the mouth of a substantial river, but the gentle flow didn't offer much resistance to the sailors. Soon after the last hut, the captain signalled to the canoes to land. They ran aground on soft mud and carried out the plan they'd formed earlier: hiding the boat under tree branches and carrying the canoes with them. Everything was done in silence.

They began to walk noiselessly along the path away from the river. Every few moments their captain stopped, listened and sniffed the air. Each man carried a weapon – a loaded pistol, dagger or sword. The four WPDs held their stun guns.

Another firework went up from the ship, unseen from their position, but the sky was suddenly flooded with blue light.

From nowhere, and without warning, men rushed at them from the shadows. The blue light revealed their glinting spears and bows and arrows, held ready to shoot. The natives wore nothing but loincloths and they began to let out the same blood-curdling screams they had hollered earlier in the day.

Before leaving the ship, the crew had made plans in case of an ambush, which their captain quickly put into operation. The sailors carrying the two canoes stepped forward, using the boats as shields for the group. From behind the canoes they fired at the approaching natives. Lotty, Sasha, Yury and Mitchi fired their stun guns. In the face of such terrifying weapons, the natives fled in terror.

The Defenders felt disorientated and afraid.

Suddenly Sasha yelled, 'Protect our backs – they're attacking us from behind!' He repeated the order in Spanish, '*Están atacando desde atrás!*'

A second onslaught of natives had replaced the first, and in the darkness it was impossible to know where to fire. The only clue was the direction of their arrows, and the only light came from the brief flash of gunpowder whenever a pistol was fired.

The sailors moved back to back so that one canoe faced

inwards towards the island and the second faced the river behind. The reinforcements of natives seemed as numerous as those in the first onslaught.

Yury yelled, 'It's up to us now! Fire your stun guns, but make sure you don't hit any of our men!'

The four WPDs obeyed. They fired outwards, and wherever they thought they saw movement or heard a holler, they fired again.

Eventually another firework lit up the sky. Now at last they could see that they had got rid of the attackers. Away to the left they saw women and children peeping from behind the huts.

The firework died and an eerie silence fell. The sailors waited uneasily. The Defenders were terrified that another onslaught would begin.

'Is that a light?' Lotty whispered.

From the direction of the huts came a small glow, which became brighter and bigger.

'Prepare the guns!' their captain said in Spanish.

After a moment it was clear that someone was heading towards them, carrying a flaming torch. A new sound went up from the huts, a quieter call made from the tongues of the natives. Lotty thought it sounded like a cry made by Native Americans in old movies.

The torch-bearer was now fully visible. He was a young native, naked to the waist and followed by what seemed to be a chief or leader. Like all the natives they had seen, the leader had straight black hair, but unlike them he wore a plain white headband and a coloured cloak. As he approached the sailors he raised his right arm in greeting.

The men spoke amongst themselves in Spanish and Sasha whispered to the Defenders, 'We're going to trust them. The captain says we should put away our weapons.'

As the chief approached, he raised his hand again. More torch-bearers came out of the darkness behind him, and after some gesturing and bowing, the sailors and the Defenders followed the chief back in the direction of the huts.

'What if this is an ambush?' Lotty asked Yury.

'Then we still have our stun guns,' he said, putting his hand on her shoulder.

The walk to the group of huts didn't take long. As they approached, several women and children appeared from doorways and stared at them with their large, dark eyes. The chief signalled for the fire to be lit in the centre of the open dirt yard. Then he motioned for the men to sit and he began to make questioning gestures.

Sasha whispered to the captain, 'I think he wants to know who is our leader, sir.'

The captain stepped forward and bowed. A naked woman came out of the shadows and hung a bone necklace around the captain's neck. He looked around uncertainly, and then held out his hat and passed it to the chief, who put it on his head and smiled broadly, his teeth very white in the firelight.

Every now and again the chief took the hat off to examine it and returned it to his head proudly. Then two young children stepped forward with cages made from cane. One contained an owl, the other a tiny bat hanging upside down. The children placed the cages in the centre of the circle and immediately the natives began to moan and prostrate themselves towards the animals.

'Are they drunk?' Lotty asked the other Defenders.

'I think they're worshipping them or something,' Yury replied.

A woman, naked apart from an apron-like skirt, brought a yucca plant over and placed it beside the cages. The owl had its head hunched into its neck and looked as if it wanted to be left in peace to sleep. The woman began to act out a little drama for the sailors. She pointed at the yucca, produced a grater to demonstrate how she would grate the roots, then motioned to a hot plate on the fire and took out a loaf of bread from under her apron. She placed the bread on the owl's cage and began to worship it.

Their captain bowed to her again and again. The woman stepped forward, broke a piece of bread from the loaf and passed it to him, gesturing that he must share it with his men. No-one resisted the offer of bread, and as Lotty chewed the flat white dough, it reminded her not of wheat but of sweet potato and nuts. It actually tasted delicious.

Their captain began to gesture to the chief and asked the Defenders to step forward into the firelight. He looked at the chief and pointed at Sasha and Yury. He held his fingers up – one, two and three – then pointed at his third finger and raised his shoulders to the chief in a question.

The chief nodded knowingly then raised the same finger of his own hand and moved as if to give it to the captain.

The sailors talked among themselves in Spanish and the captain nodded. He was going to trade the prisoners for Jamal.

The chief stood and motioned for the captain and the Defenders to follow him.

As they walked between the huts, a bird began to call. Lotty looked up and noticed that the first light of dawn was spreading across the sky from the east. The chief led them to a clearing where steps had been cut into the ground. Two large, prestigious huts were built on the raised land at the top of the steps. Light was shining from one of the doorways and the Defenders heard the familiar voice of Jamal coming from inside.

'Don't put it there! Give it to me!'

The chief stepped in through the hut door.

Jamal's voice said, 'Now get me more of that drink I like!'

The captain and the Defenders went into the small shelter. Lying on a mat in the centre was Jamal, being attended to by several young women, all naked to the waist. He was now wearing his designer sunglasses again and was drinking from a wooden cup. He appeared dishevelled and was slurring his words.

'You took your time, didn't you?' he sneered at the Defenders. 'And you needn't have bothered. I'm not going back to that hell-hole of a boat. Not now, not ever.'

The chief raised his eyes at the captain and shook his head. It didn't look as though Jamal was proving to be much of a hit with the villagers.

Jamal pointed at Sahsa. 'Ah, the geek is back, with his big, sad specs and clothes that still don't fit. The un-coolest guy in Brazil. Ha!'

Sasha looked down at the ground.

Yury asked Sasha to translate to the captain. 'Would they leave us alone with him?'

The captain nodded and led the chief and the semi-naked girls outside.

Immediately Jamal began to laugh. 'Bet you boys would like to know what I've been doing with those girls, hey?'

'Shut it, Jamal. You're a total idiot,' Yury snapped.

As he spoke, an image like a hologram appeared – three-dimensional and hanging in mid-air – above the foot of Jamal's mat. All of the Defenders could see it equally well, no matter which side of it they were positioned.

They were startled to see the face of Galileo speaking. 'Defenders, you have so much to learn. Take note of the tale that I am about to share with you, and let it speak into your hearts about the higher purpose to which you have been called.'

As he finished there appeared an image of the island they were on, but instead of the chief being in charge, the natives seemed to be working in fields, labouring while Spaniards stood over them with whips. Loaves of bread just like the ones they had tasted minutes earlier were being loaded onto a longboat and shipped away from the island. Then they saw the chief signing a treaty with a group of burly Spaniards who were all carrying guns and swords. The chief looked older and had a frightened expression, but when he signed his mark, the Spaniards laid their guns down on the ground.

The scene changed again. This time they saw hoards of murderous Spaniards rushing from the seashore to the village, pillaging, setting fire to the huts and tearing women from their homes, dragging them away by their hair. They saw the body of the chief lying dead in the village. There were children dying of malnutrition and fever, natives drunk on alcohol and trees being burned.

The last image they saw was of a single native child, left alone in the charred remains of the village. They heard Galileo's voice again, saying, 'And the sacred owl, the ashy-faced owl of the island, shall call no more. In only twenty years' time, these things will come to pass.'

Lotty began to cry quietly, Yury put his hands to his face and Sasha sank onto Jamal's mat.

'We need to get you back to the ship, Jamal,' Yury said.

Chapter 18

Much later, after their return journey to the *Nina* and after a deep sleep of several hours, the Defenders ate with Columbus in the small cabin. Jamal had rejoined the group and was unusually quiet. He hadn't spoken in the boat at all, and Lotty couldn't tell whether he was sulking or perhaps grieving for something.

As always, Sasha interpreted from Spanish to English.

Yury began, 'Sir, there is something I must say. While we were with Jamal in the hut, we were shown some kind of vision.'

'A vision!' Columbus replied. 'Was it Our Lady?'

'No, sir, not that kind of vision. We saw into the future, a bit like a prophecy.'

Lotty added, 'Of things that haven't happened yet, but may happen.'

Yury went on, 'Yes, things that will happen unless we pass on the warning to you and your people. Sir, where we come from, the world is very different from yours.' Yury paused, not sure whether to explain how the Defenders had turned up in the Atlantic Ocean in 1493. He wasn't entirely sure whether they had travelled back in time or were still in Celestxia. Either way it would all sound incredible and crazy, and he felt it was probably best not to attempt an explanation.

'Your world is unspoiled, fresh and new in a way. You're still discovering it, people live simply and the planet is healthy and strong. The vision we saw was about what will happen to this island in the next twenty years and how things will change for the worse.'

Columbus leaned forward and looked fascinated. 'Tell me, Yury, because I am so excited about the future. I have plans to take some of these natives to Spain, and to parade them through the streets, and to convert them to the true faith.'

Lotty looked down at the table and Angie stretched out her hand and laid it on Lotty's.

Yury began again. 'The vision we saw was horrible, sir. The chief lying dead in his village, children starving, the natives being forced to labour in the fields and their bread being taken from them.'

'That will not happen,' Columbus insisted, banging his fist on the table. 'But you must understand that they are not human beings like you and me. They are part animal, part human. They do not feel things like you and I.'

Lotty burst out, 'That's nonsense, sir! I'm sorry to contradict you, but I have to disagree if you talk like that!'

Yury raised his hand to Lotty and put his finger to his lips. 'Sir, we can only report what we were shown. What happens next is up to you, and up to the Spanish king or government, of course. But we have seen much further into the future than twenty years – in fact, we've seen six hundred years ahead, when the world will have nothing left to discover, when native tribes will have been obliterated and traditions lost for ever.' He stood, looking tall and proud in the little cabin. 'Please, sir, don't be a part of that destruction.'

Jamal spoke up for the first time. 'I second that, sir.'

The other Defenders turned to him and stared.

After supper the Defenders were alone. There was a commotion out on deck, the sound of sailors arguing and fighting after too much drink. After a while there were shouts of 'Yury!' and 'Sasha!' from the deck. All six Defenders emerged from the cabin door.

What they saw was a complete shock to them. Instead of the scrubbed foredeck, they saw only the round, grassy knoll of Celestxia, just as they had seen it when they first walked through the fence in the World of Splenda.

'What?' Angie shouted.

'So another part of our training is over,' Sasha said.

'But if we're in Celestxia, where's our house and Unicornio and everything?' Lotty asked.

All six were still wearing their jerkins and skirts and wimples from 1493. They stood for a few moments and then sat on the grass.

Yury said, 'I guess we just wait.'

Mitchi spoke into her communication device. 'Look how much we have changed. When we first came here, we were impatient and selfish. Already we are a team. I was so proud of you, Jamal, when you supported Yury with Columbus just now.'

Jamal looked embarrassed and turned his head away.

Mitchi spoke again. 'I'm going to search for "Columbus" on the internet to see what happened after we left. Hang on while I look.'

'I think it may depress us,' Angie said, lying back on the grass.

No-one spoke. Lotty began to pick daisies that were scattered over the mound. She made a chain from the flowers and dropped it over Jamal's head.

Several minutes passed. Yury said, 'Isn't it strange not

having a view of anywhere?'

Then Mitchi began to speak into her communicator in Mandarin. It translated into English aloud. 'It's not good. Everything that we saw predicted about the natives came true in the next twenty years. The Spaniards came back and the chief was killed. Columbus took some of the natives back to Spain and most of them died on the way. Columbus became known as a cruel and violent man who tried to force native people to convert to the Catholic faith, but later on he did become gentler as he grew older. And, listen to this... I found a letter that he wrote in April 1493 – just three months after we left him.

'It was written to a patron who'd helped fund the first voyage, and in it Columbus makes it clear that the native people had done nothing to deserve ill treatment. He wrote: "They are artless and generous with what they have, to such a degree as no one would believe but him who had seen it. Of anything they have, if it be asked for, they never say no, but do rather invite the person to accept it, and show as much lovingness as though they would give their hearts." That proves to me that he did hear what we said to him, and that for a while at least he was generous towards the people.'

When Mitchi finished, no-one said anything.

Yury let out a long and sad sigh.

Everyone jumped when Jamal spoke. 'I think that part of our training was aimed mostly at me,' he said.

* * *

All six of the Defenders lay back on the soft grass, and in turn each of them fell asleep. When they awoke, they were in their beds in the building they had imagined in Celestxia. Everything was just as they had left it: Angie's spa building,

Unicornio's stable and the locked glass building containing all the items they had imagined into being.

The Defenders met in the kitchen. At the same moment, all six communication devices buzzed as a message came through.

Yury and Mitchi's read, *Your mission is about to begin. You must deactivate Transmitter 002 in Xi'an, China. Please select the equipment you need and be ready to leave in an hour. Your outfits are ready for you in the bedrooms.*

Mitchi read and re-read the message, and her face burned red and became pale in quick succession. She glanced at Yury as often as she dared to see how he was reacting to being paired with her. He seemed calm and happy and Mitchi tried to calm the butterflies that were raging in her stomach.

The others' messages were the same, except that Angie and Lotty were directed to Transmitter 003 in London, and Jamal and Sasha to 001 in the Sub-Antarctic.

Sasha took Yury to one side in the kitchen. 'I can't do this if I'm paired with Jamal. I need to speak with Galileo about it.'

'I would feel the same way as you if I'd been put with him,' Yury replied, 'but it's a kind of compliment because the Creators must think you have the special qualities to deal with him.'

'But I can't trust him, and don't like him. He had a nasty look on his face after my chariot race.'

'I understand, Sasha, honest. I don't know what to say. I guess we just have to trust Galileo and the Creators on this.'

'That's easy for you to say – you aren't going with *him*!'

Sasha walked away dejectedly to the stables to confide in Unicornio.

The girls were outside, dividing up all the equipment for the separate expeditions. They split some items fairly into three piles, like the electrical and electronic components, wire, storage bags, water bottles, knives, lightweight rope, the three tents, tools and scouting items including compasses. But the flares, hiking boots, ice picks and polar suits they set aside for Jamal and Sasha.

Everyone was beginning to get ratty.

Angie said to Mitchi, 'I don't think it's fair that you're paired with Yury – we should be allowed to choose our partners ourselves.'

'Thanks for that vote of confidence, Angie,' Lotty retorted.

'Don't be stupid, Lotty. It's mad that two girls are together and two boys. It should be three teams each with a boy and a girl.'

Lotty replied, 'So which of us girls would have had to go with Jamal?'

'Yeah, well, I'm not happy,' Angie huffed.

Mitchi looked upset and said, 'Creator decides.'

Jamal had his hands in his pockets and hadn't engaged in conversation or sorting the equipment. Now he stepped forward to the girls. 'I know I'm the one nobody wants to be with. Stuff the lot of you,' he said and disappeared into the house.

An hour passed. All six Defenders were waiting in the courtyard and dressed in their new outfits. Mitchi had hated taking off her fifteenth-century dress and had smoothed it out and laid it in her cupboard carefully.

Sasha said to the group, 'I think this is goodbye. Will we meet again, do you think?'

'Of course, we must,' Yury replied. 'It's so important we remember everything we've been told – the power of positive thinking, of willing each other to win. Whenever we think of each other, we have to send positive energy. And we keep in touch all the time through our communicators. Okay?'

'Okay,' all five said in unison.

Jamal said, 'I still haven't seen a Glowbaby.'

'What if one of us is killed?' Lotty asked. 'Will we be dead in the real world or just dead in Celestxia?'

Angie replied, 'Oh, thanks for being so cheerful.'

Suddenly Unicornio trotted round from the back of the building and into the courtyard where the Defenders were gathered. Sasha leaped for joy. 'I guess you're coming with me and Jamal!' he said.

* * *

Everything was going well for Marduk. There had been no signs of activity on any of his monitors, and the six WPDs had gone nicely quiet. He knew they were holed up in Celestxia, and he was confident the electromagnetic fields he had created around his transmitters would prevent almost any onslaught or attack.

Mankind was doing a good job of destroying itself. Every day Marduk listened in to news from around the little planet, and it was all reassuringly bad. Wars continued, destruction of the rainforests was increasing, politicians were breaking promises and friends were betraying each other.

The range of the three transmitters was impressive. His personal favourite in London was doing a good job of covering England and Europe; 001 (Sub-Antarctic) covered most of the southern hemisphere and 002 reached out east beyond China across the entire region.

He was a little concerned about North America, where

many people were positive and encouraged success, and there was cause for concern in Scandinavia where people had set up successful health care and education programmes and avoided getting involved in wars, but he had plans to sort out these geographical anomalies.

When he was at a loose end, Marduk's favourite game was to fiddle with the signal strength on one, or all, of his transmitters. It never failed to delight him that turning up the signal strength just a fraction led to immediate and pleasing results. Although he soon had to reduce the signal again to conserve energy, the temporary effects were fun to watch.

He had recently fiddled with 003, the Globe transmitter. Had only turned the signal up from 10064 to 10068, just for fun. Later that same day, the prime minister of the UK had announced that the overseas aid budget to assist with famine in Africa would be cut by half. He explained on the TV news that the country simply couldn't afford it, especially as extra funding was needed immediately for war in the Middle East. He was, however, delighted to announce that the contract for one hundred and sixty-four armoured vehicles had been signed with a supplier in China.

The next morning, there was a radiation alert at Griffingham nuclear power station. Every British TV channel and radio station covered the story. Marduk tuned in to Radio Norwich to enjoy the fruits of his labours.

'Harmful levels of radiation have led to an evacuation of the Griffingham power plant. Higher than normal levels of radiation have already been registered in London, one hundred and forty miles away.

'There are reports that radioactive isotopes of caesium and iodine have already escaped and there is a very real danger that uranium or plutonium may have escaped – or may do so shortly.

'Radioactive iodine can be harmful to young people living near the plant and can cause conditions including thyroid cancer. The prime minister will be visiting Griffingham later today and has promised that the public will be kept informed of the situation as it develops.

'Already large numbers of local residents are leaving their homes and travelling to other areas of Britain where they hope to escape the worst consequences of the leak.'

Marduk sat back in his chair, ran his fingers through his dark hair and grinned.

Chapter 19

The Defenders were waiting in the courtyard, unsure what to do or what would happen next. Unicornio whinnied and neighed and wouldn't quieten until Sasha mounted him, bareback.

Jamal said, 'You don't expect me to join you, I hope?'

For the first time since he had left home, Sasha's temper flared. 'Yes, Jamal, actually yes. You keep telling us you own horses and go often to the Jebel Ali racecourse at home – well, now you prove it to us. Now you show you do not speak only empty words. This horse is the best you ever ride, this is great honour to ride. Shut up and get up!'

The other Defenders stared at Sasha and then broke out into wide smiles.

'For Galileo and Celestxia!' Sasha shouted as Jamal hauled himself onto Unicornio's back. The stunning golden stallion with his pure white mane and tail charged out of the court-yard. His hooves threw up chunks of turf as he clipped the grass, and in a moment he was gone.

Mitchi tapped Lotty on the arm in agitation. 'Equipment, forgot!' she said.

'OMG!' Lotty replied. 'They haven't got all their stuff.'

'Right – no time to lose,' Yury said. 'We must all think right now – focus and think and imagine the equipment being in the right place for Sasha and Jamal when they arrive at the transmitter site. Let's sit down right here and do it!'

Angie, Lotty and Mitchi joined him on the courtyard paving. Mitchi knelt while the others sat cross-legged. The boys' pile was larger than the other two as it contained all of the arctic and ice equipment, as well as clothing that would be life-saving in the sub-zero temperatures.

Lotty took hold of Angie's hand and all four WPDs followed her example.

'Think, concentrate, focus!' Yury said. 'Picture all this equipment safely stowed in the right place where the guys will need it and find it, and where no enemy can discover it before them. Go!'

When they opened their eyes, there were only two piles of equipment still in the courtyard.

'Eureka!' Lotty yelled.

***

The boys rode across land for what seemed like hours, and the sensation felt like a combination of galloping and flying. After a long way, they approached the coast, and without warning, Unicornio took off above the ocean. It still seemed like galloping, as if the stallion were running on an invisible road a few metres above the surface of the sea.

Hours later a land mass appeared on their right, which Sasha guessed would be the north-eastern coast of South America. Then there was a much longer sea ride, until ice floes and a frozen landscape came into view ahead. The air temperature was dropping like a stone, and the boys felt a sense of panic begin to overtake them.

'We forgot our stuff!' Sasha cried out suddenly. 'We'll freeze to death!'

'Oh, great!' Jamal said.

Unicornio slowed to the pace of a normal gallop and came to rest outside what looked like a low base station or encampment in the frozen landscape.

Sasha led Unicornio into the adjoining stable building and settled him in. The horse seemed unaffected by the temperature but Sasha and Jamal were shivering with cold. Sasha tried the door to the main building and it fell open immediately. Inside they found a stove already burning and two arctic suits hanging up with boots, ice picks and ropes placed neatly beneath them, and a table set for two with hot soup, fresh bread and four different cheeses. Two bunk beds against the wall were already made up with furs and pillows.

'Phew, that's lucky!' Jamal whistled.

* * *

Marduk picked up a new signal on his monitor, twiddled the controls and put the remote camera into focus. He recognised Sasha and Jamal immediately – and the stallion.

'They must think I'm stupid!' he sneered. 'Or blind – or both!

Wistfully he pushed his chair back and stared ahead, his eyes focused on nothing. For the last two thousand, two hundred years Marduk had known that the day would come when his transmitters alone would not be enough to control his personal project of planet Earth. And so he had made contingency plans from the very beginning.

'The time has come,' he said aloud, pushing his chair back and crossing the floor to his store room. He had never concerned himself with prettifying his environment and had left the steel walls bare and the floor as plain earth, hardened by centuries of padding between his living quarters, control room and stores.

He'd never been as confident of success in his Plan B and Plan C as he had been in the transmitters (Plan A), but the more he'd observed the frailty of human nature, the more his hopes had increased.

Unlocking the store room door, he switched on the light and ran his hands through his thick, dark hair as he surveyed the chaos before him. Steel workbenches were covered with tools and parts, the floor was littered with abandoned electronic circuits and the walls were barely visible behind stacks of unopened boxes.

'Where the devil is it?' Marduk muttered.

He moved from workbench to workbench, rummaging through piles of broken and discarded plastic and packaging, and then laughed. 'Got it!'

In his hands he held the prototype for Plan B. It was a computer game called *Taika*, the game that he had designed to become addictive and to destroy everyone who played it.

Marduk pressed 'Play' on the handheld console and laughed as he remembered what he had built into the innocent-looking game.

'My back-up plan!' he sneered. 'And if the Creators reckon two teenage boys can dismantle Transmitter 001, they're crazy. But I'll enjoy watching them fail!'

* * *

After the boys rode away, the four remaining Defenders felt numb and worried. They weren't sure whether to return to the house or wait in the courtyard. After a while, they heard a commotion coming from the front door.

Turning to look, Yury was startled by what he saw. Angie

and Lotty both gasped out loud. In the doorway they saw a short, squat creature with shining green fur and huge eyes, and cowering behind it was another very similar creature but with fur that was longer and deep purple.

Mitchi called out loud, 'Beepee! Teeto!'

The little creatures stepped forward a little, looking shy and nervous.

Mitchi spoke in Mandarin in encouraging tones, and both took another step forward.

'Glowbabies!' Mitchi said to the Defenders.

'Oh, at last!' Lotty burst out. 'Actual Glowbabies!'

Beepee and Teeto stepped close to Mitchi and each hid behind one of her legs, peeping at the other Defenders nervously.

'We love children!' Beepee said tentatively.

'But you are older than children,' Teeto added shyly to the Defenders.

Lotty sat down on the ground. 'Don't worry, we're not going to hurt you, and it's great to meet you at last,' she said.

Mitchi put a hand on the top of each Glowbaby's head. 'Why. You. Here?' she asked them in thickly accented English.

'We've come to send you on your missions,' Teeto said, 'which makes us sad in one way, because in our experience missions are dangerous – although we don't have much experience because we help out rather than run the missions ourselves, you see, because we're not always brave but we are very good at helping.'

Beepee butted in excitedly and stepped forward from behind Mitchi's leg. 'Do you remember the mission we helped in the desert when there was a fight against the Sand Worms? That was one of the most exciting. The children of the nomads there were being attacked by the Sand Worms and they asked for help, and if a child asks for our help, we always come – but of course you know that, don't you... Do you? So they asked for our help and the Sand Worms were surrounding them and we taught them how to use positive thought to overcome the worms, and all was well.'

Teeto jumped up and down and his fur flapped. 'Yes, yes, yes! It was wonderful. The adults couldn't even see the Sand Worms, and didn't even believe they existed. Why do adults lose the ability to see what is real and think that evil is an imaginary force? Adults are dim and witless, aren't they? That's one of the reasons we love children – only one of the reasons, of course – although, as I think we mentioned, you are older than children. But Mitchi has adopted me. Oops, was that a secret? I think it may be, in which case you must all forget we ever said it.'

Lotty stared at Angie and Yury stared at both of them, raising his eyebrows. The girls' faces broke into beaming smiles.

Lotty said, 'You're very chatty, aren't you?'

Beepee bobbed and bounced on his short legs. 'Well, there's always so much to say! But first I have a favour to ask of one of you – the first who volunteers.'

Without waiting to hear details, Yury pushed his hand up in the air immediately, ahead of both Lotty and Angie.

Beepee continued, 'Mitchi already knows about this, because she has signed Teeto's immigration papers, which are sometimes called a Pledge of Allegiance or Immigration Certificate. We have to have these signed so we can come back to Earth again. If a young human person cares enough about one of us to sign our papers then we can always come to help them, on Earth or here. It's wonderful.

'And the Pledge brings creatures together – Glowbabies like us, with humans like you – so we work better together, even when we are far apart in space and time.

'There are only four lines in the Pledge and we learned them by heart when we were baby Glowbabies, didn't we, Teeto?'

Teeto nodded enthusiastically.

Beepee went on, 'The papers say that, firstly, you agree to love and care for me. Secondly, that I will help when you are in need. Thirdly, that this Pledge will make it easier for you to develop your powers to do good and save the universe. Fourthly, that afterwards we will both work together, which is better than working alone.

'And now, Yury, I ask you most humbly whether you would sign mine – after we have talked about your mission, which I should have done first!'

Yury reached out a hand and shook Teeto's furry paw emphatically. 'Of course. I will be honoured.'

Beepee butted in. 'But we haven't even started talking about your missions yet! Yury and Mitchi – our adoptive humans – are going to China, which is a long way away, but not when we help you, of course! The signing will have to wait.'

Teeto burst out giggling at this point and Beepee continued. 'While Angie and Lotty go to London, in England – which is a very small country but people are brave and kind there, although they complain a lot of the time about things that aren't important like weather and the price of chocolate, but they are good people, and brave as I say, especially when things go wrong.'

Teeto paused and took a deep breath. 'Mmm, I seem to have lost my thread. What was I saying?'

Lotty giggled and lifted her arms towards the small, round creature. 'You're so funny!' she said.

While Teeto was speaking, Beepee appeared to be scratching himself, parting his long purple fur carefully with his short fingers on his short arms. 'The only trouble with having built-in pockets is that you can't always find them in all the fur!' he said thoughtfully. 'Aha! Found it!' he added, pulling out a small, square packet from among the thick, shiny fur.

'Teeto and I have a bit of a confession to make, as a matter of fact, don't we, Teeto? When we came to see Mitchi last time we completely forgot to give you a secret weapon for your mission.'

Teeto added, 'Glowbabies can be very forgetful, and forgetting things is one of our worst qualities, but it's also one of our best qualities because we forget all the bad things that have happened to us! So we only have happy memories! That's right, isn't it, Beepee?'

Beepee replied, 'It is right! This little packet contains the secret weapon we meant to give you. It's a pack of cards. I think you have cards like this on Earth which have hearts and diamonds and jacks and queens on them, and I think you play games with them, but our cards are different because they have real power and they're not for a game at all. And they don't have diamonds and jacks on. Oh dear, I've forgotten what I was going to say…'

'Perhaps you should give them to the Defenders?' Teeto suggested.

'Excellent plan! These cards will be useful only when you need them most, and you mustn't even look at them until the time of need comes. At that moment, you choose a card from the pack and it will always be the right one, because the right card will draw you to choose it every time.'

Yury asked, 'What's on the cards?'

'Aha! That's a very good question,' Beepee went on, 'but of course it doesn't have an answer! The right card will have the right thing on, and none of us knows what that right thing might be! Perhaps an image of a creature – an earth creature or a magic one – with the instructions, *I think you need my help, just imagine me and I will appear.* Some cards may have vital clues about how you can perform a task on your mission – maybe how to open a locked door, or avoid danger. Or they may not! As I say, it's a question without an answer.'

Beepee split the pack in half and gave a pile of cards to Angie and to Yury. 'Put them in your pockets and keep them safe. And you must never, ever, choose a card unless you're in great need. If you do, all the cards in the pack will become blank and useless ever after.'

'We won't cheat, honest!' said Lotty. 'But what if we think we're in great need and choose a card, but we're wrong, and the card turns out to be blank?'

Beepee said, 'Aha! That's not a worry at all, because if you think you're in great need then you are! That isn't cheating. We tried to help some children once who were dreadful cheats. When was it, Teeto?'

'It will come to me in a minute, Beepee, I'm sure it will, was it when… And we mustn't forget that Yury has to sign the immigration papers too… But I think we need to go back a bit to tell this story about the cheats properly, don't we?'

Yury turned to Angie and said quietly, 'I think this could take rather a long time.'

Chapter 20

Sasha and Jamal were sleeping soundly in the bunk beds, cosy under the fur wraps, and the stove still glowed. Outside, snow had begun to fall and the wind was whipping and threatening a blizzard. Within the walls of the base station the sound of the wind began to whine menacingly. Sasha heard it and woke.

'Jamal, it sounds awful out there. I'm going to take a look and check on Unicornio,' he said.

Jamal grunted and turned over.

Sasha put on a snowsuit and tightened the hood around his face, leaving a small, round hole for his eyes. When he opened the door, he was blown back inside by the force of the icy wind outside. It took all his strength to shut the door again. He remembered a trick he had learned from one of the ranchers and tied one end of a long piece of rope to the front door before stepping outside into the biting snow. In the dark snowstorm, visibility was zero and Sasha felt his way along the edge of the building, feeding the rope along behind him as he went. It seemed to take an age to reach the stable building, so long that he thought he must have lost his way. Sasha could feel his face being cut by the wind, as if a thousand knives were stabbing his eyes and temples.

Eventually he felt his way to the stable door and opened

it, making sure he took the end of the rope inside with him.

Unicornio was calm and felt warm, and the building seemed to be well insulated from the wind. The stallion snuffled his nose into Sasha's hand.

'I'm glad you are okay,' Sasha said. 'We may be here for a while.'

The noise outside was getting louder and wilder, making an unnerving and eerie sound like the screech of hundreds of women in pain.

Sasha took hold of the rope, heaved the stable door closed behind him and felt his way back along the line, praying that the end fixed to the main door hadn't come loose. The walk back was a fight of strength between him and the wind. He stumbled and fell twenty times before reaching the door at last. The rope held, and the wind threw him into the warm room.

Jamal was still sleeping soundly. Sasha pressed his back against the closed door and tried to get his breath back.

He said aloud in his own language, 'How are we going to even find the transmitter, never mind disable it in this wild place?'

He began to take off the insulated suit when he heard a knock at the door. At first he thought it must be the wind, but then it came again – a small knock cutting through the sound of the furious, icy gale.

There were no windows in the hut so Sasha couldn't look out to check whether there was someone at the door.

'Who on earth would come here anyway?' he said aloud. 'And who would survive in this weather?'

Very tentatively he went to the door. There was another knock, undeniably a knock. Sasha put all his weight behind the door and opened it. It flew open and Sasha saw the figure of a man outside. He bowed and raised his hand, as if requesting to come inside.

The man looked weary and very, very cold, so Sasha let him in. The man closed the door and leaned his full body weight hard against it.

In the light from the lamps Sasha saw that the man's face was covered in ice, but that beneath it his skin was blackened by frostbite. His clothing looked old-fashioned and thin, just a khaki-coloured jacket and pair of trousers, with large gloves made of animal fur.

'Are you okay, sir?' Sasha asked.

The man lifted his face. 'I am well, although I do not seem it judging by my appearance,' he replied.

'I can make tea for us, sir.'

'That would be more than welcome.'

Sasha busied himself with the tea and the man began to speak. 'Do you mind if I sit down, young man? Things have changed since I was in this part of the world more than a hundred years ago.'

'Are you real then, sir, or are you from history like Leonidas? Have I gone back in time?'

'I am real, and you are real, and I am here with you in your time. I'm an Englishman by birth, and was in the navy in my younger days, but became known for my expeditions to the South Pole here in the Antarctic. I am Captain Scott, known to many for the tragic journey I made a century ago, which ended in failure and with the death of my men.

'I have been called a hero, but also a blunderer; both a great leader and a terrible man who led his men to their early graves. History has judged me harshly in the end.'

'Scott of the Antarctic! I am honoured, sir!' Sasha said in wonder.

'Over a hundred years have passed since my last expedition here, when we were plagued by blizzards, equipment failure and poor clothing, and everything worked against us. I was a stubborn man, although I prefer to call it determined, and I risked everything for the mission to be the first to reach the South Pole for my country.

'The Norwegians beat us to it of course, and we lost our lives in the race. Had we lived, I should have told a tale of the hardships, endurance and the courage of my companions that would have stirred the heart of every Englishman.

'Books have been written about me and judgements have been made, and ever since I have longed to redeem myself and make amends for the actions I took. Now I have been given the chance to do so. May I?'

'Yes, sir. Please go on, sir,' Sasha said, handing Scott a steaming mug of tea.

Scott took a long, deep sip and leaned his head back in pleasure. 'That tastes so good!' He paused and stared into the warm light of the stove, then began again.

'I know the purpose of your mission, and I know what you are searching for. There are few men who know this region as well as I, after spending years of my life exploring here and every moment in the hundred years since wandering across this continent, trying to find forgiveness for the men I lost. I'm helping you now in the name of those men: Wilson, Oates, Bowers and Evans. We were the victims of starvation and exposure in the last blizzard in March 1912. Had we only known it, but we were twenty kilometres from a pre-arranged supply depot. But perhaps, if we *had* known it, we should have run mad, for we had not the strength for one kilometre in our legs, never mind twenty more.

'When we crossed the Ross Ice Shelf all those years ago, I

realised something strange was happening here. At night, when we stopped to make camp, I sometimes saw a strange greenish light coming from underground, beneath the ice and snow. I knew it wasn't natural, and I was the only one who could see it. When I lay awake, kept from sleeping by the fear of the risk we were running, I sometimes heard a deep whining coming from the ground there, quite different from the familiar noise of ice cracking and shifting, an artificial sound.

'One day I saw a strange, shadowy figure dressed in the lightest of black shirts and trousers. I was not hallucinating, and I saw him disappear into a fissure in the ice going downwards. He saw me too before he vanished and his look frightened me.

'I was not able to piece these strange experiences together until much more recently. Let me tell you what I have learned.'

Scott pulled back the hood of his thin jacket and now Sasha saw the extent of his frostbite – it made him wince but he tried to hide his shock and revulsion. From a zipped pocket in the front of the jacket, Scott pulled out a folded map.

'I will leave this map with you. It has all the details you will need of what I am about to say.

'The figure that I saw is real. He is named Marduk, and he is an enemy of God and of creation. Over two thousand years ago he planted a transmitter here beneath the Ross Ice Shelf, and ever since then it has been transmitting a powerful signal into the region and further afield. It interferes with men's minds, and with their purposes, and in this area alone it has led to ambition and greed, to fighting over territory and resources, almost to war. It has also led to a warming of the Earth so that the delicate balance of nature is being destroyed. As this ice melts, the world will flood and nature will no longer cope.

'Here at this base station, we are less than thirty kilometres from the site of the transmitter. Your job is to find it, go below the surface of the ice and disable it. The transmitter is beneath the ice, and is not defended. Marduk has been slack with it as this place is so dangerous and inhospitable.

'You must not set off until the weather conditions are right. You'll need to wait for this blizzard to pass and the cloudless skies to return. You will have only four days to complete your mission before the next blizzard sets in. You will have help, which you can call for at any time by blowing this whistle. It was left to me by Captain Oates, and his death gave special power to it. But use it only in your time of most desperate need.

'Everything is set out for you on these charts, and all that remains is for me to wish you God speed. And I have something to ask: would you do me the honour of forgiving me for the errors I made in my expedition, and for the selfish risks I ran for my country? Forgiveness is the only way I can be set free from this prison... this death in life, life in death.'

Sasha looked at Scott with wide eyes and nodded readily and enthusiastically. 'Yes, sir. You don't need me to do this I am sure, but of course I forgive you with my whole heart.'

As he said this, something quite remarkable happened. As he watched, Scott's face began to change. His skin turned from purplish black to healthy pink. Then his eyes softened from their wild expression to a peaceful yet distinguished look. And his clothing changed – the tatty, thin khaki jacket and trousers faded away and mutated into a smart naval uniform, perfectly fitted and brand new. Scott now looked well and fuller in the face, and very much younger.

Captain Scott smiled and stood up. 'It is done!' he exclaimed loudly. 'I am redeemed! Thank you, young sir. At last I am free of the weight that has hung around my neck for a hundred years. Thank you in the name of every man that was lost.

'And now your own mission will begin. Remember all that I have said to you and success will be yours!'

He shook Sasha's hand firmly and his skin was warm to the touch. 'Goodbye,' he said, going towards the door. 'And thank you!'

Chapter 21

Angie turned to Lotty on the plane. They were travelling tourist class on a charter flight full of Americans bound for their holidays in London, England.

'I really, really like him Lotty, and I don't know what to do about it.'

'You mean Yury, I guess?' Lotty asked.

'Of course! It wouldn't be Jamal, would it!'

Lotty replied, 'I like him too. In fact, since we came to Celestxia I haven't thought about Scott at all.'

'Well, that's progress. I've never been in love before.'

'Love! That's a strong word – how can you know that you're in love with Yury after such a short time?' Lotty asked, eyes wide.

'Because he's strong like a guy should be, tall, hot, and he makes decisions. My dad has never made a decision in his life. He's a wimp. Plenty of guys have asked me out, but I've always said no. Now it's the other way round – I want to go out with Yury but he isn't gonna ask me.'

'You don't know that,' Lotty said, turning her head away.

'Lotty? When you said just now that you like Yury too, do you mean like or, you know, *like*?'

'It doesn't matter, Angie. Forget it. He wouldn't look at me anyway. And we have a mission in London to concentrate on that's more important.'

Lotty turned her head away again so that Angie wouldn't see the pain in her eyes.

* * *

Sasha's heart was pounding. He crossed the room to the bunk beds and shook Jamal firmly. 'Wake up! Wake up!'

Jamal grunted.

'We have been visited by a famous person, Captain Scott of the Antarctic, and now he gave us the plans for our mission.'

Jamal opened his eyes and rubbed them.

While Sasha was unfolding the maps and charts on the wooden table, Jamal sat up in bed. 'Did you say Scott of the Antarctic?'

'Yes, he has been here to help us.'

'And you didn't wake me?'

Sasha turned. 'I tried to wake you when I went out to check Unicornio and I thought the sound of the blizzard would wake you. I tried, Jamal.'

Jamal slumped back on the wall. 'I miss everything. The rest of you see Glowbabies and meet famous people and it all happens behind my back. It's not fair.'

Sasha looked thoughtful. 'I say something to you now that you don't like. Can I?'

'Might as well – everybody else does.'

'You sleep too much. You don't be part of all that we do and learn. You are lazy. If you want to be part of a thing, you must stay awake and be in the team. We all want to like you and we want you to be there. Okay?'

'Well, it's my fault of course, how could it be anybody else's?' Jamal said sarcastically. After a pause he added,

'What did Scott say?'

'That he found the transmitter and we are very near it right here. These are the plans,' Sasha said, running his hand across the unfolded papers.

Jamal got down from the bunk.

'He said we must wait until the blizzard stops, and then when the sun comes back we have only four days to do our mission. He also gave me this whistle which we blow when we are in deep trouble, but not before.'

Jamal took the whistle from Sasha's hand. 'Okay. Let's see the map.'

'We're on the Ross Ice Shelf and Scott marked a fissure here, about thirty kilometres from this building. We must be quick and fast to reach there and disable the transmitter in only four days.' Sasha looked up from the table and listened. 'Am I imagining it or is the wind less now? Is the blizzard slowing?'

Jamal moved towards the door. 'Shall we look?

Together the two boys opened the door. The sky was getting lighter, and although snow was whirling around, the biting blizzard had abated.

Sasha said, 'We must prepare now. Today may be the right weather.'

After breakfast they laid out all the equipment they had found in the base station. When Sasha went out to check on Unicornio and feed him, he was shocked to find the stallion already harnessed and a sled beside him. It had huge runners for travelling over snow and ice, and pinned to it Sasha saw a note.

May you have more success than I, and may the world be a better place for what you are about to do.

It was signed, *Robert Falcon Scott*.

Jamal seemed to have perked up. He was fascinated by the polar equipment and spent time laying it out and organising everything. He even read the leaflet about how to erect the pyramid tent, which was: 'renowned for its outstanding ability to withstand the worst of arctic weather. Easy to pitch, even in high winds, and comfortable for extended living when travel is not possible.'

Sasha burst through the door. 'There's a sled for Unicornio, and the sun is coming out already.'

Outside, a low sun was breaking through the haze and the wind had completely stopped.

'Let's load her up!' Jamal said. 'I've packed all the freeze-dried meals, nutrition bars and ration packs, and we'll melt snow for drinking and boiling water.'

'Wow, that's good. That's very good,' Sasha said in surprise.

'It will be too cold to undress so we need to put on every layer that's provided now, and we'll have to pee into these bottles, because, well, there are certain body parts we definitely don't want to freeze!'

Sasha laughed. 'Aren't you scared? You seem excited!'

'Not scared, really, no. At home I have a lot of money and I have people to do everything for me. I've been thinking about what you said earlier, about me sleeping too much and being lazy. It is true. I've never realised before, but I'm lazy because I don't have to do anything. My dad even hired a tutor who will sit exams for me if I can't be bothered to revise. But there's something I've always wanted, and that's to make my dad proud of me. And I reckon that if I survive an Antarctic expedition, he'll be pretty made up when I tell him.'

'Wow again! I am happy to hear this, Jamal.'

It didn't take long to load the sled. Jamal put everything in place and Sasha secured it all with rope. Unicornio neighed, eager to be off. Jamal swapped his designer sunglasses for a wraparound sun visor.

'How will we keep him warm?' Sasha asked. 'He can't fit in the tent, and he must feel the cold at night?'

'I hadn't thought of that,' Jamal replied.

Sasha's communication device buzzed in his pocket. He took off his glove and read the message.

There is another item in the stable. Please ensure you take it.

He read the message aloud to Jamal, who replied, 'But there's nothing else in there – we just checked.'

Sasha went to look and came back quickly. 'There are two snow-sleds with ropes and harnesses for us to pull. We must load them.'

When Jamal saw them he said, 'If Galileo thinks I'm dragging one of those across the ice cap then he can think again!'

But still he helped Sasha load them onto the main sled.

The boys left the buildings unlocked, just as they had found them, ready for the next explorers or geologists in need of shelter. The sun was shining in an azure sky that was streaked with the thinnest of cloud trails. Its reflected light was an achingly beautiful ice blue, too bright for eyes to bear without the mirrored-lens sunglasses they had been given.

Unicornio seemed warm, despite the temperature, and once the sled began to move he had a natural instinct for finding the firmest course forward. Once or twice he was able to trot, but most of the time he walked steadily.

The sun shone down on the whiteness, and the sled whirred over the snow that muffled the sound of Unicornio's hooves. There was no noise except for the breeze, as they moved through the frozen air, and the whirring and the muffled steps. Ahead of them were the vast Transantarctic mountains that were marked on Captain Scott's charts. And they knew that somewhere between them and the foothills was the buried transmitter.

After two hours they saw a gleaming ice surface ahead, different from the snowy surface they had been covering so far.

Jamal got out his communication device and checked the SatNav. 'We've covered only four kilometres in two hours, but at least we're heading in the right direction.'

Unicornio had reached the gleaming ice and he whinnied, then stopped completely.

'What's wrong?' Sasha whispered in his ear.

Jamal's communicator buzzed and he read out, 'Snowshoes.'

'Have you seen any in our supplies?' Sasha asked.

Jamal jumped down from the sled and began to go through the equipment. 'I packed everything, so they must be here if they're being mentioned on the communicator.' He was methodical and careful, and after a while he pulled four soft pads with ties from the bundle. 'I guess these are the snowshoes.'

The boys fixed all four to Unicornio, who stood patiently as they were tied on. As soon as they were back on board, the stallion moved off, and with the new shoes and the smooth surface he was able to trot easily. The sled made a different noise here, like the sound of a sword being pulled from a scabbard, and for the first time the mission began to feel almost like a holiday.

After another hour they had covered a fast sixteen kilo-metres, but once the surface changed again progress slowed, and at one point Unicornio came to such a sudden stop that the sled spun around on the smooth snow.

'What's the matter?' Jamal yelled.

'Oh, see ahead!' Sasha said, jumping down from the sled. 'There is huge crack in the ice just in front of us.'

A few paces in front of Unicornio they saw a fissure a metre wide. It was so long that they couldn't see the end either to the right or the left of them. The boys stepped tenta-tively to the edge and looked down. Jamal picked up a piece of ice and dropped it down the crevasse. One second, two seconds, three seconds passed until they heard a chink far below.

'Phewee!' Jamal said. 'If we'd fallen down there, we'd be done for. That must be fifty metres deep, at least!'

'Do you know what I'm thinking?' Sasha asked. 'The transmitter is buried and we have to get at it down an ice crevasse, probably just like this one. So how will we do that?'

'In my country we have a saying that goes, *We will fight that wolf when we meet it.* There is no point worrying about it now. We need to get round this crevasse first.'

Unicornio walked along the edge of the crevasse for two kilometres until he reached the end of it.

'How many hours of daylight do we have left?' Sasha asked.

Jamal checked the SatNav, and then the daylight hours. 'Two, or two and a half at most, so we will set up camp after no more than two hours as we have to pitch tent and eat.'

'You are being star today, Jamal,' Sasha said.

After two hours Unicornio had covered another six kilometres and the SatNav said they had four more to cover to reach their goal. Jamal put the tent up in minutes, and they unloaded their provisions and set up camp before the light faded.

Unicornio was restless and he neighed over and over again. Eventually Sasha patted him and said, 'What is it? Try to tell me.'

The stallion rested his head on Sasha's shoulder and shook it from side to side, then pawed the ground with his front hoof. He shook his head again and began to back away. Sasha strained his ears in case the animal would whisper to him as he had done on the journey to Celestxia, but no words came.

Sasha watched and waited. Unicornio backed away a few more paces, then began to trot away from the little camp.

'Stay!' Sasha called, but the horse gained pace to a canter then a gallop, his feet no longer in contact with the snow. He made rapid progress across the frozen landscape and disappeared.

'Oh no!' Jamal said quietly. 'So we'll have to use the pull-along sleds tomorrow!'

Sasha rubbed his eyes. 'At least he will be warm now. I was so worried about him spending the night out here.'

As soon as the light faded, the air temperature dropped like a stone. The boys huddled into their tent and cooked a freeze-dried meal. When they had eaten, they climbed into the thick down sleeping bags and waited for sleep to come.

'I'm scared now,' Sasha said. 'We are very alone here – too far for help to reach us. How do we manage this?'

'Don't be scared. I have faith in the equipment, and I'm

– 214 –

not scared of Marduk either,' Jamal replied.

'How many hours till daylight?'

'Twelve.'

''Night, then.'

Chapter 22

Although Angie and Lotty had watched English films and TV coverage of the London Olympics, they had never been to England before.

As they travelled across the city towards the river by bus, Lotty enthused, 'I'm so excited to see London for real! I never expected to see actual black taxis and Big Ben – they're so cute and so *real*! I feel guilty that we got this task – it's like being on a holiday, not a mission!'

A message buzzed through on Angie's communicator.

Make your way to the Globe Theatre, Bankside. You will receive your instructions during tonight's performance of Hamlet. Your tickets are waiting at the box office.

'Cool! Have you ever done Shakespeare at school?' Lotty asked Angie.

'We did *Romeo and Juliet* and I didn't understand much of it, but I loved the romantic bits. The film of it was good.'

'We did *The Tempest*. I still remember one of the lines,' Lotty replied. 'It goes, "We are such stuff as dreams are made on... rounded with a sleep." But I've never seen *Hamlet*.'

By eight o'clock in the evening the girls were gathered in the pit at the Globe Theatre, looking around in awe at the reconstructed interior. 'It's just like *Shakespeare in Love*!'

Angie exclaimed.

'I think they filmed it here,' Lotty replied.

Suddenly the stage burst into life: actors bounded across the boards, leaping out from every entrance as well as the balconies above. The stage jutted out into the audience and it felt to Lotty as though she were part of the action. When a shower of rain fell, she didn't even notice.

Partway through the second act, something strange began to happen. Angie felt a tingling on the back of her neck, a bit like a fizzing, and her mind suddenly became very focused. She looked at Lotty and Lotty looked back. At that moment, a line spoken by Polonius jumped out at her. '"I will find where truth is hid, though it were hid indeed, within the centre."'

As he spoke the actor turned towards Lotty and Angie and paused meaningfully.

Angie hissed, 'Write that down! It's important.'

Lotty keyed the phrase into her communicator. All the hairs on the back of her neck were standing on end.

A little later on, in the third act, the strange tingling feeling returned. This time Polonius paused after he said the words, '"Behind the arras I'll convey myself."'

'What's an arras?' Angie whispered.

'Dunno – oh, look! It must be a screen – that's where he's going, that's where he's hiding,' Lotty replied, keying *Behind the arras* into her communicator.

The rest of the play passed without another tingle, until the closing scene, when Hamlet lay dead upon the stage and the soldiers had said their final words. A young actor came onto the stage and stood in the very centre. His voice rang out clearly in the evening air and the now-familiar tingle began in the back of Lotty's neck.

'I would now ask you how you like the play, and let me look upon you. I see you hear the call – gird up your courage and seek out this thing ye know of. 'Tis no blind chance you stand here – and if you both will kill the source of this great curse upon our land, men will yet be free. Now, what say ye?

'Below, beneath, this night the very earth calls you, behind the arras ye will discover what hurts this land of England.

'We are but players, not bold nor strong, but you need have the courage of a lion and a bear. And if our play has pleased you, seek us out and we shall guide your steps.

'We, and all our men, rest at your service. Gentlefolk, good night.'

Below the velvety, dark sky the crowd cheered and clapped, and some in the galleries stamped on the boards to make a thunderous noise in the round auditorium.

Lotty heard a man behind her saying, 'That's not in *Hamlet*. I don't know where that last speech came from,' and she prodded Angie in the arm.

'That bit must be for us. I'll type all that I can remember down... It's below, beneath, behind the arras. I think he means that we should go and talk to the actors now. Do you think he does?'

'Really?' Angie gulped.

'Come on,' Lotty said, grabbing Angie's hand and weaving her way through the crowds that were leaving the theatre, 'we're about to meet the actors.'

* * *

Their alarm went off at first light. Sasha was already awake and he felt colder than he had ever thought it possible to feel.

Jamal spoke from his sleeping bag. 'We're gonna need the pull-along sleds today as we haven't got Unicornio.'

'I know,' Sasha replied. 'We'd better eat and get going as soon as we can.'

Jamal was first to emerge from the tent and he saw a sky clouded over and grey, totally unlike the glorious blue skies of the day before. Suddenly he heard an almighty cracking sound beneath his feet, then some bangs, and before his very eyes the ice began to break apart. It all happened very quickly. Just beyond the tent a small crack in the ice appeared, quickly beginning to open wide and move at breakneck speed towards him.

'Sasha! Get out of the tent!' Jamal screamed.

Seconds before the fissure opened up beneath the tent itself, Sasha sprang out.

'Our stuff!' Jamal shrieked. 'Grab the sleds so we don't lose them!'

Both WPDs flung the walking poles, harnesses and sleds away from the widening crack, and then hung over the edge to rescue as much equipment as they could from inside the tent before it fell into the crevasse.

'We've lost the sleeping bags, but thank God we were wearing all our gear!' Jamal said.

'This is bad!' Sasha replied. 'Bad like hell.'

'Do you know what I think?' Jamal asked. 'This may not be bad at all. The fissure may have opened above the transmitter, and this may be our way in. I vote we should pack what's left of the supplies and go down and investigate.'

'Are you mad? And we're still four kilometres from the site on Captain Scott's map.'

'Maybe we can travel the last part underground,' Jamal went on. 'Marduk must have got in somehow. I still vote we try it. At least we won't need the tent if we're underground. And we have Captain Scott's whistle if things get really desperate.'

Sasha thought for a moment. 'Okay,' he said. 'I agree we could investigate.'

Their ice picks and head-torches had survived, and they gathered their supply packs and ropes before walking along the length of the crack to find the best place to clamber down.

'Sasha!' Jamal called out. 'Look! There seems to be some sort of path going down, almost like steps!'

Sasha saw a clear route down from Jamal's feet.

'I think this is where we should start. We need to fix a rope to the top with a strong peg and then let ourselves down.'

As they began their descent, the daylight shone down into the crevasse and lit their way with an eerie neon-like blue glow. The ice walls above their heads appeared to be almost translucent. But as the path went lower, the colour grew darker, first to deep blue and then to a dark grey-blue. The boys switched on the head-torches.

'Whoa! Look at that!' Jamal whistled as the path opened into an underground ice cavern ahead. The ice walls formed undulating curves and the path sloped away, down and to the right.

Jamal said, 'We don't need to keep tying ourselves into the rope harness now,' and he unclipped it from his waist.

'Careful, Jamal, it is slippery and dangerous,' Sasha replied.

But Jamal began to walk faster. The grips on his ice crampons dug into the ice and he seemed safe. But suddenly, as he rounded a corner, Jamal slid, slipped and scudded down a slope. Sasha watched in horror as he saw Jamal fall to another deeper fissure below, the light from his head-torch bouncing wildly off the ice walls.

'Help!' Jamal called.

There was a huge thud and the light from his torch disappeared.

Sasha followed as fast as he could on the treacherous ice path until he reached the edge of the fissure. He called down, 'Jamal, answer me! Are you okay?'

There was no reply. Sasha peered down and called over and over again. He couldn't allow himself to believe that he would never see Jamal again.

After a few minutes he sank down onto the snow and tried to think clearly. Into his head came the image of the white pebbles that he had received from Galileo, one at their first meeting and the other at the Olympics. He had never taken them out of his pockets since, and now his fingers clasped their smooth roundness.

He stood up, held one pebble above the ice fissure and said, 'In the name of Galileo, help Jamal.' Then he let the stone drop. He heard it bounce against the ice wall and then there was silence.

Moments later the voice of Jamal called from far below, 'Sasha, my leg is hurt and I'm stuck! Can you let the rope down?'

Sasha smiled with relief and delight. Immediately he uncoiled the rope and let it down into the crevasse. He wiggled it about. 'Can you reach it?'

'No, it's too high. Can you let down more?'

'That's all we have!' Sasha put his gloved hand to his head in horror and desperation, and reeled in the rope.

'Blow the whistle!' Jamal called up.

Sasha rummaged through his pockets and pulled out the

silver whistle that had once belonged to Captain Oates. He raised it to his cold lips and blew once, hard. It made a pure silver note that echoed and reverberated around the dark ice chamber. Nothing happened.

'Anything?' Jamal called. 'My leg's getting worse.'

'Not yet,' Sasha replied.

The silence seemed even deeper than before. After a few minutes, Sasha thought he could see a whitish glow coming from the direction of the path behind him. A moment later he was sure of it and the light became brighter.

A lantern appeared down the path and behind it, with its furry white arm lifted high, was a Glowbaby. He waddled a little as he approached and Sasha could hear him chattering to himself. 'Here I come, on my way, nearly with you…'

Sasha smiled with relief, and then wondered what on earth a rotund furry Glowbaby could do to get Jamal out of his predicament.

'Hello, Sasha. I'm Zizi, the Snow Baby!' he said, putting down his lantern on the ice path. 'Like all Glowbabies I bring out the best in people when they need help most. Sometimes you can't help yourselves without us, in fact! And that's why we come.

'The last time I was called by that whistle was over a hundred years ago, when I took the delightful Captain Oates home. He was lost in the blizzard, you see, and after he blew the whistle I took him to a far better place. But this time I see it is poor Jamal who needs me. Well, actually, I don't see him: he's fallen down the crevasse. These ice caverns are very dangerous. Follow me!'

Sasha called down, 'Jamal, there's a snow Glowbaby here to help!'

Zizi closed his enormous eyes and looked as if he was

concentrating. In the light of the lantern, Sasha saw a long coil of silken rope appear on the floor beside Zizi, who said, 'You can always imagine the things you need. Perhaps you've forgotten that lesson from your training?'

Sasha watched as the round Snow Baby took hold of the rope in one hand and his lantern in the other, and slid down towards Jamal.

'See you in a minute, Sasha!'

Jamal could see the light above him getting steadily stronger and closer. After a few moments, he heard a squeak and then felt a thump of soft fur as Zizi landed on his head.

'Deary me! I lost my hold. So sorry!' Zizi said as he rolled aside.

Jamal rubbed his eyes, sat up and stared and stared. Then he reached out and touched Zizi's silky white fur. 'You're real! You're an actual Glowbaby! And you came for me!' he said softly.

'Of course, that's what we do – help children when they're in trouble, and bring out the best in people when they need it most!'

Jamal felt a strange feeling welling up in his chest. It was almost as if something inside him was breaking or ripping, and as if a warm softness was springing up to soothe it. And without warning, he began to cry.

Zizi said, 'Now that's better. You haven't cried since you were four years old, have you? Although you've made plenty of other people cry since then. I've checked your files, you see. These tears will make you feel much better and much more real.'

Jamal sniffed. 'I wanted to see a Glowbaby so much, and I lied to the others and I was jealous of them, and… it's just so great to see you…'

'The other good thing about crying is that it can heal you on the outside,' Zizi went on. 'Put your hand on your leg and I think you'll get a surprise.'

Jamal reached for his leg and to his shock found that there was no longer any pain. 'I'm okay! Wow!'

'If you'll do me the honour of standing up, we can get you and Sasha back on your journey. But I have a big favour to ask you, even though we have only just met and we barely know each other…'

'Sure,' Jamal said wiping his nose. 'What is it?'

'All Glowbabies have to have immigration papers signed so that we can stay on Earth after our first appearance to a young person. The papers ask you to agree to care about us, and we need one human each to sign, and Mitchi has already signed Teeto's papers and I'd really like you to be the one who signs mine. If you please.'

Jamal looked utterly shocked. 'Me? Me! Are you sure? Shouldn't it be Sasha? He actually saw you first.'

'I would like it to be you because we seem to be very well suited. And you just need to sign with your finger because with your finger you can only write the truth.'

Zizi produced a crumpled piece of paper from his furry pocket and handed it to Jamal, who laid it on the ice path and carefully traced his name on the dotted line with his index finger. As he completed the final letter, the signature became visible in gold, and then the paper swirled into the air, spiralled up through the ice crevasse and vanished out of sight.

Zizi grinned. 'Thank you, dear Jamal. This bond between you and me will keep my molecules energised, and it means that I will always come to you when you need me. It's official!'

Then he called upwards. 'Sasha! I'll need you to climb down my rope now and join us. This path is a shortcut to the transmitter.'

A few moments later, Sasha landed beside them and put his arm around Jamal. 'Are you okay?'

'Weirdly I feel better than I've ever felt in my whole life,' Jamal said.

Zizi said, 'The transmitter is now two and a half kilometres ahead of you. I cannot come any further with you as the force field around it is too strong for anyone but human children to pass through. But I will wait here for you and I will be able to speed up your return journey.'

Then Zizi twiddled with Jamal's broken head-torch and it lit up. 'Good, that's better. One other thing: the silver whistle won't work beyond this point. But remember what I said earlier: you can always imagine the things you need, whatever they may be. And you can tap into the power of nature; it's all around you. This planet is a living thing. I'll see you soon.'

Sasha hugged Zizi and then Jamal put his arms right around him. 'Thank you, with all my heart,' he said.

'Glad to meet you, Jamal. Be safe.'

And the two WPDs set off downhill on the narrow ice path.

Chapter 23

Yury and Mitchi had sat alone together in the kitchen for over an hour after Lotty and Angie had set off for their mission in London.

They spent the time practising Mitchi's English. She was already very good at understanding people, but she was much less confident when it came to speaking herself. Yury went around the kitchen picking up objects and then typing the English name into his communicator. As he typed each word he said it aloud: 'Cup, plate, banana, paper, knife.'

'You have an amazing memory, Mitchi,' he said. 'Let's try to put some of the words together: The spoon is in the cup.'

'Zur spoon is in zur cup.'

'Good! Okay, let's try other words now – outside the kitchen. I'll find some objects from outside.'

'Zur horse is in zur stable.'

Yury turned at the door. 'Mitchi, you are amazing!'

Mitchi's face flushed and she looked away from him self-consciously. It was getting harder and harder to stop herself falling for Yury. He was so kind to her, fatherly, almost loving in the way he made sure she understood and wasn't left out. But she knew there was no chance that he would ever see her as a potential girlfriend. She imagined that he must have loads of tall, blonde girls queuing up back home in Russia, and that he would be able to take his pick of them.

Mitchi's communication device buzzed, and she read the message.

Documents printing.

Moments later, a series of documents printed on the wireless printer in the kitchen. Yury collected them. 'It's plane tickets to China, and entrance tickets to the Museum of Qin Terracotta Warriors. I guess we'd better select the equipment we think we'll need to go underground with the warriors.'

* * *

The ice path continued downhill for a while and then flattened out.

Jamal asked, 'What did Zizi say to you about imagining things to help us?'

'He just reminded me about the power of the thinking we did back in Celestxia.'

'It struck me what he said at the end about the power of nature. I reckon we humans don't understand that power. And we might be the very first people in the world who have ever seen these ice caverns and stuff. As far as I know there's never been an expedition down here under the Antarctic ice.'

'Look ahead,' Sasha said. 'The path has come to a stop.'

There was no way forward. In front of them was an ice wall, and wherever they shone their torches they saw nothing but impenetrable ice. The two Defenders discussed their strategy over a couple of snack bars from their backpacks.

'Our ice picks will be useless,' Jamal said. 'What could work?'

Sasha thought. 'A blowtorch? A massive one?'

'Yes, get imagining! One each!'

Both WPDs stood in silence and both imagined what they

would need. Moments later, two powerful, gas-fuelled industrial blowtorches appeared. They were easy to start and to use and the Defenders quickly created a huge hole in the ice wall ahead and a growing pool of water at their feet.

The hole became a tunnel and was soon so long that Jamal and Sasha could barely see the point they had started from.

'Hang on!' Jamal shouted. 'The ice is thinning out and I think we're about to break through!'

Seconds later a hole the size of his fist appeared, which rippled and opened up until it was big enough to walk through.

'Whoa!' Jamal called. 'There's a pool.'

Ahead of them, stretching beyond the lights of their torches into the darkness, was a large, utterly still body of water. Whichever way they looked, there was no path.

Jamal poked his ski pole into the water and couldn't feel the bottom. 'We're stuck!' he said.

'We could imagine a boat,' Sasha suggested.

A message buzzed through on Jamal's communication device.

Don't forget that this device contains a universe of information. Ask me what you need.

Jamal typed in a description of their situation and pressed 'Send'.

'I can see something coming through the water!' Sasha cried out. 'I hope it's not dangerous.'

Ahead of them an undulating shape was rising and falling as it approached them through the dark water. Sasha clambered back through the hole they had made in the ice, but Jamal stood his ground and watched.

'I think it's a dolphin or maybe whale,' he called out. 'It's huge!'

The creature came to the very edge of the pool and paused with its head at Jamal's feet, blowing out air from the hole in the top of its head. It seemed to be waiting.

'Do you think we're supposed to ride on it?' Jamal asked incredulously.

Sasha still hung back. 'Maybe type that question into your device?' he suggested.

A message buzzed in reply.

WPDs need to lead the way in working with nature as an ally – for the good of the planet. While humans create their own insecurities, nature worries about the actions of men upon it. Nature in all its forms is insecure about the future, especially now that the environment is on the precipice of disaster.

'I'm not sure that really answers the question,' Jamal says, 'but this whale is a form of nature, so we can treat it as an ally. I'm getting on its back.'

Sasha watched in horror as Jamal made a move towards the whale. 'Jamal, I will now say something terrible. I've been terrified of whales and sharks and dolphins since I was little boy in the water park in Rio. I cannot come with you.'

Jamal turned around and faced his fellow Defender. 'Sasha, that's okay. Maybe I have to do this on my own. There could be lots of reasons, but mainly 'cause I've been such a twit since I got to Celestxia. And mostly 'cause I nearly killed you in our training in the Olympics. You didn't know it, but I interfered with your chariot, and I knew exactly what I was doing. I was so jealous of how cool you are, and how courageous.'

'I have no courage now.'

'So it's my turn. This is what I want to do, and I choose it, to make up for what I did to you. Shake hands, and wait here for me. If I'm not back by the time you're starving hungry, go back to Zizi and do what he says. Okay?'

'Okay... And, Jamal?'

'Yes?'

'You are a good friend and a brave Defender.'

The pair shook hands and Sasha stood further back from the whale. Jamal let his body fall forward until his hands were resting just behind the blow-hole, and then hoisted himself up the smooth, wet skin until he was lying astride the whale. Then he readjusted his position and sat sideways on top. There was nothing to hold on to and it felt terrifying. He steadied himself with his hands and balanced as best as he could.

'I can't look,' Sasha said, covering his eyes.

Very, very gently the whale moved out into the centre of the pool, and every time it rose and fell, it kept enough of its body above the water so that Jamal remained dry. His head-torch threw light onto the dark surface ahead, and Jamal tried not to imagine what may be underwater or in front of them. He lost sense of time with the comforting movement of the whale's body beneath him, and eventually the creature came to a stop. The torch beam showed a flat place at the edge of the lake, and something that looked like a doorway in the ice. The whale let Jamal dismount and showed no intention of moving away.

'Wait for me!' Jamal whispered, patting the soft skin, and turning towards the doorway. He readjusted his backpack and head-torch and moved forwards.

A dim light was shining ahead. Jamal walked slowly and

silently, checking constantly for noise or movement around him.

A little further ahead he saw a closed steel door.

'Looks like I'm getting close,' he whispered to himself. Above the door was a blue electric light, giving the scene an eerie, other-worldly appearance.

There was no door handle. Jamal keyed into his communicator, *How do I open the door in Ross Ice Shelf underground ice cavern?*

Seconds later a reply buzzed through.

Place your naked hand on the ice to the left of the door. The code you need is MK002.

Jamal took off a glove, and when he placed his hand on the ice, a red keypad began to glow beneath the surface. He typed in the code and immediately the steel door swung open.

Jamal felt no fear as he entered the corridor beyond the door. He found it opened into a small room, four metres by three, containing only a desk, a chair and a control panel. The wall behind the panel was made of glass and beyond it he saw a transmitter tower, no more than five metres high and made of a metal skeleton frame with a wide base and topped off with a round head covered in mesh. A series of lights at the top of the transmitter were going on and off in sequence.

'There's no security or anything!' Jamal said aloud. He sat down at the desk. The controls and lights were labelled and there was grime on the panel. It didn't seem to have been used for a long time.

Suddenly there was a whirring noise above his head and Jamal looked up. A CCTV camera was pointed at him, its red light blinking like an electronic eye.

'Damn!' Jamal said. 'I need to hurry. Think, Jamal, think

what you need!' He guessed that Marduk would be watching now at the other end of the camera, although he suspected he would be many miles away. He hadn't seen any other CCTV cameras anywhere above or below ground since he had arrived in Antarctica.

Jamal put his head in his hand and imagined some explosives, using the same thought technique he'd employed in the chariot stables at Olympia. But however hard he thought, however much he tried, he couldn't make anything appear.

'Don't panic. Remember everything you've learned,' he said to himself. 'My thinking is probably blocked by the force field Zizi mentioned, so I'll start with that.' He typed into his communicator, *How do I disable the force field around Transmitter 001?*

And the reply came at once.

Impossible. Look in the desk drawer.

Jamal pulled open the drawer and saw a box of paperclips, an old calculator, some pens and – to his amazement – a user guide labelled, *Transmitter 001 Operating Instructions*.

Despite the seriousness of his situation, Jamal laughed. Quickly he flicked through the contents until he came to a section at the back.

Disabling or destroying the Transmitter. In extreme circumstances the transmitter can be disabled by...

Jamal ran his finger down the page until he came to part he needed.

WARNING! This action is irreversible. If needed, the transmitter can be destroyed by built-in explosives. You will be given five minutes to exit the control room after selecting this option.

Jamal read the instructions carefully, hardly believing his luck. He selected the series of commands and pressed the right buttons until the screen flashed with the command, *ENTER MASTER CODE.*

'I bet he's written it down somewhere,' he whispered, glancing up at the CCTV camera briefly. He turned to the back of the instruction manual. Nothing. Then he rummaged in the desk drawer and pushed his hand right to the back. His fingers found a scrap of paper, and when he pulled it out, Jamal saw *M123* written in pen. He guessed immediately what that would mean and typed *MARDUK123* into the control panel. A message flashed up.

Are you sure you want to destroy the transmitter? This action cannot be reversed.

He typed 'Y' for yes, and pressed 'Enter'.

Immediately a red timer appeared on the display, and began rapidly counting down as the seconds ticked away: 5:00; 4:59; 4:58.

Jamal didn't waste a moment. He grabbed his backpack and ski pole and legged it out of the control room, down the corridor and back to the pool. He was overwhelmed with relief when he saw the whale waiting in the same place. This time Jamal flew onto its back and the whale moved swiftly and dived much deeper into the icy water, so that Jamal was soaked by the splash.

'That went far too well,' he said aloud, and glanced at his watch. He reckoned it would be less than a minute until the explosion.

When it came, it was deafening. The sound was trapped underground, making the ice crack around them and creating a mini tsunami in the water of the pool. The body of the whale shuddered beneath him but it kept on swimming.

'Thank you, thank you,' Jamal said to the creature. He watched tensely for the sight of Sasha's torchlight.

When he reached the ice hole they had made earlier, Sasha peeped out nervously and called, 'Well done!'

Jamal climbed off the whale's back and said, 'Please find me again one day,' and the two Defenders hurried along the ice tunnel back towards the place where they knew Zizi would be waiting.

'Hurry, hurry,' Sasha said. 'Marduk will be on his way.'

'Nothing he can do now!' Jamal called out.

'Oh yes there is!' came a menacing voice behind them.

The boys turned and saw a tall, dark-haired man dressed in black leather and carrying a gun.

Jamal spoke first. 'Hello, Marduk. You're too late.'

Marduk seized him by the arm, twisted it behind his back and held the gun to Jamal's head.

'I'm not scared of you!' Jamal shouted. 'Even if you kill me now, you can't bring back the transmitter, and you can't take away the good thing I've done. And because of this I'll die a better person than I was. And now there are at least five people who care about me. And one Glowbaby.'

'One *what*?' Marduk growled.

'Glowbaby. *And* he asked me to adopt him too!'

'So you've fallen for the myth, you sad little boy,' Marduk sneered.

'It's no myth. He's waiting for us just ahead. I can call him any time I need because I signed his papers,' Jamal added.

'Prove it!' Marduk laughed.

Sasha tugged at Marduk's arm. 'Stop it! Leave us alone, please!'

But Jamal called aloud, 'Zizi! I need you!'

Immediately a light gleamed along the path ahead and the Defenders saw Zizi trotting towards them, carrying the lantern in one hand. 'I'm on my way, coming!' he was saying.

'There! Now do you believe me?' Jamal challenged Marduk.

'There what?' Marduk said, looking around. 'Where?'

'Coming towards us, right here!' Jamal replied. 'Zizi, the snow Glowbaby!'

'Deary me,' Zizi said as he reached the group. 'This will be tricky.'

'Oh, an *invisible* Glowbaby!' Marduk said sarcastically. 'Of course!'

Jamal asked Zizi, 'Can't he see you?'

'Of course not! Only children can see us, or very special adults, like Captain Oates, who have the heart of a child.'

Marduk spoke to Sasha. 'My argument is not with you, the coward of Cuiaba. You may go free. It's *this* one I want!' And he dragged Jamal away by the hair, the gun still held to his head.

Chapter 24

CNN Newsflash
In an unexpected move today, heads of government from the G8 nations have signed a treaty on future exploration in Antarctica. Full agreement has been reached on major issues including a ban on oil exploration, whale hunting and mineral exploitation.

BBC News headlines at nine a.m.
The president of the United States today authorised a research project into the impact of global warming on the polar ice caps. He has allocated a budget of six billion dollars for protecting against further damage to the ozone layer. In a statement he said, 'We have reviewed our arms budget and been able to allocate funds from a reduction in nuclear capacity to this vital work to preserve the planet for our children's children.'

TV Brasil News
South American heads of state met today to agree a total ban on further timber extraction from rainforests throughout the continent. All wood products will now be sourced from sustainable sources. This unexpected decision came after a short and amicable meeting in Rio de Janeiro.

* * *

Angie and Lotty made their way around the side of the Globe Theatre to the stage door. There were three people waiting outside for autographs.

Angie pushed her way to the front and spoke to the security man at the door. 'Excuse me. One of the actors has requested to see us,' she said.

Lotty's eyes widened and she swallowed hard.

'And who will that be, miss?' the guy asked.

Angie seemed prepared. 'Ben Jenkins, who said the epilogue,' she replied.

Lotty's eyes widened even further.

'Wait here, miss,' the man said and he disappeared inside.

Moments later he reappeared and beckoned the girls inside. 'Up the stairs, along the corridor, third dressing room on the right,' he said.

Lotty whispered, 'How did you do that?'

'Dunno! Just a hunch!' Angie replied.

They knocked on the dressing-room door and immediately the young actor opened it. He was already free of make-up and dressed in jeans and a T-shirt. 'Oh hi!' he said. 'You must be the girl I had the message about.'

'That's me!' Angie said confidently.

'I'm Ben and I had a message that you need a tour of the undercroft for your college project. I've had a chat with security but there's no way you can have a key tonight. You'll have to come back in office hours, and with a teacher or someone with the authority to give you access.'

'But that's such a pity,' Angie replied, ''cause I'm doing this project to attract more young people back home to the theatre. There's a lot of interest in Shakespeare where I come from in South Africa.'

'It's great to hear that, but there's nothing I can do to help.

Security is security, and we can't just let anyone in – you might be terrorists. Not that you look like terrorists. I don't know any beautiful blonde ones, anyway!' Ben said slimily.

Angie smiled and moved a little closer to him. 'Oh go on, just for me?' She tilted her heart-shaped face towards his. A strand of hair fell across her cheek seductively.

'I wish I could,' Ben said, 'but I can't. Gotta go, but I really hope you'll come and see me again.'

'Damn it!' Angie said after Ben shut his dressing room door. 'What do we do now?'

They heard someone talking further down the corridor. Lotty looked in both directions, and they scooted in the direction of the voice. In the passage ahead they saw an actor still in costume, wearing the rich russet and gold brocade of Elizabethan dress. The actor had his back to them and was saying, 'I can get you backstage, or allowed in the hall; I outdistance a cart that is stuck in a crawl. I succeed in a class, relinquish the ball, or can opt out when you have no interest at all.'

'What a coincidence that he's talking about going backstage!' Angie whispered to Lotty.

The man turned to them, and Lotty's jaw dropped, then Angie's eyes widened as they both realised that the face on the top of the body was, without a doubt, that of William Shakespeare. He looked exactly like the famous portrait they had both seen in school books: swarthy, with one earring and a sensuous mouth.

'OMG! OMG!' Lotty said under her breath.

'Greetings, my ladies!' Shakespeare said, dropping his right arm before him and stooping to make a low, gracious bow.

Both Defenders gave their best attempt at a curtsey.

Lotty's wasn't bad, but Angie lost her balance and toppled sideways.

Shakespeare repeated, 'I can get you backstage, or allowed in the hall; I outdistance a cart that is stuck in a crawl. I succeed in a class, relinquish the ball, or can opt out when you have no interest at all.'

There was silence.

'Is it a riddle, sir?' Lotty asked, her eyes staring wide.

'Most certainly,' Shakespeare said, his dark eyes laughing. 'All of life is little more than a riddle. We are born, we make play to understand the riddles of life and then we fall into our ready graves. But this riddle is for you alone and holds the key!'

He held up a golden key in his right hand, and Lotty noticed that his fingers were dirty and stained with ink.

OMG! she thought. Perhaps he's just finished writing *Romeo and Juliet*!

He smiled. 'But the key remains in my hand until you answer my riddle!'

'Could you say it a third time, sir?' Angie asked, her eyes melting.

Shakespeare repeated the lines again, more slowly this time.

'Is it a key?' Lotty asked. 'To get backstage or in the hall?'

Shakespeare shook his head.

'"To succeed in class" – do you mean an exam?'

He nodded and tilted his head.

Angie giggled like a schoolgirl, then shrieked, 'Pass! Is it "pass"? You pass the slow cart, have a pass to go backstage and pass a class!'

'You have the measure of me!' Shakespeare said, taking Angie's hand and lifting it to his lips. Lotty noticed that as he did it, his eyes held Angie's gaze and burned into her.

Shakespeare dropped the golden key into her hand. 'You have earned your reward, and it was a very great pleasure to meet you, my lady,' he said. 'I will pen an honour to you in my next play: I will create a character that I shall name Angelo. And as you have the measure of me, I shall call the play *Measure for Measure*. Perhaps I have met my equal in you.'

'H-how do you know my name?' Angie stammered.

'I know many things, and I bring them all to the stage,' Shakespeare said. 'Now do what you must and return the key to me in time.'

As they walked away, Angie said, 'OMG, Lotty! He's the most gorgeous, hot, lush guy I have EVER seen. Compared to him, Yury is a numpty.'

'But he's *ancient*!'

'He's experienced!' Angie laughed.

'Er... teeny problem,' Lotty replied. 'He died hundreds of years ago – which could make dating difficult!'

'Now I know why he was so good at writing about women!' Angie said. 'He's a girl's guy! I hope we meet him again!'

'Focus on the job!' Lotty said, slapping Angie on the arm teasingly.

The backstage areas were well signed and the girls found the door to the undercroft easily. The key fitted the lock and they let themselves in, locking the door again behind them.

Angie said, 'I guess we just head downwards as far as we can. The actors said it's in the centre and beneath, and behind some kind of screen – that's our clue.'

One door was marked, *Electricians only*; another, *Stores*; and the last, *Archaeology Area*. They were all locked. Angie tried the key in the door for the archaeology area and, to her surprise, it turned in the lock. She flicked a switch and a series of strip-lights came on, revealing that they were among the foundations of the Globe Theatre, surrounded by building props, earthworks and trenches. In various places there were archaeological markers, measurements and numbers.

'This must be the dig they had to do when they were building the theatre,' Lotty said.

'We need to go further down,' Angie replied, looking around.

'There!' Lotty said, pointing to a set of metal steps which led down into the darkness. There were hard hats and boots and torches at the top of the stairs, and the girls put on the safety gear and grabbed torches before they climbed down.

'It smells weird – earthy and a bit musty,' Lotty said. 'And I'm not that keen 'cause I'm a bit claustrophobic.'

At the bottom of the steps they found themselves in a small chamber in the earth, held up by steel builders' props. There were no entrances or exits.

'Help!' Lotty said.

'Guess it's time for one of the playing cards the Glowbabies gave us.'

'Are you sure this counts as a time of great need?'

'We've got no tools, we're wearing normal clothes and we're facing a dead end. I reckon so,' Angie said, taking the cards out of her pocket. She turned them face down and held them out in a fan to Lotty. 'Go on, pick one.'

Lotty whistled and slowly pulled out one card, which she handed to Angie.

'It's an instruction. "Remove the earth from the dead centre of the floor. A trap door will be revealed. The transmitter is behind the screen which holds back the water of the River Thames."'

The instructions resulted in success. Below the trap door was a metal ladder down to a much larger excavated area. One entire wall was made of concrete. 'Guess that's the river defence,' Angie said. 'Now what?'

'We can't get in there, and we can't cause any damage to that wall or the water will break in. What do we do?' Lotty replied.

Angie looked around. 'We need more information', and she typed into her communication device, *Ground plans of Thames barrier beneath Globe Theatre*. 'Here's the reply,' she said reading aloud. '"At this time, we cannot locate any information on how access can be obtained."'

Lotty said, 'I reckon Marduk is on the warpath. Maybe he's prevented information from Galileo and the Creators reaching us down here.'

'So we try another card,' Angie replied.

This time, as Lotty selected a card, something remarkable happened. Both girls experienced an all-over body shock, as if a bolt of electricity had gone through them.

'You're glowing green!' Lotty cried.

'So are you!'

Lotty was still clutching the card she'd selected, and she turned it over to find the words: *You are now able to pass through any solid matter in the universe. You are invisible to all life forms.*

'OMG! I guess that means we can walk through the concrete wall?'

Angie began to move forwards, and when she reached the wall, her hand, arm, shoulder and body passed through it until she stood on the other side. Lotty followed, both of them with their eyes wide in shock.

'It feels a bit like wading through a current in water,' Lotty said.

On the other side of the concrete wall was a glass chamber, like a large fish tank, containing a transmitter just like the one Jamal had found, but a little smaller. On the top of the narrowest part of the frame was a round mesh top from which a series of lights glowed.

The girls passed through the glass easily and stood right beside the transmitter.

Suddenly they saw movement beyond them, on the other side of the glass chamber. A man stood there. He was dressed in dark clothes, and had dark hair and a scowling expression. He appeared to be attaching something to the far wall.

'What is he doing? Could that be *him*?' Lotty breathed.

'Oh no! Explosives!' Angie said. 'Marduk's trying to breach the river wall!'

'But that will destroy the transmitter and him and *us*!' Lotty squeaked.

Before she had time to think, Angie passed back through the glass wall. At first she forgot that she was invisible and was surprised when Marduk didn't look round at her. Sure enough, he was applying demolition charges to the defence wall, and unreeling some sort of cable which was attached to the charges. He took no more notice of Angie than if she had been a fly, and she realised how much power it could give her to be invisible at this moment.

She thought quickly and watched to see what Marduk was doing. She beckoned to Lotty to go back through the concrete wall into the earth chamber below the theatre, but

- 243 -

Lotty was still standing transfixed beside the transmitter and didn't move.

Marduk was now fiddling with a control switch on the end of the cable. He began to head off towards a steel door to the side of the area. It was obvious he still had no idea he was being watched.

Angie returned to Lotty. 'Go back the way we came and alert the police and the river authorities – there's going to be a heck of a flood.'

'Will you be okay?'

'I want to do this, Lotty. For the first time in my life I feel needed. It reminds me of when I did the long jump in Olympia. The feeling then was great – and it's even better now.'

Lotty kissed Angie on the cheek and returned through the wall to the theatre undercroft.

Stealthily Angie followed Marduk through the steel door and into a lift shaft. Her mind was clear and sharp, and she knew exactly what she had to do. She had no intention of letting Marduk get away from the explosion and press the detonator after he was safe. Just before he closed the lift doors, Angie leaned forward and pushed the red button on the control panel.

Marduk let out a groan as he heard the detonation alarm begin. Angie held the lift door open and counted the seconds: one, two, three, four... And at ten she heard an almighty explosion, followed by a great roaring sound. A wave of water smashed down the steel door they had come through and gushed into the lift.

Marduk yelled as the river water, stones and debris smacked into him, but Angie had already climbed onto his shoulders, passed through the ceiling of the lift and was scampering on up inside the lift shaft. She emerged in the very centre of the Globe stage, in the exact spot where Ben had delivered his epilogue just over an hour earlier. With huge relief, she heard emergency vehicle sirens and knew that Lotty must have delivered the message.

'I hope he's drowned,' she breathed as she fell flat on the stage floor.

Chapter 25

Marduk crawled back to his control room like a wounded beast to its lair. He was bruised, bleeding and exhausted, but grateful to have survived. He made it as far as his chair and slumped over the desk, panting.

His monitors were showing a sorry scene. Transmitter 001 (Sub-Antarctic) was no more. The only monitor on the Ross Ice Shelf that was still working showed a huge crater in the expanse of polar ice. Dotted among the debris in the very bottom of the crater were pieces of twisted metal that had once formed the tower of his first transmitter.

He turned his attention to Transmitter 002 in Xi'an, China. There, all was well: the Terracotta Warriors were still protecting it with their radioactive coating and the dangerous chemicals they contained. Marduk was relieved to see that nothing had been disturbed.

But the images of Transmitter 003 broke his heart. The river flood had destroyed his transmitter tower completely, but the inner defence wall had held the Thames water back from the foundations of the Globe Theatre and engineering work had already started to repair the breach. All Marduk had achieved with his explosives was to destroy his own creation and almost kill himself. His plan to keep people away had backfired.

'I still don't know what happened,' he breathed. 'I never saw a Defender. No-one was there... The damn detonator just set itself off! It's a complete disaster – and after all my careful planning.'

He rubbed his head with his hands. 'But no animal is more dangerous than when it is wounded. I will recover from this and destroy those idiot children.'

Marduk took a pack of pills from a cupboard and swallowed several at once. He flung the packet on the floor and turned back to his monitors.

'It's time!' he said angrily.

Ever since he had installed the three transmitters on Earth, they had been transmitting in standard mode to affect human behaviour, sending out a signal of which he often varied the strength. But they had been created with the capacity to transmit in super mode, or even nuclear mode.

Now he had lost two of his three transmitters, the decision was simple. Marduk keyed in the commands to switch Transmitter 002 in Xi'an, China, to super mode. He knew the effects on mankind would be immediate and devastating.

'You didn't expect this, Galileo! Your favourite little planet will pay a high price for you sending those kids to mess with my plans,' he snarled.

Smiling, he turned out of the room into the corridor. After a few metres he reached a door, which he unlocked. 'Jamal?'

No reply came out of the darkness within.

'Get up!' Marduk growled, switching on the light in the corridor.

Jamal squinted and sat up from his position on the floor. The room was empty apart from a piece of matting, and there were no windows. 'I need a pee,' he said.

'You'll need more than a pee when I've finished with

you,' Marduk growled.

'You don't scare me!' Jamal said, rubbing his eyes.

Marduk seemed thoughtful. 'Maybe you and I can do a little deal,' he suggested slowly. 'Come with me.'

Marduk allowed Jamal to sit on a chair in his control room, and passed him a plate of crisps and chocolate bars. 'It occurs to me that I may have been a bit harsh, Jamal. You and I have always seemed to be two of a kind, haven't we? Ambitious, strong… and intelligent.'

Jamal munched crisps and watched Marduk carefully.

'You're aware that I have a great deal of power, here on Earth – obviously – and in much of the created universe too. I share that power with no-one, and have had no ally… until now. Imagine how much fun we could have if we worked together, as a team of two, like brothers in arms.'

Jamal spoke with his mouth full. 'What's in it for you?'

'Because two can achieve so much more than one. I'm sure you learned all about that in your training, didn't you? And mine is a lonely kind of power; it would be good to pool resources. You know a lot about the Defenders and Celestxia, and you can help me in my campaign to make the world a better place, while I can give you access to privileges you've never dreamed of.'

'Actually,' said Jamal, 'I've already had those in my life at home, and it was no fun. I've been happier since I haven't had the privileges.'

Marduk tried again. 'But you've never had *real* power, have you? That's what I can offer – a chance to influence world events, change the future, and for your name to outlive you!'

Jamal broke into a chocolate bar. 'Give me an example of what you've got in mind about us working together.'

Marduk rubbed his chin, and decided he would chance his luck. Since the WPDs had begun training he had tried endlessly to pick up signals to track their whereabouts and overhear their mission plans. On all but two occasions he had failed. Only twice had he tuned in and picked up sound and pictures of the Defenders, both at times when they were being negative about each other. Frustratingly the signal had broken down very quickly and he hadn't been able to get a precise or long enough lock on the WPDs to enable him to achieve full tracking. He guessed that when they spoke critically, their negative energy broke down the protective shield that surrounded them during training. But he thought the snippets that he'd recorded may be enough to motivate Jamal to defect.

'Well,' Marduk began, 'your former WPD colleague, Yury, has disappeared from view. I assume he's on the way to Transmitter 002 in China to try to disable it. You already know the kind of guy he is – arrogant, good-looking, a hit with all the girls. Imagine how unbearable he'll be if he succeeds in his mission. But if we work together, we have time to stop him. And you can help me increase the effectiveness of the transmitter to make great things happen. It's a once-in-a-lifetime chance for a guy like you.'

Jamal raised a final objection. 'But I was happier in my last few days as a Defender than I've ever been – why should I walk away from that?'

'Because they don't like you. Never have. They've all been nice to your face, but… Do you want to know what they've been saying behind your back?'

'What do you mean?' Jamal asked quietly.

'Take a look,' Marduk said, flicking switches on his control panel. 'These videos were taken during training – and even since.'

An image of Yury and Sasha appeared on one of the monitors, and Marduk turned up the volume. The film was taken outside Unicornio's stable door.

Yury was saying, 'He's the weak link in the team, and I don't know why he was chosen by the Creators to be a WPD.'

Sasha replied, 'I just hope I don't get paired up with him for the missions. If we were not under orders, I would punch him in the mouth.'

Marduk selected another clip and Angie and Lotty appeared on screen, speaking on board Columbus's ship, the *Nina*.

'When we left the island, I actually wished Jamal had never been found and that the chief had kept him as a slave or something,' Angie said.

'Me too,' Lotty replied. 'Especially 'cause he's so lazy; he's not done a thing to help since he arrived. I guess he's been ruined since he was little by having rich parents and servants and stuff.'

Jamal held up his hand. 'That's enough,' he said. 'And to think I actually risked my life for these little gits. Especially Sasha – I wish I'd chucked him in the water with the whale he was so scared of.'

'It can't be easy hearing that,' Marduk went on, 'and it must hurt. That's why I thought you may want to help me scupper Yury's plan to make himself the greatest.'

Jamal paused for a moment and then said, 'I do. I'll help in any way I can.'

* * *

China Central TV News
The most powerful earthquake ever experienced in China occurred late last night close to the city of Hebei. Measuring 8.7 on the Richter scale, the quake lasted for over a minute and almost a million people are feared dead, with thousands more missing. It has been impossible for emergency services to reach the worst hit areas as the damage is so extensive. The Chinese government has appealed for international assistance.

BBC News
An unexpected outbreak of violence has occurred in the Pacific Rim. Further details to follow as soon as we receive them. An international commentator in the region has stated that several nations are on the brink of war.

CNN Breaking News
The prime minister of Anatolia has admitted responsibility for a massive explosion in the western zone of the capital city of Timor with a death toll estimated at forty-nine, including women and children.

Channel 7 Australia
The world is holding its breath after an atomic bomb was discovered hidden underground in the central deserts last night. The Australian nation is in shock, demanding an answer to one question: how did this happen? How can something of this nature have gone on under the nose of the government in a modern democratic nation? The prime minister will make an address on TV at noon.

* * *

On their flight to Xi'an in China, Yury and Mitchi tried to take in the conversations buzzing around them like flies. As soon as they reached the airport they had heard the dreadful news stories that were consuming the world. The Chinese were shocked about the massive earthquake – the effects of which were even being felt in Beijing – and were worried about the conflict in Korea, but were talking most of all about the nuclear bomb discovered in Australia.

'What's happening to the world?' Yury asked Mitchi. 'I've never known a time like this in my whole life.'

Although her home in Chengdu was far, far from the centre of the earthquake, Mitchi felt that all the certainty of her world was shattered. She was worried about her family, terrified about the effect on her nation and afraid for the future.

Yury said, 'I guess our mission is even more important now than ever.'

During their flight, the Defenders read as much information about the Terracotta Army as they could get from their communication devices.

'There are thousands of warriors and horses, all uncovered since the peasants found the first pieces of pottery in 1974,' Yury summarised. 'The figures are in three main pits, and it's all open to the public. The experts believe the figures are guarding the tomb of Emperor Qin Shi Huang Di, but we've got to assume that they're being used by Marduk.'

Mitchi tried out her rapidly improving English. 'My communicator many time say the "Final Battle". What that?'

'I dunno, but it sounds worrying. Do you mind if I watch a film for a bit – clear my head?'

'Okay,' Mitchi said quietly, hoping Yury wasn't bored by her company.

Yury selected an action adventure on his in-flight monitor and sat back to watch. As soon as the adverts finished, he was shocked to see the face of Galileo appear. Yury tapped Mitchi on the arm and they both began to listen as Galileo spoke.

'Welcome, Defenders. You have heard of the terrible things that are happening on Earth at this very moment, but you do not yet know that these events have been caused by Marduk for his evil purposes.

'Mitchi has already noticed that your project has been named the Final Battle. This is because Lotty, Angie, Sasha and Jamal have already been successful in their own missions. Marduk's great anger is a reaction to the success of the first two WPD missions and it is now critical that you are able to destroy his third and final transmitter. Unless it is stopped, it could mean the end of planet Earth.

'Once you get close to the Terracotta Warriors, we will be unable to reach you, as the force field around them is too strong. But you have the cards given to you by Teeto and Beepee, and you have dormant powers which you have not yet released. Even acting alone, the extent of these powers is amazing, so long as your thoughts are true and intended for good. Positive thoughts are the ultimate power in the universe.

'But when two or more of you act together, your powers are far, far greater than when you are alone. Working together is the only way you will be able to win the Final Battle ahead.

'When you find yourselves alone and in danger, do not forget to call out for others to help you. The ones who come to your aid may not fully understand what they are part of, but when they return to their own lives they will know they too are special and will spread the belief in themselves – a power that will one day save the world.

'All of us who shared in your training are with you in spirit – do not forget that. And remember that evil will never defeat goodness; that is an unbreakable law of the universe.'

Then Galileo disappeared and the movie began to play.

* * *

Lotty, Angie and Sasha were back at Celestxia. Now that they had completed their missions the place was the same and yet utterly different.

Outside they had found sensational new experiences: a water park, ski lifts, motorised toboggans and a whole new building which appeared to contain electronics, games and equipment that in normal circumstances they wouldn't have been able to wait to try out.

But all they could do was think about Yury, Mitchi and especially Jamal.

Sasha talked over and over again about the last few hours he had spent in Antarctica. 'Jamal became a different guy – he's the bravest, most good Defender with all courage. He did the mission; I only waited. And now he is prisoner with Marduk and I could not stop it.'

Lotty repeated what she had already said fifty times: 'Don't feel bad, Sasha. You couldn't have done anything to stop Marduk taking him prisoner.'

Angie added, 'It was much easier for Lotty and me. We were so lucky to be invisible, so he couldn't grab us. If only you'd had the cards before you set off on your mission, you would have had a chance.'

Lotty ran her fingers through her hair. 'Why do you think the Glowbabies only brought the cards after you'd left? It bothers me.'

Angie replied, 'We just have to trust that the Creators know what's best. And it isn't the end of the story yet. Yury and Mitchi are still out there. We have to keep sending out positive thoughts and willing them to win, just as we did to help each other in the games at Olympia.'

Whenever he felt lowest, Sasha went to the stable to spend time with Unicornio. The stallion moved close to him and even lay down in the straw to let Sasha curl up next to him at night. Sasha couldn't bear being in the empty bedroom without Yury and Jamal.

Each night he took the second white pebble from his pocket, held it to his lips and said, 'For Jamal. Be safe and come back to us.'

All three WPDs knew they could do nothing now but wait.

Chapter 26

Marduk was beginning to like Jamal more and more. He thought they had turned out to be surprisingly well suited and was relieved that his new protégé didn't eat much and slept until late in the morning. Their days began late and ended in the small hours. Entertaining him was easy – all he seemed to need was a new computer game.

'I have a little job for you,' he said to Jamal one afternoon after they had checked the monitors on the Xi'an transmitter. 'It's a pilot of a game I want you to road test.'

'Yeah, 'course!' Jamal replied.

'It's only a little thing I designed a few hundred years ago – a game, but not a game. I think you'll understand when you play it. The name's *Taika* – which means *magic spell*,' Marduk said. 'I'll set it up on the console in here if you like.'

'Great,' Jamal replied.

Marduk loaded the software and watched Jamal's face as he hunched over the screen, ready to play. The game's strapline flashed up.

TAIKA – Where nice guys finish last.

The play page loaded, with its complex graphic of a warrior, naked to the waist, and the pulsating words, *TAIKA – IT'S MORE THAN A GAME.*

Choose your level, the screen prompted. *Return or no return.*

'What does that mean?' Jamal asked.

'Exactly what it says,' Marduk replied.

Jamal chose 'Return'.

Select your player identity.

Jamal looked for his options. 'I can't see any identity choices. This game needs a lot of work yet,' he said to Marduk.

'Whichever identity you select, there are no real choices in *Taika*,' he replied. 'You play as yourself or not at all.'

Jamal pressed 'Next' and watched as the graphics swirled and changed. Suddenly it seemed that the screen grew larger in front of him and he experienced an indescribable force dragging him towards the monitor. Jamal held on to the arms of the chair to stop himself being tugged forwards. 'What's happening?'

'Aha, it still works then!' Marduk replied. 'I just wanted to check that the game is functioning correctly. If my last transmitter is destroyed, the world will be discovering a whole lot about *Taika*, where nice guys finish last!'

* * *

Yury and Mitchi arrived in Xi'an without a hitch and made their way to the entrance to the museum of the Terracotta Army.

The place was quiet and Mitchi suspected it was because of the dreadful news of the earthquake. She wondered whether people were staying home with their families.

At the ticket office Yury smiled at her. 'I'm so glad you speak Mandarin!'

They began by going around the main exhibition, seeing the plans and models of the pits that contained the warriors, and learning about the battle formations of ancient Chinese armies and the weapons they used.

Mitchi was fascinated by the objects in glass cabinets, examples of the metal that had survived since 200 BCE when the army was first buried – triggers from crossbows, whole arrows and bronze halberds. Wood and leather and fabric had rotted away, but the harder materials had survived in a remarkable state of preservation.

A message buzzed through on her communication device.

A bag is waiting for you in Lost Property. It has your name on it.

The bag turned out to be full of electronics, and Mitchi's eyes grew as wide as saucers as her fingers searched through the items inside. There were locks, timers, alarms, flashing LEDs, sensors, lasers and two laser guns. She wanted to investigate right away. The bag also contained a set of overalls branded with the logo of the museum.

Yury was studying the plans of the three main pits. 'I reckon that Marduk's transmitter will be behind the warriors. They're all facing the same way, as if they're protecting something, and the junior rank soldiers are at the front. We need to get down there and find our way through to the back.'

Mitchi was totally absorbed by her bag, but Yury continued. 'This has got to be a night job – we can't go poking around in the daytime. But getting past security will be impossible.'

'Me make thing here?' Mitchi asked him.

'You want to build some equipment for our mission? Of course. I'll meet you back at the picnic area when I've scouted around the site,' Yury replied.

The museum tickets gave Yury access to all four pits where the warriors had been excavated by archaeologists. At each pit he walked around the viewing platform above the warriors and looked carefully for any possible exit points towards the back of the pits.

He noticed a multi-coloured costume draped over the rail ahead of him, and hanging from it he saw a label marked *Yury*. He scooped it up and went to the visitor toilets. Once inside the cubicle, he unfolded the garment and found it was a reproduction of a costume worn by a warrior. It came complete with an arrow on a pole, saying *'Can I help?'* in English and in Chinese characters.

'I'll look just like a guide in this!' he whispered and changed into the costume.

Before he came out of the cubicle, he sent a message to Mitchi's communicator. *Put on your overalls – security will think you are an engineer.*

This time Yury was able to leave the crowds of tourists and go through doorways and into areas clearly marked *Staff Only*. He checked out the layout of Pit One, the largest of the four, and wasn't challenged once. Suddenly he spotted Mitchi, who was now wearing the branded overalls and carrying the bag of equipment. She looked exactly like an engineering worker.

A little crowd was gathering around Yury and asking him questions. He felt obliged to say something. 'I am wearing a reproduction costume of one of the senior ranking officers displayed in Pit One beneath us.'

As he spoke he noticed that Mitchi was talking to a member of staff and pointing towards the back of the pit. She moved quickly along the viewing platform and disappeared through a door marked *Staff Only* at the far end.

Yury continued to speak to the gathered tourists. 'If you would like to buy a replica warrior dressed in the costume I am wearing, you will find one in the gift shop in the exhibition hall.'

The group nodded enthusiastically and began taking photos of themselves standing next to Yury.

As soon as he could, Yury excused himself and went through the door he had seen Mitchi use moments earlier.

Mitchi was waiting for him, and she spoke into her translator. 'I have found the route we need to take to get down to the back of Pit One. We should wait until the museum closes and then begin our search. I told the member of staff that I'd been called to test the lighting on the warriors in the pit and he was fine about that. We have forty-five minutes till the tourists leave.'

'Well done,' Yury said to her.

Mitchi looked so small and cute in the navy overalls. Yury noticed her, almost for the first time, and admired her glossy, bobbed hair, her smooth skin and dark, almost black, eyes. The top of her head reached to his shoulder, and he wondered what it would feel like to have his arm around her... protective but appealing?

'Mitchi?'

'Yes,' she said quietly, wondering why he was staring so hard at her.

'I'm glad we got paired up to do the mission together. And I promise to look after you as best as I can.'

'Tank you.'

While they waited for the museum to close, the Defenders planned their strategy. Mitchi had already scouted out the entrance to the excavations beyond the part of the pit that was open to the public. Yury proposed that they explored as far as they could get, and said, 'Marduk must have made an access route to the transmitter somewhere. There may be a tunnel.'

When their watches said six-fifteen p.m., they peeped back through the staff door into Pit One. The display lights had been turned off and there was no sign of anybody.

'Okay. Let's go!' Yury said.

Steps led down into the area behind the warriors. Yury scanned for an exit or corridor that might lead further back.

Mitchi said, 'What izz noise?'

Coming from the main pit was a rumbling, churning noise, a little like the sound of distant thunder.

'This isn't good,' Yury said to Mitchi. 'Get out the laser guns.'

The noise became quieter and then a few moments later, without warning, the wall leading to Pit One exploded, sending a stream of debris through the air towards the Defenders.

'Lie down!' Yury yelled, and they flattened themselves on the earth floor in blind fear.

A new sound now began, the blood-curdling yell of men mixed with the neighing of horses and clinking of chariots, just as they had heard in the hippodrome in Olympia.

'The warriors have come to life!' Yury shrieked. 'We're done for!'

'Follow!' Mitchi called above the din, and she ran as nimbly as a gazelle towards the back corridor.

They ran for their lives, and Yury understood her logic and realised that in the narrow corridor they would only have to face one or two warriors at a time, rather than the full force of a battle formation. Both Defenders stood their ground, pointed their laser guns towards the onslaught and began to fire. Chinese arrows were falling at their feet, missing their targets because the low ceiling made accurate enemy fire impossible. Mitchi and Yury continued to shoot at the approaching warriors, who lunged forward in their multi-coloured battledress. The way they moved and the inscrutable expression on their faces made them robot-like.

But as each warrior fell, several more climbed over the fallen bodies and pushed towards the Defenders, so that they were forced ever further back down the corridor.

Suddenly Yury thought of the advice Galileo had given them on the in-flight film, that the Defenders could call for help from the Educators when they were in need. 'Leonidas!' he called aloud. 'Columbus!'

Immediately he sensed that he and Mitchi were not alone. The huge bulk of Leonidas appeared beside him, cutting through the air with a sword and holding a shield to protect himself. Beside Mitchi, he saw Christopher Columbus fire a musket straight at the Chinese warriors.

Mitchi glanced backwards and saw what was happening – the warriors had already pushed them back down the length of the corridor and they were about to be forced into a wide open space in the archaeology area. She knew that without the advantage of the corridor they would be dead in moments, and in desperation she reached inside Yury's pocket for one of the cards the Glowbabies had given them.

The card she pulled out had a picture of an elephant on it. She tucked the card inside her overalls and carried on fighting. Everything happened very quickly: the Defenders were forced backwards out of the corridor, and even though the warriors now had to climb over a hoard of fallen soldiers in the corridor, their number began to grow. For every four that were felled, another eight appeared.

Again Mitchi looked behind her. She now saw a line of terracotta elephants, so lifelike that they almost looked as if they were breathing. Then one moved, and she realised they were coming to life, just as the warriors had done. The elephants filled their lungs with air and pawed the ground, sending up clouds of dust, then began a stampede towards the stream of soldiers coming out of the corridor. They bellowed, trumpeted and trampled, making mincemeat of the approaching enemy. The archers' arrows bounced off their thick hides as if they were made of paper.

'How many more are there?' Yury yelled to Leonidas.

'Up to eight thousand,' he replied breathlessly as he fought on with his sword.

An alarm sounded in Mitchi's bag, and she stepped back to check inside. Her Geiger counter alarm was showing that the levels of radiation were now dangerously high. She stepped back from the fight and leaned against the wall, her hands pressed to her head. She imagined a hooded radiation-proof suit with a mask to filter out hazardous chemicals and prevent radiation. Then she imagined three more, in the right sizes for Yury, Columbus and Leonidas.

Moments later four suits appeared and she gestured urgently to the others.

Yury understood what was happening right away, and he and Columbus acted swiftly to put them on, but Leonidas wouldn't stop fighting. He refused to put down his sword and carried on slashing at the warriors as they advanced.

'Leonidas, stop!' Yury called, but to no avail.

At that moment Mitchi's Geiger counter started to screech in red alert. From within the safety of their suits, Columbus, Yury and Mitchi watched in horror as the dreadful effect of extreme radiation acted upon Leonidas's naked torso. His skin turned darker, then black, and began to wrinkle like a sheet of plastic in a bonfire. He screamed as the radiation burned him, then fell to the ground, twitching, writhing, and finally still. The mighty Leonidas, Olympic champion and warrior, was destroyed.

Chapter 27

'Do you think you can persuade any other WPDs to defect to our side?' Marduk asked Jamal.

'No chance. They're all soft, and all fans of Galileo,' Jamal replied.

'Then we'll succeed without them.' Marduk grinned. 'Things are going very, very well for us on Earth, and we're wreaking havoc.'

'What do you mean?'

'Just that my last transmitter is doing its job better than I dared hope. It's always been easier than I expected with humans – they carry the seeds of their own destruction within them. They can be so noble and brave, but with just the tiniest temptation they become greedy and oh-so selfish.'

Jamal looked away with a slightly wistful expression on his face. 'What is it you want from planet Earth?' he asked. 'Why did you choose us?'

'Because it's full of natural resources and is peopled by creatures almost as intelligent and fascinating as the Creators themselves. But the silly fools are ignorant of this, not least due to my efforts! And I had to find a new home after our planet Aurea Cura was destroyed, and this was the best option. In fact, it was the Creators themselves who drew this place to my attention. They had already begun to invest in the creation of Celestxia, and to make their own plans here. But I decided over two thousand years ago that I wasn't going to let anyone else have this planet.'

'What's your vision for Earth, then?' Jamal asked.

A shadow passed over Marduk's face and the frown on his brow deepened, 'Mastery. Complete control. Most of mankind will be unnecessary to my plans, obviously. I intend to preserve only the intelligent, the inventive, the geniuses. And of course the mob, that great body of people who can build and farm and produce the goods I need. And they need to be the ones with the smallest brains of all, so that they never question or object, or – Great Creators! – rebel against me.'

'It sounds like fun!' Jamal said a little unconvincingly. 'And where do I fit in?'

'You'll be my junior, my apprentice, and eventually my Number Two. Stay close to me, stay loyal and the world will be yours.' Marduk paused and slammed his fist on the desk. 'And now we have a job to do in Xi'an – the job of destroying your ex-friends, Yury and Mitchi!'

* * *

'Call on help!' Yury yelled. 'G said we can ask for anything … anyone.'

The warriors were increasing in number and were slaying many of the elephants with their spears, halberds and battle-axes.

Mitchi keyed into her communicator, *A fearsome creature, immune to radiation, ferocious*. A picture came up immediately with the name *Lorcan* underneath.

In Mandarin Mitchi cried out, 'I call upon Lorcan to come to us,' focusing her mind on the image.

Above the din of the soldiers began a new noise, and Mitchi turned to see a huge creature, as big as an elephant. It reminded her of an enormous hairy warthog, with two huge and sharp tusks coming out of its mouth, each as big as the prongs on a fork-lift truck. As the Lorcan approached, it appeared to be half-asleep and Mitchi heard it muttering in Mandarin, 'I didn't agree to come out of hibernation for another three weeks; this is all highly irregular.' But after letting out a huge roar, the Lorcan charged at the oncoming warriors. The effect was immediate, and many of them turned and tried to get back into the corridor, while others tried to impale it on their swords, but the blades rebounded as if its body were made of rubber.

Mitchi called out again. 'More Lorcans. Angie, Lotty, Jamal and Sasha – come to us… wearing radiation-proof suits and with weapons!' she added almost as an afterthought.

This time the noise behind her was deafening as a herd of sleepy but very angry Lorcans appeared, and behind them, to the utter joy of Yury and Mitchi, were Lotty, Angie and Sasha, suited and armed with rapid-fire guns.

'Where Jamal?' Mitchi shouted to Angie.

'Marduk took him,' Angie yelled back.

At that moment there was a crack of falling bricks and a cloud of dust so thick that for a while it was impossible to see even a metre in front of their faces. When the air cleared, the Defenders saw a breach in the side wall through which a new army of warriors had burst, followed by horses and chariots. They were letting out bloodcurdling cries which chilled the Defenders to the core.

'How many more?' Yury cried out in desperation.

The Lorcans began to impale, Columbus fired, the remaining elephants trampled and Sasha, Angie and Lotty took out hundreds with their guns. But still the warriors came, line after line of them, through the breached wall.

The fighting went on for an hour, two hours, until Yury suddenly thought that perhaps the number of new warriors might be getting less. The whole area was now packed with fallen bodies.

A little later Angie called out, 'There are less of them coming, I'm sure of it.'

The fight was so much less fierce that Sasha took a breather and spoke to Columbus in his native language, and then to Yury. 'Columbus says that of all the warriors he has shot, not one bleeds. They are not like humans.'

Yury hadn't even had time to think during the heat of battle, but now he saw the fact – there was not one drop of warrior blood anywhere.

There were so few new fighters that Lotty and Mitchi were able to provide fire cover without help from the others. Yury stepped up to a body lying close to him and examined the corpse. The brightly coloured costume with red and black epaulettes and patterned breast-piece was undisturbed. The tightly coiled topknot of black hair was smooth and only the little black slippers and bottom of the turquoise trousers were dusty. The warrior's face was as inscrutable as it had been before he fell. Yury switched his communication device to scan mode and passed it over the body of the warrior. Immediately information appeared on the screen.

Robot type E-37tYYTX-3800. First seen on Aurea Cura six million years ago. Regularly used in situations considered too risky for created life, e.g. installation of equipment in sub-zero temperatures or in deep-water exploration. Note: If needed, may be useful in battle.

Radiation detected – dangerously high levels of gamma radiation present. Protection with PPE suits essential.

'They're robots,' Yury called to Sasha. 'They must have been programmed by Marduk to protect the transmitter. And all the time people on Earth thought they were created by the first emperor of all China. It's so spooky!'

Lotty felled the very last warrior and the place became eerily silent. There were no more roars, no more firing, just a sound of weapons rolling away from bodies as gravity took its course. The Lorcans and elephants were no more; those that hadn't been destroyed had limped away in wounded defeat.

The Defenders huddled together to plan the next move.

'Where's Columbus?' Sasha asked the others.

Everyone looked around but there was no sign of him.

'What's this?' Sasha asked, looking down at his feet. He picked up the dusty but familiar tricorn hat that Columbus had worn throughout their training on the island. 'His hat!' Sasha said sadly. 'I think we shall not see him again.'

'It's for you,' Lotty said softly. 'He has left it for you; that's why it was at your feet. He was a kindred spirit to you.'

Unseen beneath his radiation mask, tears fell from Sasha's eyes. Carefully he put the hat in the pocket of his protective suit.

'Guys, there's a door in the wall behind us,' Angie said, pointing her finger. 'Maybe it leads to the transmitter.'

Yury asked, 'Does it face west from here?'

Angie checked her communicator. 'No, it's south. Why?'

Yury replied, 'Because the tomb of the Chinese emperor is west of us, and I'm certain the tomb is a decoy – the archaeologists are still digging west of here thinking that's where they'll find more buried stuff. I think the transmitter could be south.'

They tried the door, which was locked.

'Okay, wait,' Mitchi said, taking a small detonator from her bag of electronic goodies. She fiddled with the controls and set off a controlled explosion that blew away the lock.

One by one, the five Defenders walked through the smoking door. They found themselves in a very dark chamber, almost like a cave. Scattered about were piles of discarded tools, boxes and surveying equipment.

Mitchi said, 'No more suits,' and pointed to her Geiger counter, which was showing that radiation levels had returned to normal.

'What a relief!' Yury said, shedding the awkward clothing and smiling at Mitchi when he saw her now-familiar, almost perfectly heart-shaped face. Her hair was tousled from wearing the head mask, and he wanted to smooth it with his hand.

Angie set off into the cave. Only a second after she had stepped forward, the Defenders heard a ripping, metallic sound and suddenly a sword blade three metres high shot up through the ground in front of Angie.

'What the...?' Angie shrieked.

Lotty screamed and put her hands to her mouth.

'Nobody move!' Yury commanded. 'Sasha, can you reach that box near you?'

Sasha leaned forwards and pulled the box towards him.

'Pick it up and throw it ahead of Angie.'

Sasha lifted the box above his head and lobbed it forwards. The box rolled once, twice and stopped. Nothing happened.

'Okay,' Yury began, 'I'll move next. He stepped alongside Angie. Nothing happened.

Very carefully he moved again. The searing noise of metal

happened immediately and an identical sword stabbed up through the floor. It had missed Yury by no more than a whisker.

Sasha stepped forward, following Yury, then took a pace to the right and one more. Two more swords shot up ahead of him.

'Oh no!' Lotty whispered.

Angie sprang forward and sprinted across the cave floor.

'No, don't!' Yury screamed. Fast as lightning, three swords, then five and then eight more burst up at her. The very last one ripped through her tunic and she yelped.

'Stop!' Mitchi cried. 'Sir Isaac Newton, help, help!'

'Isaac Newton?' Yury said quietly to himself. 'What possible use is he?'

Immediately the familiar figure of Sir Isaac appeared through the door behind them, his long, fair, wavy hair falling on his shoulders, his body wrapped in the brown velvet cloak that had always reminded Lotty of a dressing gown.

'Greetings, greetings,' he muttered, stepping forward in his pointed shoes and tapping his long chin with slender, pale fingers. 'Ah, the young pupils. Ah,' he said again, looking at the swords, 'how delightful, the Fibonacci sequence.'

'Delightful?' Lotty said, pulling a face at Sasha.

Sir Isaac walked around the swords with complete confidence.

'No! Don't,' Yury called out.

'Whyever not?' Sir Isaac replied. 'An excellent gentleman was Fibonacci. He discovered one of the most beautiful mathematical truths of creation, the perfect sequence of numbers that are now named after him. Born 1170, and he discovered the sequence before he reached thirty. A genius.

Excellent, beautiful mathematics. So you know exactly where the swords are buried, my dear friends.'

'Do we?' Lotty asked blankly.

'But of course. You have all the information you need already. God speed.'

'Sorry, sir, but we don't understand,' Yury said.

'A brief lesson in the Fibonacci sequence, then!' Sir Isaac clapped his hands. 'Excellent indeed. Each row of swords contains the sum of the two numbers preceding it. So in the first row you have one sword, then one more, then two, then three, then of course five – which is three plus two – then eight – which is five plus three. Isn't it beautiful? You see how they are spaced equally in each row? How many will be in the next row? Tell me, please!'

Lotty looked blank again, but Mitchi said, 'Is why I call you. Thirteen. Twenty-one. '

'The young lady has it!' Sir Isaac cried. 'Such a pity that in general terms ladies are so lacking in mental faculties, but of course you are correct, my lady,' he said, taking a deep bow.

Yury began thinking aloud. 'Eight plus five is thirteen, and thirteen plus eight is twenty-one, so the next would be twenty-one plus thirteen, which is thirty-four. I think I get it.' He stepped forward through the rows of five and eight swords very carefully.

There was a screeching sound as thirteen swords rose through the rock floor, in a perfect row, equally spaced from the rows behind.

He stepped again and the screeching multiplied, as twenty-one and then thirty-four more swords erupted.

'Sir,' Sasha said, 'now the swords are so close together we cannot pass through them!'

'That is certainly true, good sir, and would remain true, unless you knew another beautiful fact about Fibonacci's sequence. I will help you. Nature has shown us that wherever these numbers form, they prefer to cluster in the pattern of spirals, just as they do in a seed head. But of course you will have observed this.'

'Will we?' Lotty whispered to Sasha.

Sir Isaac went on. 'And so just by tilting the last sword on the final row towards its neighbour, like so...'

As he did, the thirty-fourth sword leaned towards the thirty-third, which tilted to the thirty-second until, like a set of giant silver dominoes, the entire collection of swords swirled to form a beautiful circular cluster, like the petals of a flower in the centre of the cave.

'Beautiful,' Mitchi whispered.

'And now this sequence is complete and you may move on in safety,' Sir Isaac said, bowing courteously to the Defenders.

Mitchi bowed from her waist and Sir Isaac disappeared through the doorway.

'Somehow maths and nature overcame Marduk's defences,' Yury said, ruffling his short blond hair. 'Amazing. And what a genius!'

'Beautiful,' Mitchi said again. Then she stepped towards Yury. 'I thinked.'

'Use the translator,' Yury replied.

Mitchi's device translated after she spoke. 'We must find the transmitter. We need explosives, torches and geophysics equipment to see where the transmitter may be.'

'Yes! Do you think we can imagine all those things?'

'Go for it!' Lotty said. 'We managed it in Celestxia.'

The Defenders sat on the ground, with their backs to the

spiral of swords, and put their heads in their hands. Lotty peeped once or twice, Angie peeped several times, but after a short time everything they needed surrounded them on the cave floor.

'We done it!' Sasha said. 'Galileo will be proud. He says we must fulfil our potential. We are doing that.'

'Fulfil our potential,' Lotty giggled. 'I guess we're learning.'

'Ready,' Mitchi said, handing a geophysics instrument to Angie.

The girls stepped towards the back of the cave. Mitchi reached it quickly, but Angie felt herself come up against some form of invisible barrier.

'I can't move,' she said.

'I'll help,' Sasha said, coming forward. But he could get no further than Angie. 'It's like my feet are stuck with glue,' he said, turning back to the others.

Lotty and Yury came over. Yury walked right past Angie and Sasha, but Lotty was rooted to the spot where Angie and Sasha were already fixed.

'I understand,' Lotty said, shaking her head until her curly red hair shook. 'We're not meant to do the next bit. It's Yury and Mitchi's mission and they'll be going without us.'

'No!' Angie objected. 'Pass me one of the cards, Lotty; they're still in your pocket.'

'Okay, but...' Lotty said, passing the pack of cards.

Angie selected one. 'It's blank!' she said in surprise. She pulled another, then turned over the rest of the pack. 'They're all blank.'

'It wasn't a time of great need,' Lotty said. 'We were warned. We've got to wait here.'

'Be safe,' Sasha said to Mitchi and Yury.

The Defenders watched as the two of them tracked along the cave walls with the geophysics equipment until the instruments showed they had reached a place that was not backed by solid, natural material.

'Here!' Mitchi called. She seemed to know exactly what to do and she attached explosives to the wall, prepared the detonator and set the timer.

'We move,' she said, leading Yury into the safety of an alcove in the rock. The others sheltered behind the silver swords.

When everyone was safe, Mitchi pressed the remote detonator switch. After the sound of falling rock subsided, she and Yury ventured out to find that a door-sized hole had been created in the cave wall.

Yury led the way through, and for a moment Mitchi paused, looking back at her fellow Defenders. She lifted her hand in a small wave and Lotty blew her a kiss back. Then she followed Yury, through the smoke and rubble fresh from the explosion.

As they blinked and looked around they saw immediately that they were in the right place. But in front of the transmitter, in its cage, stood Marduk and – with a gun in his hand pointing straight at them – Jamal.

Chapter 28

Yury screamed, 'Jamal, what are you doing?'

'Keep quiet. If you speak, I'll shoot,' Jamal said menacingly.

Mitchi looked shocked and white. 'Jamal, why? Why?'

'Silence!' he replied. 'Hands above your heads!'

As soon as the Defenders raised their arms, Marduk stepped forward with handcuffs, which he fitted to their arms roughly.

'Don't hurt her, there's no need,' Yury barked at Marduk.

'Shut it!' Jamal added.

Marduk dragged Yury, and Jamal pulled Mitchi.

'At least tell us where we are going,' Yury said.

Neither replied. They continued to drag their prisoners along a corridor until they came to a door in the wall.

'Stand still!' Marduk commanded, and then he and Jamal wrapped blindfolds around the captives' heads.

The door opened into a disused cupboard, less than two metres by two metres, and Jamal pushed the Defenders inside. Marduk tied their legs together with tape, and Mitchi and Yury fell to the floor.

Marduk reached inside their pockets, pulled out the communication devices and tucked them into his coat. 'There's no point trying to move,' he said. 'The door is metal and will be locked. You will be here until you die, or until we capture the other three WPDs. Your mission is over, guys.'

The door slammed and Mitchi and Yury heard the lock turn.

'Are you okay?' he asked.

'Yes. You okay?'

'Let's try to get as comfortable as we can. At least we can talk to each other. Wriggle until it hurts less.'

Mitchi seemed to understand and moved about until she was on her side, rather than lying on her handcuffed arms. Yury did the same.

'Better?' he asked.

'Yes. Think. Imagine help,' she said.

'Right, let's imagine all we need to get out of the cuffs and blindfolds, and then the door,' he replied.

Both of them imagined, forced pictures of the equipment they needed to mind, but there was no tingling sensation. Even though they were blindfolded, both knew that if they could open their eyes, there would be nothing to see.

'Why it not come?' Mitchi asked.

'There's something stopping us from focusing... some force field or negative energy,' Yury replied. 'We need to think and remember everything Galileo ever told us about our powers. There has to be a way out of this.'

'I will,' Mitchi said, and despite the pain she was thankful that in the darkness and discomfort, she could feel the warmth of Yury's strong body beside her.

* * *

'I'm not happy,' Lotty said to the others, rubbing her fingers through her red curls. 'I feel worried – I haven't felt as bad as this since we came to Celestxia. I think something's wrong.'

'Okay, we've got to think. Maybe we'll get a clue about what's wrong and how we can help Mitchi and Yury.'

The three Defenders focused their thoughts. After a while Lotty said, 'All that's coming into my head is Jamal. What about you?'

'Nothing,' Sasha said. 'I can't think at all.'

Angie said slowly, 'Something has just come to me – we've been forgetting about Jamal, and he's in deep trouble. And I keep remembering how we hated him and were mean about him sometimes, 'cause he was a total pain. Maybe we should be focusing on him and not on Yury and Mitchi.'

'Yes, I agree!' Lotty said. 'That feels right. Let's send positive energy to Jamal.'

After a few moments Sasha asked, 'Anything?'

Lotty said, 'I keep seeing Jamal with some kind of aura around him, but I've been imagining him having everything he needs and that he'll be okay. Maybe that's the best we can do right now.'

'Maybe it is,' Angie replied.

* * *

Marduk patted Jamal on the back. 'Good work!' he said.

'What's happens next?' Jamal asked.

'This Xi'an transmitter is on maximum output already, and it's creating havoc out there – which is very, very good. Now we need to stop the last three WPDs from reaching it, and then move on to phase two.'

'Phase two?'

'To destroy Celestxia. Phase three is obvious – the world is overpopulated, and mankind is using up the planet's resources too quickly, so the population needs to be downsized.'

'Downsized? You mean people have to die?'

'It's not as difficult a problem as you may imagine. The signal has already caused several outbreaks of international conflict – huge numbers of deaths will follow. A couple of well-placed molecular rearrangement devices to make humans less troublesome creatures will be very effective too.'

Jamal swallowed hard.

Marduk went on, 'Celestxia is a tricky one, and it was vital that the WPD missions weren't successful, or the Defenders would have returned to find the place was bigger than imagination – and full of potential for personal development. All completely counter to my purposes, and giving away far too much power and opportunity. That's all dealt with now, of course, and I owe you a debt of thanks already.

'You can imagine how much attention I've given to the problem of Celestxia. Its existence seems connected to the push and pull of energy fields. While the WPDs were being trained, and as each mission succeeded, Celestxia expanded. But as soon as the negative energy in the world grew, as soon as my transmitter switched to maximum output and man's selfishness richened and deepened, then Celestxia got smaller.

'It seems that the space occupied by the matter that builds Celestxia gets bigger or smaller depending on the decrease or increase of negative energy in the world. Which is more wonderful than I ever dared hope.'

Marduk patted his stomach as if he'd just finished a satisfying meal. 'So with the work of the transmitter, I believe we'll see the end of Celestxia.'

'And the destruction of the WPDs?' Jamal asked.

'Exactly. And on that subject, we need to make a plan. We have the perfect opportunity to seize the other three – they're still in the cave of swords. No time to lose.'

Marduk led Jamal back down the corridor to the cave and, sure enough, Lotty, Angie and Sasha were sitting with their backs to the beautiful curved spiral of swords left by Sir Isaac Newton. Each of them had their eyes closed and their head in their hands.

Jamal felt a lump come into his throat as he saw his former colleagues, but he swallowed hard and made sure his face would betray no emotion.

The Defenders opened their eyes as soon as they heard the noise of footsteps approaching.

'Jamal!' Sasha exclaimed, rushing to his feet, but he was held back immediately by the invisible force field. 'Jamal, buddy! Are you okay?' he went on, as if he wasn't at all afraid of Marduk.

Marduk and Jamal pointed their guns at the three Defenders and moved through the force field, taking hold of Sasha and Angie and pressing their weapons straight at their heads.

'Jamal, what are you *doing*?' Sasha breathed.

'Shut it!' Marduk barked. 'There is no point protesting. We have Yury and Mitchi already and you are all being taken prisoner. Lotty, if you don't follow, your friend Angie dies. Okay?'

It had all happened so quickly. Lotty was in shock and fear, and she called aloud, 'Galileo! Help us! Beepee, Teeto, come to us!'

'STOP THAT!' screeched Marduk and he pulled the safety catch on his gun. Angie shuddered as she heard the terrifying click.

But then she heard a far more welcome sound – the buzz of a message coming though on Lotty's communicator.

'Give that to me!' Jamal said icily. Like Marduk, he now clicked off the catch on his gun and bent Sasha's neck back in an arm-lock.

Very slowly, Lotty took the device out of her pocket and then threw it onto the ground in front of Jamal.

Jamal manoeuvred it towards himself with his foot and glanced down at the screen. 'Your friends Beepee and Teeto can't reach you here – bad luck, guys!' he said aloud to the others. 'Sasha and Angie, we need your communicators too!'

Equally slowly, each of the two WPDs put a hand in their pocket and tossed their device onto the ground.

As soon as they moved, Lotty made a run for it, dashing back out of the cave entrance the way she had come in.

But Jamal was too quick. He turned his gun on her and shot her in the right foot.

Lotty screamed and Angie hollered, 'No! No!'

Lotty crumpled and fell to the ground, crying out in raw pain. A pool of dark blood oozed out of her trainer and onto the sandy floor of the cave. Angie and Sasha wrestled but couldn't free themselves, and Sasha spat a gob of spittle at Jamal's face. It glistened on his chin and dripped to the ground.

'Now MOVE!' Marduk ordered. 'And you, girl, you drag yourself and your bleeding foot behind us!'

He whispered to Jamal, 'We need a different location for these three. There's a lock-up beneath the transmitter that'll be perfect.'

Now Marduk was with the Defenders, the force field seemed to have faded away and all four were able to pass through the cave, along the corridor where Yury and Mitchi were silently imprisoned and into the transmitter hall. The entrance to the lock-up was beneath them, down a set of concrete steps.

As they descended, Lotty whimpered in agony at each step. Her face was greenish-white and she was swaying in a near faint.

'You rat! You scum of the world!' Sasha spat at Jamal. 'This will be a stone of guilt you carry to the end of life. May you never be free of it!'

Marduk smiled. 'You are the ones who will never be free! Nothing will work here, not thought power, not mind games. And any positive energy you try to muster will be sucked up and evaporated by the negative power in this place.'

As Marduk threw them forward into the lock-up, Sasha said, 'Jamal, how could you do this to us? We were friends, and you were so brave in Antarctica. Think of your dad!'

Sasha thought he saw Jamal wince very slightly before he turned away.

This time Marduk used tape around the WPDs' legs, arms and mouths, and as he tied Lotty's legs, she screamed out in pain. Marduk left her lying on the ground, but tied Angie and Sasha standing to fixings on the walls of the lock-up.

Marduk switched out the light, then slammed the metal door and locked it from the outside.

'How long will you leave them?' Jamal asked him.

'I'll come back and shoot them as soon as I know they can't tell me anything useful,' Marduk replied.

'Don't you think a painful death would be much more satisfying?' Jamal asked. 'Why not leave them till they starve?'

'I like it!' Marduk said. 'It's not as if they can escape. You're improving fast! And I think I may have come up with a way to increase the power of the signal that's being transmitted, but it means a bit of tinkering. If we replace the transmitter tip with zyphonite, we should be able to get a more powerful output. It can be done quickly, only losing a minute of transmission time. I already have the parts I need.'

'I can help,' Jamal said. 'Maybe if you do the part replacement, I can control the output from the desk.'

'That's a plan. But there's something else I want to do first,' Marduk said. 'I hate a lot of creatures, but the race called Glowbabies are the ones I hate most. I told you they were only a myth, but the truth is I've never come across more infuriating life forms in any part of the known universe. And it occurred to me that you can help me destroy them, as you have a special bond with Zizi, the snow Glowbaby.'

'How do you mean?' Jamal asked.

'As far as I understand it, Glowbabies are genetically programmed to help young humans, and if someone has signed a Glowbaby's immigration papers, it can't refuse to come whenever their adoptive human calls. Of course, I know about you adopting Zizi, so we could use him to draw in the others.

'Oh, I think this will be a perfect plan if we can pull it off – we can implant a small explosive device in Zizi, and when he returns to his compatriots, we can detonate it remotely. That way we get rid of all of them and their stupid, furry bodies and endless chatter.' Marduk shuddered.

'Where do they live? Where are they the rest of the time when they're not here, I mean?' Jamal asked.

'No-one really knows. They were found on Aurea and a

planet called Aasta. It's a very small planet actually, but every creature on it is furry and affectionate. Nauseating,' Marduk replied.

'I rather like Glowbabies,' Jamal said. 'Couldn't we convert them to our side?'

'Not a chance!' Marduk replied. 'They're full of positive energy and predisposed to be selfless – which makes them absolutely useless for our purposes.'

'Then I'll do it,' Jamal said, 'but only on one condition.'

'What's that?'

'That you grant me special powers of jurisdiction on planet Earth. I want control of half of the Earth, divided by natural resources, not by geographical size, and I want my own HQ with huge numbers of staff and servants.'

'Deal!' Marduk replied. 'But only when the Glowbabies are destroyed. Call Zizi now!'

Jamal pressed his hands to his temples and called aloud, 'Zizi! Zizi! I need you!'

One of the monitor screens flickered and an image of Zizi appeared. 'I can't reach you where you are, Jamal,' the Glowbaby was saying. 'The force field is too strong, which I think I pointed out before, but I'm not completely sure. I can meet you just outside the Xi'an museum if that helps? We all hope you are okay. We've been thinking of you lots.'

'I'm fine,' Jamal replied, turning the volume dial up on the screen microphone, 'but I need you to bring Teeto and Beepee too… It's an emergency.'

'Will do my best,' Zizi said. 'We always help when we can. We'll be there in a few minutes, so long as I can stop them both talking. Glowbabies do have so much to say!' he added, before the picture disappeared.

Marduk butted in. 'I'll get the explosive device. It needs

to be tiny so Zizi doesn't feel it in his fur, and the detonator will need to work across time and space.

'I know I've got something like it in the store room. Hang on. While I'm sorting that, you need to start making copies of the *Taika* game. I want it ready to distribute to every games store and retailer in the USA, Russia, China, UK, Australia, Canada... you can add more countries to that list. Once it's packaged, it'll retail at half the price of similar games. That should make it irresistible to the global teen market.'

Zizi was as good as his word, and when Marduk and Jamal emerged from the Museum of the Terracotta Warriors, blinking at the startling brightness of the daylight outside, they spotted all three Glowbabies jiggling up and down. Jamal noticed at once that none of the tourists seemed to be able to see them.

'I'll hang back,' Marduk said to Jamal. 'You know what you have to do.'

As the three creatures jumped and jiggled they looked like three giant pom-poms – purple, lime-green and snow-white. Jamal walked cheerfully towards Zizi and opened his arms for a hug. Zizi enfolded him in white fur and made a sound half like a giggle and half like babbling water. As Jamal tightened his arms, he slipped the small device snugly into the thick fur on the Glowbaby's side while releasing the adhesive to ensure it couldn't fall off.

'What can we do for you?' Zizi asked.

Teeto and Beepee stepped forward nervously and each of them tried to hide behind the other, which involved a lot of stumbling and mumbling and was as unsuccessful as it was amusing to watch.

'The other Defenders have all been imprisoned by Marduk and I've no idea how to locate them,' Jamal said. 'I know you can't get through the force field down there, but I want you to pass a message to G to see if anything can be done to help them. Marduk may be holding them near here or at his HQ. I have a plan to find them, and I'll let you know as soon as I have news.'

'You are so good and brave,' Zizi said, 'and I'm so very proud that you're the one who adopted me. There was a boy from Bolivia who lost his mother and he wanted to sign my immigration papers, but something made me hang back – almost as if I was meant to meet you.'

'No, don't be silly. I'm nothing special,' Jamal said, and he looked away in embarrassment.

'So good to see you again,' Zizi said. 'We all hope it won't be too long till the next time.'

Teeto stepped forward shyly. 'And if you do see or hear of Mitchi, before you say anything else at all, tell her I love her and I think of her every minute.' His huge eyes were bright with tears.

When Jamal turned his head to say a last goodbye, there was no longer any sign of the purple, lime-green and snow-white creatures.

Marduk peeped out from behind the wall, holding the detonator in his hand.

Chapter 29

It was impossible to tell how many minutes or hours had passed. In their dark prison, Yury and Mitchi lay as still as possible, talking most of the time and sleeping for a short snatch when exhaustion overtook them.

At first, their biggest problem had been the discomfort of lying on the hard floor, tightly tied and blindfolded. Every part of Yury itched but he couldn't scratch, and sometimes an itch was so overwhelming that he thought he wouldn't be able to bear it. He was amazed by the power Mitchi seemed to have in lying still and calm.

After the first few hours, thirst and hunger had become their biggest problems.

To distract them from their pain and empty stomachs, Yury was teaching Mitchi new English words. The challenge of explaining the meaning of a word when blindfolded was immense, as Yury couldn't gesture or show a picture of an object as he spoke. He had only the power of language, using the limited vocabulary that Mitchi had already learned. But she was a very quick pupil.

Her stillness kept Yury sane, and he felt certain that if he'd been imprisoned alone, he would have gone stark, staring mad from fear in days.

'Do you think we may not get out?' he asked at a

low moment.

'Not think it,' Mitchi said. 'Think happy. Think Celestxia. Think love.'

'I wish I could get a drink of water for you.'

'Not think water. Think strong. Remember why here. And keep think Jamal.'

'You're right, of course, but you are so focused and strong, even though you're small and look fragile. You're a very special girl, Mitchi.'

'Not understanding,' Mitchi said.

'It doesn't matter, Mitchi. Well, it matters a lot, but if we get out of here, I'll show you what I mean,' Yury said sadly.

* * *

In their lock-up, Lotty lay in the dark in silence, the tape cutting into the flesh around her mouth. Meanwhile Sasha and Angie stood tethered to the wall, hurting and afraid.

* * *

Marduk rubbed his eyes and let his fingers trail through his greasy black hair. 'That's a job very well done, my little apprentice,' he said. 'Copies of my game *Taika* are on their way to every computer games retailer in every city on the planet. And I've got adverts scheduled to start on TV, in magazines and on commercial radio. The world's teenagers won't be able to resist it. Ha! That's one way of preventing any more WPDs being nurtured by Galileo to mess with my plans.'

'But it's only a game,' Jamal ventured.

'That's where you're wrong. It's *so much more* than a game!'

'Meaning what? I couldn't even get the set-up commands to work,' Jamal said.

'Remember how you felt yourself being pulled into the screen?'

Jamal nodded.

Marduk laughed. 'That's what will happen to everybody who plays. They will be pulled into my world, into the virtual universe I have created from which they'll never escape. It's a game without an end that will suck out every gram of positive energy from potential Defenders. So my Plan B is already in operation.'

* * *

Message to the Creators:

How could this have gone so wrong? The Glowbabies have just met Jamal and discovered that, since we lost contact with them, the remaining five Defenders have been imprisoned by Marduk. Was it the training that failed? Was it inadequate? How can Marduk's force field be strong enough to overpower our positive energy? How can one individual hold so much power over this dear planet?

I have become extremely attached to these young people and feel helpless in the face of this great evil that they are fighting. Please reply as soon as you receive this.

Galileo

* * *

To Galileo, from the Creators,

The training programme put together for the WPDs was carefully designed, appropriately targeted and successfully completed. Trust us that ALL WILL BE WELL. The power of positivity and of love will always overcome negativity and evil. This is not yet the end.

* * *

Jamal swigged a large mouthful of cola and scoffed the final piece of the cheeseburger he was eating at the desk in the control room.

Marduk took the final sip of his double rum and let out a belch.

'I can't help feeling sorry for Zizi,' Jamal said. 'I do think Glowbabies are cute.'

'There's still a long way to go to toughen you up,' Marduk replied.

'Actually I've got a request.'

'Go on.'

'I want to be the one who presses the detonator to destroy them when we're sure they're back at their home planet. Can I?'

Marduk's dark, unshaven face broke into a grin. 'Yes, if you want – but why?'

Jamal thought for a moment and frowned. 'Because I hate them now as much as I liked them before. From the very start I hated the way Galileo taunted me with the Glowbabies, and then they wouldn't appear to me, even after everyone else had seen one and… that's why.'

Marduk passed him the detonator and Jamal steeled himself.

At that exact moment, a loud, buzzing noise sounded from the transmitter beyond the screen. A stream of white sparks was pouring down from the transmitter tip like an upside-down firework. The buzzing increased to become a fierce electrical spitting.

Marduk sprang forward. 'Help me! It's overheated. I need to replace the tip. I was worried this might happen.'

On the control panel in front of them several warning lights and messages had appeared. A graph showing the transmission strength changed from a green line to a red one. *ALERT* and *DANGER* flashed across the screens.

'Let's do as we discussed,' Jamal said. 'You get up the transmitter with the replacement zyphonite tip, and I'll wait here and switch the power off for a minute while you do the job.'

'We've got no choice,' Marduk said angrily. Very quickly he showed Jamal what to press, and in what order, and then got ready to enter the transmitter area. 'You'll have to switch the signal off as soon as I step in there; it's far too dangerous while it's still live.'

'Will do!' Jamal said. 'And remember I want *half* for doing this. Half of the power on Earth.'

'You've got it.'

Jamal slapped him on the back and said, 'Good luck.'

Marduk took down a hard hat, ear protectors and a hi-vis jacket from the wall and put them on hastily. He slung the backpack containing the zyphonite tip and the tools over his shoulder. Then he let himself into the transmitter chamber through the steel door. For the few moments that the door was open, Jamal heard the deafening sound of the electrical storm. Then Marduk swung the door shut and made his way to the scaffolding, his shoulders hunched into his neck.

From behind the reinforced glass wall in the control room Jamal watched Marduk, his fingers ready on the controls.

Marduk climbed onto the first rung of the ladder. The stream of sparks was raining down on the top of his hard hat and bouncing off the yellow jacket. He climbed a few rungs higher. Jamal watched intently, utterly still and focused on the task in hand. Marduk stuck his thumb up and climbed higher.

When he reached the top of the scaffolding, and before he

entered the round structure on top that contained the transmitter tip, he looked down at Jamal and motioned for him to switch off the transmission power. Jamal could barely see him through the shower of bright white sparks.

At the split second when Marduk's head disappeared from view inside the enclosed sphere, Jamal acted.

He turned off the power and the sparks reduced to a trickle before stopping completely. Then he grabbed the detonator connected to the Glowbaby explosive device, Marduk's set of keys, a knife and cutters from the toolbox. With lightning speed, he locked the door to the transmitter chamber and bolted from the control room.

He crossed the floor to the set of steps leading down to the lock-up beneath the control room. He fiddled with the keys and let himself in. Inside he saw Lotty on the floor, a pool of congealed blood around her legs, and Sasha and Angie tied to the wall.

With swift but gentle movements, he cut the tape around Sasha's mouth and arms and passed him the knife. 'Free the other two. I'm fetching Yury and Mitchi so you can carry Lotty out of here. I'm about to destroy Marduk, but *get out* – get out fast. You have thirty seconds.'

Then he raced down the corridor to the store room and searched for the right key. Yury and Mitchi shuddered and pressed themselves closer together as the door burst open. Jamal cut Yury's bonds and handed the cutters over to him, saying, 'Free Mitchi, then turn right down the corridor, join Sasha and help him carry Lotty out. I'll follow.'

Jamal ran back to the control room. Glancing up at the top of transmitter, he could see no sign of Marduk.

He retraced his steps along the corridor to check that the Defenders had got out, and then raced to the exit that led into the cave of swords and through the devastation of the piles of warrior bodies. When he reached the exit into the museum, he stopped and took the detonator out of his pocket.

He pressed 'Set' and then 'Detonate'. There was a fifteen-second pause before anything happened. Then came a sound like a mighty explosion in a quarry and the very ground reverberated.

Jamal ran for his life and didn't look back.

Chapter 30

'He did it, he did it, my human did it!' Zizi jumped up and down.

'Jamal did it! The greatest Defender of all, the one we love!' Beepee giggled.

'Although we love ALL the Defenders, and all human children, of course,' added Teeto, twirling round and round so that his lime-green fur splayed out like a ballerina's skirt.

'My Jamal did it!' Zizi repeated, pressing his little hands to his furry, round chest.

* * *

Jamal was lying on his back on the grassy knoll outside their home in Celestxia. He knew that at that moment he could choose to be skiing, space surfing, learning to dive to a depth of three thousand metres without breathing apparatus or eating a meal fit for a king. But he didn't want to do any of those things. Staring up at the perfect blue above gave him more joy than he had ever felt in his life. And it meant that he could go and check on Lotty every few minutes, to see how her foot was healing.

He didn't know it, but Galileo had already given Lotty the option of taking an instant healing pill. But because she'd seen how much pleasure it was giving Jamal to tend to her and help her recover, she refused the pill. 'I can always take it if the pain gets worse,' she said.

Two days had passed since the Defenders had been transported back to Celestxia. They had found it recognisable but utterly different. It was bigger in size, and in fact Yury was beginning to wonder whether it was infinite. They were astounded by the wealth of opportunities and objects available for them to experience and experiment with – everything from sports to software, to action and live animals.

Indoors in her bedroom, Lotty braced herself and levered her body out of bed and onto crutches. Very slowly she made her way to the grass outside. Jamal looked blissfully peaceful and serene lying there, and Lotty noticed that for the first time he wasn't wearing his designer sunglasses. He's actually really good-looking, she thought.

Gently she lowered herself onto the grass beside him.

Jamal turned to her with a start. 'What are you doing? You should be in bed!'

'I wanted to be out in the sun, and I wanted a chat,' Lotty replied.

For a few minutes they sat in comfortable silence. Lotty watched a pair of butterflies performing an intricate and delicate dance in the air close to them.

Eventually she said, 'Can I ask a few questions?'

''Course.'

'You won't be offended?'

'I might be rude or abrupt, but it doesn't mean I'm offended,' Jamal laughed.

'The first one is why did you shoot me in the foot? Or maybe I need to go back a bit further… At the time when you shot me, were you planning to stick with Marduk?'

Jamal sat up on one elbow and stared ahead. 'I never, ever

planned to side with that vile creature, no.'

'Then why did you go as far as you did with Marduk? Are you lying to us now? And you haven't answered about my foot.'

'I need to tell you in my own way, in the order it happened. Can I?' Jamal asked.

'Please.'

'As soon as Marduk captured me I began to plan. He kept me locked up for a while and I bided my time, waiting for the opportunity to behave like the old Jamal and to convince him I could share his selfish ambition. It amazed me how easy it was to take him in — maybe 'cause he was self-absorbed, or maybe he was just lonely. I dunno.

'Pretty soon he let me join him in the control room, and then he showed me a couple of bits of film of you lot being honest about me. Yury was calling me the weak link in the team, and Sasha said he wanted to punch me in the mouth. Then he showed me when you and Ange were onboard Columbus's ship, saying you wished I'd been left behind on the island, and that I was lazy and spoiled.'

'I remember that. I'm sorry,' Lotty said.

'But you didn't say anything that wasn't true. Think of all the bad stuff I said about Sasha, and I actually tried to kill him for God's sake. What could you have said about me that I didn't deserve?'

'Didn't you hear what I said next, though?' Lotty asked.' Straight after we said all the stuff about you being spoiled, Angie and I said how proud we were of you when you stuck up for Columbus.'

'Trust me, it doesn't matter. And in fact seeing the bits of film of you all gave me the chance to show Marduk I hated you. It was dead easy to convince him of my ambition, but I knew I had to convince him I'd truly detached myself from you five if I was going to have a chance of overpowering him. Evil only understands evil, and in a way I knew that from my behaviour back home.

'I didn't plan to hurt any of you, *especially* you,' Jamal said, looking down. His olive cheeks coloured slightly. 'But I knew that if I shot you right then, I would have Marduk's total trust for what I had to do. I wished over and over again that I had shot one of the guys – they might have been able to bear the pain better – but you were the one who was making a run for it. I'm so sorry.'

'It's cool. In fact, G has offered me a healing pill that will cure me instantly.'

'Have you taken it?'

'Er, not yet,' Lotty replied.

'Why?'

Now it was Lotty's turn to colour up. 'Tell me about the Glowbabies. What would you have done if you'd had to press the detonator and Zizi had exploded?'

'You don't understand. First I nicked one of your communication devices after Marduk had made you chuck them on the ground in the cave of swords. I typed a message to Zizi on it telling him everything that had happened and what I was planning. I couldn't send the message the usual way 'cause of the force field around the transmitter. When I met Zizi, I took the explosive device *and* the communicator with me. Marduk hung back so he wouldn't be seen, and instead of fixing the explosive to Zizi, I actually stuck the communicator in his fur when I hugged him. I whispered in his ear and told him to retrieve it and read the message on it.

'I kept the real explosive hidden in my pocket until

Marduk told me it was time to detonate it. So if I'd set it off at that moment, I'd have blown myself up, with Marduk beside me and the transmitter next door. I honestly was ready to do it, although I was truly, wholly scared.

'But at that same moment, the transmitter failed and a heap of sparks started pouring out of the top. It was seriously overheating 'cause he'd had it on maximum output for a while. I saw my chance and the rest was easy. Before he went out of the control room I slapped him on the back to say good luck, and that's when I fixed the explosive to him. I did panic when he put on his hi-vis jacket, but he never felt the device.

'I turned off the power to the transmitter, knowing that would keep him busy for long enough for me to free you and the others, and then I detonated the explosive as soon as I was at a safe distance.'

Jamal paused. 'I don't know if I've destroyed him, but I must have done 'cause he was at the top of the transmitter, the exit door was locked from my side and the whole place is now annihilated.'

Lotty's eyes were as wide as cupcakes. 'You were amazing, incredible – braver than anyone ever,' she said.

'I owed it to all of you, for being such a brat. I owed it to G, to my parents and especially to you,' he said.

'Well, you sure paid your debts!' Lotty replied.

Jamal put his arm around Lotty's shoulders and squeezed her.

At that moment, Sasha and Yury returned from interstellar hockey and emerged behind them.

'Lotty's out of bed! Let's join them!' Sasha said.

Yury put out his hand and stopped him. 'No, I think we should leave them. This is their private moment.' As he turned towards the house he looked back and saw that Jamal's arm was still around Lotty's shoulders.

* * *

That evening was the first mealtime that all six Defenders had been together for since their return. Lotty couldn't stop giggling, Sasha played the fool and Yury impersonated Sir Isaac Newton. 'How delightful, the Fibonacci sequence... of course you all know what the Fibonacci sequence is... what's the next number after thirty-four? What *do* they teach you in school?'

Even Mitchi had to wipe tears of laughter from her cheeks.

Yury was standing on a chair and performing when the door opened and Galileo walked in.

'G! G!' Lotty shrieked, hobbling over to hug him.

Galileo patted her shoulders and moved straight to Jamal. 'Well done, bravest of all the Defenders. Your goodness will be for ever spoken of in the Creators' halls. To us your name has come to mean "courage".'

'Please don't make a fuss,' Jamal said. 'I had a lot to make up for.'

Galileo turned to them all. 'I come with a heavy heart, as it is time for your return home.'

'No! Please don't send us home!' Angie shouted aloud. 'We've only just got back here!'

Galileo smiled at her. 'I can't help but remember the trouble I had getting you to come here in the first place – you were a very reluctant pupil!'

'But that was when I didn't know anything about me,' Angie replied, 'or about what was possible, or what my potential could be. I was so focused on myself and my problems… My dad always said I couldn't see beyond the nose on the end of my face, and I realise now that was true!'

'You have all learned much,' Galileo said, 'but you and Jamal have perhaps grown most of all. It has been a privilege to see you develop your full potential.'

He looked around from one Defender to the next and went on. 'Because your missions were successful, when you return home you will find that time in the world has stood still. That means that the consequences of Marduk's transmissions have been avoided. And one particular joy is that the mighty Leonidas has been restored to us.'

At this point Lotty began to cry. 'Sorry, G,' she sniffed, 'but that's so brilliant.'

Sasha, Jamal and Yury gave each other high fives.

Galileo said, 'If you had failed in your missions, time in the world would have moved on, along with the evils done by Marduk.

'Your missions have proved to me and to the Educators that you now understand your special abilities and powers. Because you acted together, you were able to defeat Marduk, and you learned that with imagination and self-belief, you can achieve anything. You learned to see nature as a powerful ally, and that all of life on Earth is interlinked. '

'Has Marduk been destroyed?' Lotty asked.

Galileo replied, 'Yes, and no. Although we told you enough about Marduk to understand his evil purposes and the power of his transmitters, we did not reveal the full extent of the evil forces behind him.' Galileo paused and looked out of the window. 'If this were a game of chess then Marduk was only ever a pawn on the evil side. The king is still out there, and he has other pawns. That is why your job is not yet over.

'Once a WPD, always a WPD – so we will never be out of contact with each other. And the Glowbabies can be called into the world by you at any time.'

Yury asked, 'Will we ever be back here… all together?'

'But of course. This is now your true home. The time that you have spent here in Celestxia will enable you to develop abilities and reach heights you have never dreamed of. If you remain true to yourselves, to each other and to all you have learned then you will soon be ready for your return.

'That is all I will say for the moment, except that there is already an even greater evil threatening this planet than the transmitters. But that is for another day. It is time to say your goodbyes now.'

Chapter 31

Hi Yury,

OMG I miss you all. Being home is hell. I can't believe it all really happened and I miss you tooooo much. Anyway, can we meet up??? ☺ Mum says she'll pay for me to fly over to Russia for a couple of days. Hope I'm not being too OTT, but anyway, let me know. I can do any time in the last week in October, can you?

LOL Angie xxx

Hi Angie,

Great to hear from you. All day at college I can't wait to get home for the group chat on our communicators. The mission was the best time of my life and I can't wait to be in Celestxia again. Think it's only fair to tell you that I'm going over to see Mitchi soon, and that I'm hoping, though it seems so arrogant to even think it, that we might start seeing each other. You're a great girl and will find a better guy than me! LOL

WPDs for ever, Yury xx

* * *

Sasha watched the still waters at his favourite fishing spot, where he had the clearest view of fish in the shallows.

Smiling to himself, he let his fingers clasp the white pebble from Galileo where it nestled, safe and secret in his pocket.

* * *

Lotty tossed aside her game console and logged into the chat facility on her mobile phone. She giggled when she saw Jamal was online and clicked to begin their daily chat.

* * *

Mitchi was sitting cross-legged on the floor of her sitting room at home, tinkering with the inner workings of an old mobile phone that a boy at school had been throwing out.

Her mother called from the kitchen in Mandarin, 'Mitchi Wang, I wish you would show as much interest in boys as you do in wires and plugs and all that rubbish. How will I ever get you married off?'

Mitchi put down the circuit board, raised her eyes to the window and smoothed her jet-black hair with a dainty hand. From the bottom of her being, a smile rose, bubbled up and spread across her face.

* * *

In a bedroom in Tokyo, fourteen-year-old Kisho sat at his computer, holding his brand new copy of the computer game of *Taika*. Very carefully, he peeled off the polythene wrapper and prepared to insert the disc into his games console.

His finger hovered over the controller and he pressed 'Play'.